Callen's Girl

Red Eagle Ranch, Book 5

Alyssa Bailey

I0667850

Love the inside scoop?

Sign up for my Newsletter with special offers, bonus content, and fun.

https://www.alyssabaileyromance.com

Cover Design by Joe Dugdale
Manufactured in the United States.

Description

First loves were never forgotten loves

Bella's first and only love was never far from her dreams. When Callen broke up with her because of a misunderstanding, Bella was done with forever love. She threw herself into her art and tried to forget that Callen held her heart. Done with the city life that had turned cruel, Bella was relieved when she was called home to care for her dying mother. Then she saw Callen and suddenly, she believed in second chances.

The minute Callen saw Bella at the ranch, he knew rough waters were ahead. He never stopped loving her, but he was older and wiser now. She either accepted him or rejected him as the possessive, loving man and daddy he was, but he would be done holding his heart in wait for her.

Callen reluctantly agreed that Bella accept a huge commission for a series of paintings. But creating this art was far from the nurturing experience painting always had been for Bella. Before the dust settled, protective Red Eagles landed and crime bosses clashed over whether Bella's commission would cost her not only her freedom, but possibly her life.

Prologue

Little Sister Schemer

The cozy restaurant seemed noisier today than most Thursdays. Renee was feeling a little guilty for pushing her brothers into their respective relationships. She knew she didn't make them fall in love, nor did she even introduce them, and yet she hadn't even screened them as a sister should. Luckily, she loved each one of them and, more importantly, so did Ma and Atè. Still, there was a hint of guilt. Just a hint.

"Wow," said Renee's friend Janna. "It seems almost eerie how you wanted the guys to get girlfriends to take their focus off of you and they got girlfriends."

"Actually, they got fiancées," replied Renee. "That's even better. It worked just like I'd hoped. They've been forced to divide their time between us, and I'm not the center of their over-protectiveness anymore." *Win-win.*

"You're almost done with the first stage of your plan."

"I honestly haven't done much, but I like their choices and made my future sisters-in-laws and future cousin feel comfortable. Now, with all of them engaged, it's time for Callen. He's the last holdout."

"He said he likes to hook up and then go home," Janna reminded Renee. "And that is his major appeal to most. He isn't interested in exclusivity or ties. He's the one you go to when you need to scratch an itch but don't want someone on the regular. Do you know that he,

4

I mean, I've heard that he makes the woman agree to only one night? No strings attached?"

"Who told you that?" asked an indignant Renee. "He isn't cold or unfeeling. He was hurt. I think he feels too much, really."

Janna shrugged and took a sip of coffee. "I hear things in the gym locker room, that's all."

Renee didn't pursue why her friend's face was heating rapidly. Renee didn't want to know.

"So, he might be a little harder, but he did mention a girl he went on a date with a month back. I don't really know her, but by reputation, which isn't good. Maybe I'll see how the temperature is in that direction."

"Good luck. I'm thinking he is going to go down a lot harder than the others."

"Maybe. And now that Jacob is here, it was nice that he seamlessly fell into the program of finding his mate. He can be as difficult as the rest of the men in my life. I was prepared to just wait and see. You know, if he didn't bug me, then he could remain single. Nice to not have to work on him, though. He came home with a plan and pursued Sage hard." Bella shook her head and sipped her coffee. "But that brother of mine, the holdout, might make me work at finding him forever after. Not sure who that might even be, so I'll just keep an eye out."

"Didn't he date Bella Thompson in school?"

"Yeah, but don't you remember? We overheard that conversation when she was telling her friend that she was hoping to get out of her home situation... she'd finally have breathing room because the Red Eagles had money, and everything that came with that."

"Vaguely. It meant more to you than me, really. I was a freshman. Everything was drama."

"Well, I wonder if Bella will come back to see her mom, Vanna, before she dies. People are saying that will happen soon. I never knew about their lifestyle. I mean, the house was nice, if small. But I guess we all thought, in high school, that Vanna had some insurance she and her girls lived off of."

"I heard that, but do you really think Bella would return? I mean, after everything that happened?"

"If she has any love left for Vanna or this place, probably. Out of curiosity, if nothing else."

"Hmm. Good luck with Callen, anyway. You'll have to work for him, I fear. Now let's order. I'm starving."

"Janna, you wouldn't be interested in Callen, would you?" Renee asked casually, not entirely as a jest.

Janna sputtered and then laughed. "Look, he's close to my age, and he's got hot cowboy written all over him, but I haven't really found my forever. I mean, I'm honestly still looking for the one and I promise you, your brother isn't him."

Renee shrugged nonchalantly. "Well, when I get Callen taken care of, we can both go on the prowl."

"Deal."

Chapter 1

Going Home

Bella Kaye Thompson, known in the art world as Bella Gregoria, was a talented painter and sketch artist, or so the people who purchased her work said. Moving to New York City was her mentor's suggestion. It was a good place until it wasn't. But today, Bella made the comforting decision to return to her childhood home in the northwest corner of South Dakota.

She sat looking out of her apartment for one last time, knowing she wouldn't be returning to this city, probably not the east coast. Gary had stolen everything from her when he'd used her to get to the money she brought in for the galleries. It was horrible enough when he stole from the very businesses who showcased her work, but to add insult to injury, he'd stripped her operating bank account. There wasn't much in that account, for a reason, but the violation and humiliation caused her to fold into herself.

New York City was a hard and unforgiving place to live. She never felt safe there alone, but she was able to paint and sell her art in many places. She found success in a few fashionable galleries and was becoming known in some notable circles. Today, she was trying to stay out of the limelight without much success. Not to sound crass, but news of her mother's declining health came at the perfect time in her life.

A month ago, Bella would have been devastated to leave her bohemian community to attend to her mother's needs, but recent events changed all that. Last week, Garrison (Gary) Gold, a stupid name for a stupid man, her now ex-boyfriend, was arrested. It wasn't for something unrelated to her, and that is where the rub came in.

Her ex-boyfriend was found, literally, with his hand in the till of an exclusive gallery that was hosting a selection of Bella's work. She was going to end things with him that evening after the showing. It turned out to be one day too late. Bella rued the day she met Gary Gold. He'd been charming, and she'd been lonely and evidently an easy target.

She was forced to prove she wasn't part of the theft and luckily, she had done enough things and been to enough places that she was cleared quickly. The immediate humiliation, when she discovered what he being arrested for, was devastating. It was also profitable. She sold out and all her back stock in local galleries throughout the city within a week.

She was left with a few bits of unfinished art and a stack of business cards of people interested in her next paintings when completed. She'd left twice as many of her own cards in the hands of interested buyers. And she felt an odd sense of defeat, worry, exhaustion, and some shame now it was all over. Callen Red Eagle would have been a force to reckon with if he'd still been her boyfriend. She missed that feeling of being precious to someone and protected from all things that could cause her pain.

Art enthusiasts found strange reasons to decide whether an artist's work was worth purchasing or not. Evidently, the painter being in the gallery when it was robbed by an ex-boyfriend was exciting. It made the art a piece with a personal story. The Gallery owner immediately had the prices removed from her work and any work not yet displayed was doubled.

Bella was glad everything sold because she didn't want to have to store any of them. The money had been excellent, but the devastation to her life was immeasurable. She didn't know when or even if she would return to this community. She kept her favorite works because they meant something personal to her, like the portrait of Callen Red Eagle sketched in pen and ink. Anytime someone saw it on her wall at her studio apartment, they wanted it.

In one way, her ex had done her a favor by taking from her daily account because it showed investigators that she wasn't in on the robberies, but her pride and trust in her ability to read people was damaged. Her sister Tracy, who had also become her financial advisor, showed her how to diversify and that meant that she wasn't nearly as vulnerable as Gary had thought. Still, the emotional damage was no less severe. And her thoughts ran to Callen.

Tracy told her years ago that Callen had seen the error of his choices in high school, but it had been too late. She'd forgiven him the best she could. They were good together as teens. Bella often wondered how they would be now if things were different. Now, after everything with Gary Gold-digger, she was surprised to find herself yearning for Callen and the connection they had. She wanted that comfort and care he always provided her because she was important to him. She knew it was discontent and disillusionment that made her mind go to Callen. She pushed her budding thoughts away. Callen had gone on with his life, as had she, sort of.

The Red Eagle Ranch was the main employer in that part of the state. There was little else there. It was situated some fifteen miles out of Buffalo Township and was a place where her spirit held a love-hate relationship. The clean air and soul freeing summers were what fond memories were made of, but the dramatic breakup of Callen Red Eagle and herself was something that her heart still bled a few drops over, even now.

That traumatic event in New York demanded she slide back out of the public eye for a while, both to regroup and paint more. Thank goodness at home she was known by a different name. Not trying to keep up with the very few friends she still had by high school graduation suddenly would allow her to hide out and begin again. Luckily, she could take some time, figure out her mother's needs and how things would proceed from here.

Bella hated making decisions about anything but her art. She made all kinds of decisions about color, brush strokes, the brushes themselves, the emotion of the piece and so much more. She always figured she was suffering from decision fatigue, but really, she just shied away from decisions because, in the rest of her life, Bella had a hard time trusting her choices. If it involved anyone other than herself and Tracy, her younger sister, it was an absolutely paralyzing event.

Because of that very problem, she surrounded herself with good judgment so they could advise and all but make them important decisions for her. It is what attracted her to Gary in the first place. He took over when she needed it. But that brought its own problems. He took over areas when she didn't want to acquiesce to him as well.

So much of her life was spent forcing herself to do things for her and her sister out of necessity. Anxiety was her dastardly companion in those days, creating her life now. She shied away from more than the most mundane decisions. Except when she was with Callen Red Eagle in high school. Callen made all the decisions she would allow him to make, and she allowed him a free hand. No use crying over unreversible choices.

Bella gathered her fears, her meager personal items, and all her art supplies wrapped in hope and headed for her inspirational solace in the familiar surroundings of her childhood ranching community. She got in her late model SUV her friends had told her she didn't need to buy. She was glad she ignored them.

"We don't need cars in the city. Public transport is great, and everyone uses it," her friends said.

Bella did use community transportation often. But to get out of the city and find some freedom in the green part of the state, she needed a vehicle, and she preferred it to be her own. Besides, she always felt insecure, as though she might need to get away from danger. A danger she could never quite identify.

That overdeveloped sense of watchfulness and hypervigilance learned in childhood when dealing with an alcoholic mother made reading the room automatic. She still reacted so strongly to anything that felt out of balance. Bella didn't exercise a fight-or-flight response during those stressful times. She simply flew away to hide herself in her studio-slash-apartment. Her past was the impetus behind her being seen as a shy, almost reclusive artist at times. Not that she wasn't an introvert, she was. She liked her own company. Even with the bohemian friends she had, they all knew that Bella Gregoria was sometimes a recluse. But she was a dependable friend, and that's what mattered.

She hadn't felt entirely safe anywhere since she had South Dakota. Even though the last few months of high school were accomplished without Callen Red Eagle at her side, he was always watching over her. She knew it. She counted on it. She hadn't seen him since graduation, but she had dreamed of him. Often. Putting him out of her mind hadn't worked because he was never far from her thoughts. Memories flavored everything she did or said on some days, and certainly her art reflected her heritage and Callen's world.

Bella had run into Stryker soon after arriving back home. Nothing much had changed about this man. He had demanded she go to the ranch and let them all know she was back in town. She knew he meant, *let Callen know*. That family took care of each other and those that belonged to them. It was well known. She had been one of those chosen few until the "great misunderstanding." Her status had vanished in an instant.

"I'm sorry to hear about your mom, honey. I assume that's why you're back in town."

Stryker waited for her to fill in the blanks, but she didn't feel she could right now, so she didn't. The thing about Stryker Red Eagle that everyone knew, he wasn't a man you put off or ignored. He never had been. Much like all the brothers. Richard Red Eagle led his family by example, and they had all learned well.

"Stryker, nice to see you haven't changed." She smiled as his eyebrow raised, encouraging her further disclosure. "I just got here yesterday. I'll come by soon. Okay?"

"Should I tell anyone or let you surprise them?"

Decisions. She shrugged, making the decision Stryker's, not hers. It was an old trick she had used to get by when the answer didn't really matter to her or the stakes were too high.

"I'll let you be a surprise. Don't take too long to come out or I'll sic Callen on you. You don't want that. He basically hasn't changed much either. How about tomorrow? You know you can't keep a secret long in this part of the world."

"I'll try."

"Try real hard, honey." He leaned over and kissed the top of her head. He was such a bossy sweetheart. She missed this more than she would ever admit.

Stryker had become more of who he already was as a young man. More bossy, more muscular and gentler. Sweet even, but she knew he wouldn't appreciate that adjective. It made her smile. It was nice to be home.

Taking Stryker at his word but wanting to exert her independence, she'd waited two full days, but on day three, she drove onto the road leading to the Red Eagle Ranch. As the dust settled behind her car, Bella's hands gripped the steering wheel with a force that whitened her knuckles. The old iron gate of Red Eagle Ranch loomed before her, its familiar silhouette etching a mix of anticipation and anxiety into her heart. For the hundredth time, she hesitated. It was a return charged with memories that clung to her like shadows at dusk. She wondered if Callen ever thought about them and what had gone wrong that fateful day when everything that was right in her world had crumbled.

With a steadying breath, she killed the engine and put her forehead on the wheel to steady her nerves. The silence that followed was punctuated only by the faint sounds of dogs barking and cowboys yelling in the distance, and ranch life in full swing. She sat there for a lingering moment, steeling herself against the swell of emotions churning inside. No one had seen her. Maybe she would come back in another six or seven years.

Shaking her head at her lack of backbone, Bella pushed open the door and stepped out onto the well-trodden earth over the grooves embedded in the drive made by workers, vehicles, and horses. And lovers. Her boots met the ground with a crunch that echoed the weight of her arrival. She was an adult, a successful artist.

Why was this so hard? Hadn't she dreamed of putting their relationship right so many nights since she left? Having this opportunity should have been a relief…. but it wasn't. It was terrifying. Bella cringed as her boots continued to crunch on the gravel of the driveway, announcing her presence as she made her way toward the heart of Red Eagle Ranch. She knew the sound of her arrival was intensified in her mind, but she tried to go quieter, nonetheless.

As she closed the car door behind her, the scent of hay and horses greeted her. The familiarity of earlier days calmed her racing pulse. She allowed the comfort of those smells to wrap her in its reassurance. She'd spent countless hours here in her teen years. The familiarity almost choked her in lost time.

Her eyes traced the outlines of the weathered barns and fences and remembered dozens of sketches of those same structures. And now, as then, she acknowledged their need for a new coat of paint. Bella smiled to herself. Color was something she was intimately acquainted with and those out buildings needed some. She also knew that was the last thing on the minds of Red Eagle men.

The ranch seemed to exhale around her in greeting. The sounds of the working ranch wrapped around her, a welcoming embrace from an old friend. A protector. Callen. She searched for signs of movement, a shadow against the barn doors, a flicker of fabric in the wind, anything that might signal the presence of Callen or the family she once knew so intimately.

Again, she thought, *maybe this wasn't such a good idea*, but the mid-afternoon sun cast long shadows across the expanse of land where bison were mere spots in the landscape. Where horses dotted the fields, their coats shimmering with a golden hue. She paused, taking in the tranquil scene, filling her, grounding her in the moment. This is what she painted when she wasn't lost in the hustle and bustle of life in the Upper West Side of New York City. It is also what more and more of her patrons wanted. The lure of city life seemed distant already. She took a deep, cleansing breath before moving.

As she approached the main barn, the heavy doors swung open. Callen Red Eagle appeared; his tall, muscular frame silhouetted against the dim light within. He was wiping his hands on an oil-stained rag, his movements deliberate and sure—a cowboy at ease in his domain. He exuded confidence of place and position, and Bella tingled all over at the sight of him. Fear mingled with pure joy.

He used to claim her with that same swagger and certainty he had now. She loved that about him. His possessiveness and protectiveness were a bit high-handed at times, but she never doubted she was special to him. Did she want that again? Maybe. His dark hair brushed his collar, his tanned skin and the stubble lining his jaw spoke of long days spent working in all kinds of weather. Callen took after his mother in hair and eye coloring, but in every other way, he was a Red Eagle. Strength of character was a hallmark of this family.

Their eyes met, and for a second, the world seemed to stand still. Callen's gaze widened in surprise. The deep-set lines around his eyes that weren't there eight years ago softened as he registered Bella's presence. The air between them crackled with a tension that spoke of a history marked by passion and pain laced with longing and something else. Doubt? Fear? Regret?

"Callen," she said simply, her voice carrying across the distance, betraying none of the whirlwind of emotions that surged through her at the sight of him.

She sizzled as though she were struck by lightning, but she had learned to hide her reactions if needed. She rolled her bottom lip between her teeth. Nerves raced in her veins like thinned blood, carrying her desires and regrets. Her emerging hopes that this might be the beginning of something good. Callen took another step toward her.

Chapter 2

Old Wounds and Hope

His name hung suspended in the air, a bridge across the chasm of time and misunderstanding. It was a sweet melody after all those years of separation. But it also gave Callen pause. He didn't take another step. He stopped and stood as if rooted to the spot, the bridle in his hand forgotten. Sweat coating his brow.

Callen's palms felt suddenly clammy as he clutched the metal bit, his fingers tensing around the cold metal. He wrapped the reins around his hand absently. The sight of Bella standing there, as if conjured from the very dust of the ranch he loved, sent a jolt through him that was almost buzzing with life. Not entirely unwanted.

Memories surged like a torrent—the way her laughter used to echo in the barn, the warmth of her touch on cold mornings, and the crushing void that followed their parting. Involuntarily, his chest tightened, each heartbeat sounding out the rhythm of what they once had and his fear of the pain that he thought he had healed clawing to the surface.

"Hey." Bella ventured, her lips curving into a small, tentative smile.

It was a careful gesture, one that seemed to reach across the years and pull at something he thought he'd buried deep beneath layers of resolve and ranch work. Her voice held a tremor, betraying her nervousness, yet it was laced with the familiar warmth that had once wrapped around him like a blanket on those long, shared winter nights.

"Hey Bella," he echoed back, his voice unexpectedly hoarse, as though dredged up from the depths of his own surprise. He figured he wouldn't see her again and yet, here she was.

HE NOTICED THE FAINTEST quiver in her stance, the way her hands clung to each other, seeking solace or perhaps strength. It was clear she felt the gravity of their reunion just as intensely as he did. He took a deep breath and almost forgot to let it out until his chest burned in protest.

Callen's eyes remained locked on Bella's. His hand swung the leather reins against his leg with seemingly no sting. *Damn, she was even more beautiful than she was as a teen. I want to spank her ass, claim her, and take her hard. I'm fucked.*

He took another step and had to swallow a smile when he watched her watch the reins in his hand. He'd threatened to use them on her rear once, but he never did. She had always been his sweet Baby Bella and had never done anything to call for that kind of discipline. He wondered if her sweetness tasted better in her maturity. If she was sassy enough to earn the leather across her fine ass. Would she want it? Want him?

Bella watched Callen as he got closer to her. Was she battling the turmoil inside like he was? Was she hating not being in control right now because he knew he did? She seemed to be uneasily waiting for him to do or say more. He wasn't sure what he wanted in this moment, either. He watched as she shifted weight from one foot to the other again and she had to have seen the edge of his lips tip upward, then wrestled back to a straight line. It was like a dance. Lean into then pull out of the emotional movements.

He'd held his spontaneous grin. He loved that he remembered her habit because it gave him the information he needed: she was nervous. She'd tried to erase that habit in high school, but she never had been able to do it because here she was again. It didn't appear to ease the tight knot of anxiety in her stance. It was the signal that cued him to take charge, that she wanted him to take over.

"Never thought I'd see you back here," he managed to say, his voice steady despite the storm raging within. She wasn't his Bella anymore, and he wasn't her daddy, but he wanted to be. That thought stopped him. Did he?

He watched her carefully, searching her face for any hint of the pain they'd both endured when their paths had diverged. Again, he realized it was with some effort that he didn't stalk over to Bella and take her over his knee for a good spanking in penance for all she had put him through. Then, Callen make love to her until exhaustion took them both. But there was so much that had been said and gone unspoken.

A shadow flickered across Bella's features, perhaps a reflection of his own turmoil. He liked thinking this was affecting her as much as it was him. "Life's full of surprises," she replied, her voice carrying a hint of resilience that didn't quite mask the undercurrent of sorrow and uneasiness.

A little sass, which brought a welcomed pressure in his jeans. Yeah, he knew what that was about. He was more than attracted to her smile, her beauty. She was perky, sassy, and intelligent. All that and more attracted him to her. And naughty. Disobedient. Secretive. Avoidant.

The air between them grew heavy, charged with the weight of unsaid words and unresolved history. These stilted responses were not getting them anywhere. He should say something to get the conversation going forward and to make her more at ease, but he wasn't sure he could do that successfully.

"Callen..." The name escaped her lips again. Despite the years and the distance, their connection thrummed alive, a testament to the enduring bond that not even the wildest storm could wash away.

Without a word, Bella stepped forward hesitantly to bridge the space between them, but Callen figured they were both desperate to be accepted and received. She reached out her hand, and he stared at it. Too soon, her arms dropped, and she took a step back. She turned back toward her vehicle.

And that was the outside of enough. "Bella Kaye, stop." She slowed but didn't stop. "Dammit, I'm tired of you walking further away from us–me, instead of talking about what you want, what you need. You're here and I want you here. You belong here. So, if you take one more step away from me before we have a chance to talk, you will be eating lunch standing up."

Bella stalled at the manly, stern voice. It froze her movements for a tick before she slowly turned toward Callen again. She watched him with a wary hope as his long strides brought him to her. He dragged her tight to his hard body as though she had no ability to stop him. His arms encircled her petite frame, pulling her close until there was no space left for regrets or doubt. He didn't realize how petite she was until she wound her arms around his now broad shoulders, letting her fingers thread through his hair, shorter than it had been when she last saw him. Tears coursed down her face as he felt his own eyes water.

"I've been waiting for what seems like a lifetime to hold you again. You aren't going to deny me this pleasure. If nothing else, we have to use this time to clear the air and settle our differences. It's important. I feel like I've been stuck in this longing for an eternity. Whatever comes from this after we have our say will be of mutual agreement. What do you say?"

"It's past lunch," Bella said with a seriousness that accentuated her guilelessness and how uncomfortable she was.

He dipped his head and grinned. "I meant tomorrow."

Her lips formed a silent "O" as she leaned back to see if he was serious. The heat of his body seeped into hers, the solidness of his presence grounding her fluttering heart. She could feel the steady beat of his own heart against her chest. Her breath was labored.

"God, I've missed you," Callen murmured, his voice muffled by her hair before putting a little distance between them.

He looked as though he was about to kiss her but thought better of it. She wanted that kiss from him. He was like her shield, her mountain, solid, dependable, protective. *Bella, you are a weak woman. You don't need a man.* Bella was well aware that need and want were two different words.

"Me too," Bella confessed, the words barely audible. "I've missed you so much."

"I know we both played a part in this little drama, but I've been worried about my baby girl for a long time. And I am torn between kissing you senseless and spanking you till you are hot and achy then taking you hard so you never doubt how much I want you."

She allowed his embrace to fill her soul for long minutes. Reluctantly, they parted, but only enough to allow Callen to take her hand firmly in his. With a gentle tug, he led her towards the ranch house. He pushed open the heavy front door, its hinges singing a familiar tune of welcome.

"But you won't, right?"

"Oh, I plan on doing all of those things multiple times. Just not at this moment."

The hallway stretched before them, adorned with photographs framed in rugged wood and burnished metal—visual echoes of the Red Eagle legacy. Images of stoic ancestors, youthful exuberance at rodeos, and milestones marked by smiles and embraces watched over them as they passed. And there on the wall amongst all the others was a photo of Callen and Bella, young eyes full of hope for the future. A future that never happened.

"Your family always took the best pictures," Bella commented, her gaze lingering on a photo of a young Callen, his face smudged with dirt but eyes alight with triumph, a fish in his hand.

"Only because we had a good reason to smile," he replied, his thumb caressing the back of her hand. "Today is another good day to smile."

A comforting aroma drifted from the kitchen, where the scent of freshly baked bread promised a soothing balm for weary souls. It was a smell that spoke of homecoming and the simple pleasures found in the heart of this home.

Callen watched her drink it all in, an affectionate glimmer in his eyes as he saw her reconnect with the space. "Mam is in Ireland, so it's Libby who's been baking," he said, the corner of his mouth lifting in a half-smile. "Libby and Mam say the house isn't alive unless it's filled with the aromas of good cooking."

"Feels like it's alive with much more than that," Bella murmured. "I've eaten plenty of warm cookies and snacks in this kitchen."

"And dinners," added Callen.

"Remember how we used to camp out here during storms?" Callen asked, his thumb brushing over her knuckles gently.

"Yup, because your parents wouldn't allow us to go into your room alone. I remember when your father was pretty upset with us for bringing all the available blankets and pillows on the floor with us."

"He wasn't really upset about the blankets as us being out here without any other kids. Even then, I guess they noticed we stuck pretty close after we met."

Bella laughed softly. "So, we did. And then..."

"And then, one morning, we were more than friends. So much more." He paused as though he was weighing his words. "Bella, we need to figure this out, so we aren't away from each other like we have been. I can't tell you how much I've missed you. How much I want us again. I know the reason it happened, but now we need a solution."

Bella took a deep breath, the weight of the resurgence of unshed tears making her chest feel tight. The warmth of Callen's hand in hers provided a small anchor in the storm of emotions she was battling. He sensed her hesitation, turning toward her with eyes that asked silent questions.

"Callen," she began, her voice quivering slightly, "there's something I haven't told you about why I came back." Her words hung between them, laden with the gravity of untold tales.

"Mom's health is failing," she admitted, the raw truth of it making her voice break. "It's been a slow decline, but these past months have been rough. And then..." Bella hesitated, gathering the shards of her resolve. "And then there was New York."

Callen's grip on her hand tightened. A silent promise of support. His jaw tensed, a telltale sign of his concern as he waited for her to continue. "I've heard about your mom, and I'm sorry. We can work through whatever is necessary there. But what about New York? I thought I might have read something, but I wasn't sure if it concerned you or you just witnessed something."

"I guess it was too much to ask that it didn't reach all the way out here." She took a cleansing breath.

"There was this guy," she whispered. The memory of his flagrant abuse of their relationship to steal from the very people she made her living from was still too vivid in her mind. A tear escaped, tracing a path down her cheek.

Callen reached out, his thumb brushing away the tear with a tenderness that belied his rugged exterior. His protective gaze never wavered from her face. "Are you okay? Do I need to take care of anyone? Do I need to go hunting for bear?"

She gave him a wet smile. When the Red Eagles went hunting for bear, it meant they were going to take someone down a peg or three. "No, nothing like that. I've got it handled. Well, the police do. I left it to them. But thank you for offering to protect my honor."

"Darling," he said, his voice imbued with a fierce protectiveness that resonated deep within her, "you're not alone in this. Whatever you need, I'm here. If it's for your mom or any other situation, you've got me, Bella. Always. And the whole damn lot of us if you need us."

Bella leaned into him, allowing herself to be enveloped by his strength. In his embrace, she found the solace that had eluded her in the chaos of the city. Here, amidst the quiet creaks of the beloved ranch house, healing seemed like a possibility—at least with Callen by her side.

"I've been thinking about staying here for a while," she said. "The city... it's too much now. I need space to breathe, to create again. I miss the open skies, the smell of earth after rain, the way life moves with a purposeful slowness out here. I want to be part of this community again, to find myself in the rhythm of life."

"Then do it. This town, hell, this ranch has always been your home, Bella," he said, taking her hands in his calloused ones. "I'm sorry I was such a kid that I didn't know you were made for me and this place back then. But I do now. If you want to be here." His thumbs traced circles over her knuckles, grounding her with his touch. "You'll always have a place here, with me, with us. We're your family now as much as we were then, and we'll help shoulder your burdens."

His eyes held hers, fierce and unyielding, yet filled with a gentleness that reached into her very soul. "You can find peace here, paint to your heart's content, ride until you can't remember what sorrow feels like. I'll be right here, every step of the way." His voice was steady,

"Thank you, Callen," Bella whispered, the knot in her chest loosening as she allowed herself to lean on his promise, to accept the sanctuary he offered. "I have to go back to mom's for a couple more days to make sure everything is set up first. I know my mom was not a great mother after dad died, but she's the only parent I have left. Tracy is in Germany and can't come back even if she wanted to. I doubt she would if she could. I thought I could walk in and take care of things and leave again, but..." she shrugged as tears flowed down her cheeks.

"You don't have to do things alone."

"I don't want people thinking I came back home, *here*, because I needed bailed out of any situation. I can't handle that right now. Not after... everything."

"Bella, baby, I'm not sure how we're going to deal with all of this, but we will. There is no way you're going it alone unless you tell me to back off. And I have to tell you, sweetheart, I'm not a kid any longer and I'm not likely to listen. I'm more likely to help you, anyway."

"Callen, I'm an adult. *We* are adults and we ask permission and accept other's decisions."

"Oh, baby, you have to remember that refusing help you need never worked with a Red Eagle. We never leave our people standing on their own."

"Cal, I'm not one of your people." That hurt saying and hurt hearing.

"No, you belong to me. We've lived separate lives for eight years, but you have always been mine. Stay with me. I'm hoping we can work everything out but even if we can't see our way clear to being together as a couple, you are always going to be mine, part of this family... Always."

"I have a hotel room for now, but I'll think about it."

"Why would you waste money when I have a lonely bed that is looking for a companion?"

"I can't just sleep with you."

"Why not? If I promise not to do anything you don't want me to do, can you do it?"

She gave him a sad smile. "That is a very dangerously tempting thing to say, Callen Red Eagle, and you know it." She put her hand on his chest. "Look, can I think about it?"

"Of course. And we have a place for you if you don't want to share with me. We would be hurt if you didn't stay here, but I understand. I feel I need to warn you that everything's changed here," Callen added, his voice resonant with the quiet authority that always seemed to underscore his words.

"Change isn't bad," she replied. She withdrew herself a little as she said that.

"Never said it was," he responded, his smile genuine, if a bit wistful. "Just different."

"How?"

"Well, you know Ma and Até are in Ireland until the end of April. Stryker, Declan, Seamus and even Jacob have all found their forever loves. Carson is still here. I run the dude ranch program we have. Seamus and Carson still take care of the animals and the running of the day-to-day ranch. Stryker and Renee, with some help from Declan, do the background work involved in running a spread this big. Oh, and there's a lodge now. And fiancées. Yeah, I guess we have changed somewhat."

"Some? I'd say there have been huge changes. It sounds like you have kept tabs on me, so you know I'm an artist with paintings that I have sold. I don't really want people to know, especially outside of the ranch, that I have a pseudonym. I have begun to find some success, selling quite a few, actually. Thanks in part to my asshole ex. I'm known for a certain realistic warmth, I've been told. But it all comes at a price."

Callen made a grumbling sound deep in his chest. "You find that price is getting too steep, you just let me know. I can manage things like the old days. Now, I have a couple of things I need to take care of quickly and then you are going to tell me everything you have done since leaving me in your dust after graduation. I shouldn't be more than a few minutes."

There was a measure of excitement mixed with old hurt in his eyes, but it quickly vanished. The sadness was something they both could feel and, hopefully, they could find a place somewhere between the past hurt and the future goal of happiness. Time would tell.

Bella followed him out of the house and into the barn, then watched as he went about methodically putting away equipment and checking on the horses. He spoke to a stable hand, nodding and smiling. She remembered that smile directed at her. She missed it. Bella cooed to the nearest horse.

"That one has a temper, so be careful you don't get too close."

"He seems to be calm."

"Bella, I know you love horses, but don't ignore my warning. You don't know this fella the way I do."

She didn't respond to Callen but continued to speak soothingly to the horse. Callen went back to his conversation, but she could feel his eyes on her. Soon he was interrupted by the sound of approaching footsteps and voices. His siblings Renee, Stryker, Declan, Seamus, along with his cousin Jacob and family friend Carson, filed into the room one by one. Their curious gazes shifted between Callen and Bella as the tension in the room ramped up.

"Fuck."

Bella's thoughts exactly.

Chapter 3

Acceptance

The sound of approaching footsteps broke the stillness, and one by one, Callen's siblings appeared from various parts of the ranch like elements of a gathering storm or some bad horror movie. Both brought trouble. Callen hoped life didn't imitate either instances. He sensed Bella was too fragile right now for either.

"Looks like we've got company," Callen said, breaking the silence that had settled over the group. The muscles in his jaw flexed as he prepared for the barrage of questions he knew would inevitably come.

"Indeed," Bella responded, her voice tinged with a barely concealed apprehension.

Stryker only raised her insecurities in that department. "Family meeting in fifteen," he'd said with the confidence of someone who was used to running the show.

"I'd better go," said Bella.

"Nice try, sweetheart," said Seamus, "But you are part of the family. You won't be going off before we all talk."

Callen leaned down close to her ear. She shivered as his warm breath blew across her cheek and neck. "I said you belong here and now you know I wasn't just saying those things to get you in bed."

She nodded at Callen but didn't reply to Seamus. The rest said hello as they joked with each other as though they were in a good mood. Not about to rake them over the coals, about not connecting again, or it was too late for Bella to come back, or whatever her active imagination could conjure up in the next fifteen minutes. Callen ushered Bella into the barn as confident as he ever was. Bella felt like she was that teenager so long ago, following Callen like a little puppy dog. It irked her and gave her comfort.

"What do you think Stryker needs a meeting about?"

"You baby. Don't worry, if anyone steps out of line, I'll set them straight, but I don't think anyone will. They will be excited to see you with me."

"Maybe."

Finally, they entered the family room that looked nearly the same as it did a decade ago, except there were several new females in the group. If she were to interpret where they were in proximity to everyone, she could name which woman belonged to which man. Thankfully, no one seemed to have claimed Callen. *Of course they haven't. He offered you his bed.* When everyone had settled down, Stryker spoke.

"We have a little issue of misunderstandings and possibly hard feelings concerning our Bella, and it's time we deal with them so we can go on as a family."

The response to Stryker was complete silence. Then, simultaneously, Bella and Callen spoke. Bella would have laughed if this wasn't a serious situation she wanted to have dealt with and be done. She continued before Callen could.

"I feel I should start off by apologizing for those early days of letting you sit in your misunderstandings." She turned to Renee. "It hurt me that you knew me and thought I was only after Callen for his money. The reality was I wanted his lifestyle. The ranch, sure, but even if he wasn't part of this ranch, I wanted him and the security he represented. I had a kind of love for him that teens have. You know, all-consuming and focused. Then, when you misinterpreted the conversation you overheard," she shrugged, "I was too devastated to correct your misperceptions. I couldn't disclose my home life because my sister still needed to finish high school at home. I wanted to hide, so I did. Before I knew it, we were graduating, and my art was discovered, and I was gone."

Callen took it up from there. "And she's had her work sold all over the world. She's here because her mother is ill, not because she needs me or what I have. I want to help her get through these few days, and I intend to do it." His voice hardened and had a hint of challenge in it. "Then possibly more, if she'll have me."

Stryker spoke again, looking straight at Avery and Renee. "Sounds like enough. Anyone have unanswered questions?" Both women shook their heads. Avery was shame-faced and reached over to hug Bella. It took her by surprise, but she allowed it and smiled. "I'm sorry, Bella. Please forgive me."

"Of course. There isn't anything to forgive. I just want to go forward."

"Me too."

Callen joined Stryker in the stare down of Renee, who wriggled under the undisguised demand.

Renee spoke. "I'm so sorry if it was me who caused you so much pain you left for so long, but I'm glad you came back."

Callen's girl hesitated. He watched Bella closely and saw the second she released her pain. "Thank you. It worked out for the best. Honestly. But I'm glad I'm back, too."

Renee sat in her place, tears streaming. Callen pulled Bella in tighter. His sister wanted to get past the pain, and he hoped his other brothers would see that and give her their physical support. Carson drew closer to Renee first. Callen saw Bella understood as well. She left his arms and walked into the younger woman's outstretched ones and soon both women were crying. Callen didn't need anyone to tell him these were good, cleansing tears.

Stryker smiled and nodded in Bella's direction. Declan's calm demeanor did little to hide the surprise etched on his face. Renee never cried. Seamus's easy-going manner brought a palpable energy that had, at first, seemed out of place amidst the tension. Now, it matched the group's relief.

Carson settled his hands on his hips and tipped back his cowboy hat, surveying things as though he didn't know what to make of the scene in front of him. Lastly, there was Jacob, who always seemed mature for his age. He watched, his silent assessment resonating louder than any words could.

"Good thing we got all that out of the way before Sage and I left on our trip. I'd hate to miss the good stuff and Sage would have been livid. It certainly saved her butt from being uncomfortable while sitting in the truck."

"Jake, stop it," said a red-faced Sage. There was much needed laugher in response.

Their collective gaze danced between Renee, Callen, and Bella, each sibling wearing an expression that spoke volumes more than any dialogue could. The women separated. Renee backed into Carson's waiting arms and Bella into Callen's, which made him feel ten feet tall.

Stryker spoke. "Glad you paid attention to our conversation the other day, Bella, but I expected you by yesterday. Good thing you made it today, because I was going to let the cat out of the bag at dinner tonight. Nice timing, honey."

"I said I'd try."

"That you did. Proud of you following through. You always were a courageous girl. Most women don't challenge me."

"Except your Avery," said Seamus with a laugh.

"Sounds like we'll get along," replied Bella with a smile in Avery's direction.

"That you will, darling." Stryker looked over Bella's head to connect with Callen, as he often did when she was in high school. "This one is old enough now, so I anticipate you paying as much attention to her backside as I do to Avery's."

Stryker was the undeclared, or maybe now declared, leader of the group. He'd said his parents weren't home right now, but she hadn't processed what that meant. Before she could shoot back a smart response, Stryker winked at her. "Glad you're home, sweetheart. We missed you." He drew her into his strong arms and while they weren't Callen's, they were comforting.

"Good to see you again, Bella," Declan added, his easy smile attempting to bridge the gap of years and unspoken words that lay between them. Declan seemed even more mature and gentlemanly than he had as a young man. Gentleman scholar.

"Thanks, Declan," Bella replied. She didn't know Declan as well because if he wasn't doing chores, he had his nose in a book.

Callen's gaze stayed fixed on Bella, his blue eyes searching hers for any sign of retreat. But she held his gaze steadily, finding an unexpected solace in his familiar presence. Despite the history, despite the pain, there was a sense of homecoming in standing beside him once more.

"Let's clean up," Seamus suggested, his words directed more at his siblings than Bella. "We have a lot of catching up to do, and I'm starving. We need to get dinner going."

"No," said Renee, "Libby does." It was an indication of how out of sorts she still felt. Colt swatted her butt, and she gave him a look of irritation but otherwise ignored it, and so did everyone else. Seems some things hadn't changed. They all stood.

In the months before the defining high school incident, Callen had been experimenting with the "daddy" concept. They had fallen into the roles very easily then. Now? She didn't know. Bella wondered if he still played with it. A possessive side of her hoped he didn't. The practical side hoped he did. At the time, she was embarrassed and curious... and relieved. Now she was intrigued in a more intimate way. She dreamed of turning things over to someone she trusted. The man she trusted. Maybe she had a chance to do that now. Second chances did exist.

"It's been what, six or seven years?" asked Jacob.

"Almost eight," replied Bella.

Carson, not one to mince words, said, "Don't do that again. We didn't know where you were for most of that time. Friends and certainly family don't treat each other that way."

She smiled apologetically. "I missed you too, Carson."

He grunted and headed off in the direction of the barn Callen had first come out of.

"Welcome back, Bella," said Jacob, his voice hinting at the camaraderie they once shared. The familiarity in his tone brought a swell of gratitude to Bella's heart. She was thankful for this semblance of normalcy, despite the storm of emotions churning within her.

"Thank you, Jacob," she replied, her voice steadier than she felt. "It's good to see you all." She wasn't sure how much was a truth or a fib, but it sounded like what she should say.

"Well, I echo Carson's sentiment. Don't do it again or we will come and find you. Then take turns pounding on your backside as we bring you home." He settled his hat back on his head. "But honestly. We all know about your mom's failing health. If you need anything, you call one of us or all of us."

"Thank you, Jake. I will."

But she knew, at least for now, she wouldn't. Jacob seemed to get that message too.

"Remember, there are consequences to not asking for help or waiting until it's too late for a good outcome." His stern tone made her smile. *Bossy much?* Although he was technically Callen's cousin, Jacob was Red Eagle through and through.

"I'll try to remember that."

Jacob grunted. These men were predictable.

As the last echoes of polite and chastising conversation faded, Callen took a step closer to Bella, his tall frame casting a protective shadow over her. Jacob backed away immediately with a grin. His hand found the small of her back, ushering her away from the group under the pretense of showing her something outside.

"Are you alright?" Callen's voice was low, the timbre resonating with concern.

"Callen, I..." Bella hesitated, her heart caught between past hurt and the lingering affection she held for the man before her reigniting strongly. She looked up into his face, searching for the boy she had once loved within the contours of the hardened cowboy he'd become.

"Hey, it's okay," he said, his voice softer now, laced with an emotion she couldn't quite place.

There was longing there, but also something deeper, something that spoke of sleepless nights and roads not taken. And more fear of the unknown that was echoed in her own heart.

"Thanks for looking out for me," she managed to say, her words barely audible when mixed with the horses being brought from the paddock into the stables. The warmth from the sun had disappeared.

"Always," he murmured, his eyes never leaving hers. "They're all housebroken, so I didn't expect any accidents of the mouth."

She laughed. "Good to know." Her heart prayed that perhaps there was a possibility of mending fences long thought beyond repair. Maybe there was actually something like a second chance in her life. Her heart lightened as she began to contemplate being with Callen. Her life was so different now. This time last month, she was finishing some paintings and preparing for her art exhibit. Now, she was thousands of miles away, contemplating staying with Callen on the ranch she thought never to return to. The twists and turns of life were dramatic sometimes.

Callen leaned against the worn wooden fence, peering through the slats, then up at the darkening sky. Bella stood a few paces away, her arms wrapped around herself as if to ward off more than the evening chill.

"We need to go inside. It's getting pretty cold out here now. I just wanted to give you some breathing room."

"Just a little longer? I'm going to need to leave soon."

"Remember that summer?" he started, voice hesitant, as if testing the waters. "The one where we camped out by the creek nearly every weekend, just you and me against the world?"

Bella nodded, a faint smile touching her lips at the memory. "How could I forget?" she replied. "And your Até would have someone ride by at crazy times. We were so sure we could handle anything together."

"Yep," Callen echoed, the word laced with regret. "Until we couldn't."

Bella hugged herself tighter, her gaze drifting to the ground, the darkening sky and surroundings, to anywhere but his face. Callen's jaw clenched, the muscles working as he grappled with the weight of what came next.

"I thought I knew best," he admitted, pushing himself off the fence to stand closer to her. "I thought I was protecting you... from everything. But I was just... scared. Scared of losing you, I guess. And scared that what Renee said was true. That it wasn't me you wanted, but what my family had. It made more sense than you wanted it all, me included."

Her eyes finally met his, and there was a depth to them that spoke volumes. They held pain, yes, but also an understanding that only time could grant.

"Callen, we were both scared," Bella said softly. "I didn't make it easy on you, either. My past, my walls, my insecurities and let's not forget pride... I kept you out when I should have let you in."

"We were young."

She chuckled. "We were doomed."

He took another step, close enough now that he could see the delicate freckles dusting her nose. A detail that time had not erased from his memory. "Maybe. I'm sorry, Bella. For not listening, for the pride that got in the way. For letting you go when I should have fought harder. It's good to see you, touch you," Callen finally said, his voice tinged with both longing and regret. "I wasn't sure I ever would again or if I deserved to."

Bella gave a sad half-smile, the memories of their painful breakup still touchy. "I wasn't sure either. But here I am."

An awkward silence fell between them. So much left unsaid and unresolved. Callen ached to pull her into his arms, to pick up where they left off, but uncertainty held him back. The scars they had inflicted on each other wouldn't heal so easily.

"I'm sorry, Bella," he said heavily. "For so damn much. For the way things ended between us. I should have trusted you more. I should have..."

His voice trailed off. He shook his head. Bella's eyes glistened with tears as she absorbed his apology.

"I'm sorry too, Callen," she replied softly. "I said some terrible things out of anger and pain. But I never stopped..." She shook her head. "We have to stop apologizing. Because of what happened between us, I followed my dream when the opportunity presented itself, and I don't regret that. You have your permanent place at the ranch, and we might have gone in a totally different direction. Maybe this is what was meant to happen."

She faltered, emotions welling up. Callen reached out and gently caressed her cheek. They gazed at each other, the possibility of reconciliation hovering tentatively between them. There was still a chance to mend what had been broken if only they were brave enough to try again.

"Well, this is where we are now. What should we do with now?"

Bella leaned into Callen's touch, her heart aching with longing and regret. There was so much history between them - a deep love marred by pain and distrust. A future filled with hope and longing.

Callen gently brushed away a tear that escaped down Bella's cheek. "I've missed you so damn much," he murmured. "Having you here, it feels like I can breathe again."

Bella gave a shaky laugh. "I know the feeling. Being back at the ranch, seeing you and your family...it's overwhelming."

She paused, searching Callen's face. "But it also feels right, somehow. Like I'm finally home."

Callen's eyes lit up at her words. Home. This was where she belonged, by his side. If she was willing to try again, he would spend every day proving himself worthy of her trust and love.

"Stay with me, Bella," he implored, his voice rough with emotion. "We can take things slow, rebuild what we had into a better us. All I know is that I can't lose you again. You're my girl."

Conflicting emotions showed as they flitted across Bella's face. The urge to protect her heart battled with her enduring love for this complicated, commanding, wonderful man.

Finally, she lifted her hand to cover Callen's, where it still rested on her cheek.

"I'll stay," she whispered. "But I don't know if I can promise anything else. I have my mom's care to settle."

"We will make that happen."

Callen exhaled in relief, then drew her into a fierce, tender embrace. They still had a long road ahead, but now they would walk it together.

In the dusk, his features softened, and something like hope flickered across his face. "Is there any chance you could forgive a stubborn cowboy who's realized his mistakes? Who wants to see if maturity and life experiences can right the wrongs of the past? Could you give us a chance for a future?"

The question hung in the air, mingling with the scents of earth and grass and the distant scent of burning wood from a chimney. Bella looked up into the sky, now a canvas of stars beginning to pierce the dusk, and exhaled a breath she seemed to have been holding for years.

"Maybe," she whispered, the single word carrying the weight of a thousand possibilities—a second chance just out of reach but drawing nearer with each heartbeat. "Maybe," she repeated, her voice barely louder than the rustle of the wind through the grass. "But Callen, we can't just erase the past. I still have to reconcile the pain."

He nodded, as he began walking them back toward the house filled with light and warmth. "I don't expect us to forget, Bella. I just... I hope we can learn from it. Build something stronger. Something lasting. I didn't think this was something that I would ever want, but the moment I saw you, I knew why I had never committed to anyone since us. Never told another woman I loved her. Never thought I could love another. I have to try to work through the past as well and see if we can carve out a future."

"Learning from it sounds good," Bella murmured, allowing herself a small smile that didn't quite reach her eyes. Her gaze flickered to the barn where they'd shared covert kisses, stolen moments away from watchful eyes, then moved forward to the porch they had lazed many evenings on. "We were just kids back then, thinking we knew what love was."

"Maybe we didn't know much about love," Callen conceded, his voice rough like the gravel paths that crisscrossed the ranch. "But I knew enough to know I'd never stop loving you, Bella Thompson. And I didn't. Not for one damn minute."

A shiver ran down her spine, not from the cool night air but from the raw honesty in his words. She could see the remorse etched into the lines of his face, the determined longing in the set of his jaw.

"Callen Red Eagle, you always did have a way with words," she said, the ghost of her former sass making a fleeting appearance. "Even though some things aren't as simple as you liked to make them, they always sounded good."

"Only when it comes to you," he replied, his mouth lifting in a half-smile that hinted at the teenager he once was—the one who could make her laugh and dream without effort. She hoped it was a glimpse of the man he was now.

"I'm not sure you understand. I've got a lot to do with mom, Callen. I don't know how much free time I'll have for a while."

"And you'll have to go home to New York at some point."

"There isn't a return date, so I wouldn't put too much thought into that right now. I let my place go." Bella got serious. "But it will take time to get care set up. Then I must start painting again. I'm hoping being home will help with that. You have your own work to do and I know it's a busy time of the year."

It sounded as though they had a lot to think about, but Bella was willing to wait because she wasn't lying. There was a lot on her plate right now. But now that the dreaded trip to the ranch was over. The rest seemed much more doable.

They topped the porch as Bella rubbed her arms with the cold. The cool night breeze playing with the loose strands of her hair suddenly irritated her. She took a step closer to Callen. "Listening or understanding my side of things was always a challenge for you."

"I thought I did," he said quietly, his words slicing through the space between them. "But seeing you here now, Bella, I realize I didn't fully understand. I didn't listen to you through my own haze of perceived betrayal and the hit to my immature pride. Not until this moment do I think I truly understand."

She blinked away the sting of tears, her sassy nature warring with the vulnerability that made her chest ache. "And yet, despite it all, I can't extinguish what I feel for you, Callen. It's like trying to douse a wildfire with a single cup of water. But I don't want to become vulnerable again in the same way I was. I can't be that kid in woman form."

"And I wouldn't want you to be something you aren't. I want you, as you are, here with me today."

The warmth from his fingers seeped into her skin, spreading a heat that coursed through her veins, reigniting old flames that she thought were long extinguished. Bella felt the walls she'd built around her heart begin to crumble, stone by stone, leaving her exposed in a way only Callen Red Eagle had ever managed.

Bella's gaze held Callen's, a silent urging passing between them, an echo of Callen's plea. Her breath caught in her throat, each inhalation sharp with the weight of the decision. The surrounding air seemed charged, electrified with the tension of what remained unsaid. She took a tentative half step closer. *Could she do this without throwing caution to the wind?*

"Callen," she began, her voice a whisper. "I..."

He waited, his body taut as a bowstring, every muscle coiled in anticipation. Callen's eyes searched hers, dark and fathomless, reflecting his hopes and regrets.

"Can we really go back?" she asked. The breeze picked up, playing with strands of her hair, sending them dancing around her face—a stark contrast to the stillness that gripped Callen. It didn't bother her in the same way this time. She swiped at her hair. He cupped her cheek.

"Back? No." His voice was firm, decisive. "But maybe we can start anew. A second chance doesn't mean repeating the same mistakes."

A lump formed in Bella's throat, and she swallowed hard, trying to dislodge it. The scent of earth and growing things filled her senses, grounding her in the moment, in the reality of Callen's unwavering presence. His confident earnestness.

Her heart hammered against her ribcage, a drumbeat of possibility. "Starting anew..." she repeated, tasting the words, rolling them around her tongue as if they were the ingredients to a potent spell. Maybe they were.

"Only if you're willing," he said. His voice was barely above a hoarse murmur. His hand lowered from her cheek. But the warmth lingered, filling her with hope.

Was she? One minute she was all in, the next, she was too afraid to try. Bella's eyes stayed locked on Callen's, the setting sun painting their faces in hues of fading light. The surrounding ranch took on a hushed quality, as if the world held its breath, waiting for her answer. Bella knew her decision would change everything.

"I...

"It's getting chilly out here. Let's get you back inside where it's warmer. And where is your heavy coat, woman?"

She shrugged. "Didn't think I'd be here this long."

"Didn't you just. Good to know I surprised you. I know I've got a lot to make up for," he said quietly. "Losing you...it tore me apart, Bella. I was too proud and stubborn to admit it, but you walking away left a hole in me I didn't know how to fill."

Bella's eyes glistened with tears. "It wasn't easy for me either," she admitted. "I loved you so much, Callen. But you had this...this need to control everything. I needed it sometimes and other times... it felt like you didn't trust me to make my own choices."

Callen closed his eyes, pained. "I know. I thought I was protecting you, taking care of you. But I see now how I smothered you instead. I'm so sorry, Bella."

"I'm sorry too," Bella said. "I should have tried harder to make you understand how I felt. I was confused too. The feelings were so strong. Maybe if we'd just talked..."

She trailed off. They couldn't change the past now. All they could do was move forward and try to rebuild what they'd lost.

Callen brushed a strand of hair back from her face tenderly. "No more big mistakes," he vowed.

"I wish it was that easy," she said, her voice trembling. "I'm willing to make this work or know we did the best we could."

"People are going to say we are doomed because we haven't taken time to work through this longer. We didn't agonize more over the decision."

"Only eight years. Besides, we never cared what other people said."

Bella grinned. "Nope, we didn't."

"Then this is real? We're doing this? You'll be my girl again and I'll be the man you need?"

"I guess we're doing this."

Callen drew Bella in close and lowered his head, waiting just long enough for her to step back. But, if possible, she stepped forward, her arms wrapping around his neck, as he softly brought his lips to hers in a tentative kiss. The pressure increased as both became more deliberate and confident in their touch. Callen had been a good kisser, but she had only kissed one boy. Now her experience told her that Callen was indeed an impressive kisser.

Tongues tangled, breathing stuttered as the kiss became more physical. Until, just when Bella thought she would fall into his soul with him, he raised his head. Dropping down to give her a few small slow kisses as a cooldown, he stepped back.

"That was, incredible."

He smiled. "It was perfection, like you."

"I need to go back to mom's tonight and check on her, then my hotel room."

"I know. I just don't want to let you go now that I have you."

"Promise I'll come back."

"After dinner. Stay for dinner. Stay here, on the ranch."

Bella hesitated, but then shook her head sadly. "I can't, but I will be back soon. I promise."

Callen added her number to his phone and texted her, listened for the ping before he let her go back outside, into the cold, into her car, and waved her off. He hated it, but it wouldn't be long until she was back for good. That sounded like heaven.

Chapter 4

Accident

The red flashing lights intermingled with the blue and occasional white lights alerted Callen that there was an accident ahead long before the officer with his flashlight swinging came into view. This many of the county's finest safety and rescue vehicles might have indicated a huge accident, but in Northwest South Dakota, it could mean anything from a dinged fender to loss of life. He held his breath to see which one it was.

As Callen tentatively approached, the lights were overwhelming his vision, and he slowed even further so he didn't add to the chaos by hitting something himself. Arriving at the flagged stop, he wondered who was involved in calling the whole county out on Wednesday evening. This road wasn't traversed much. Mostly farmers and ranchers. It didn't go anywhere interesting, and it wasn't the way through to anything interesting, except the locals going to Buffalo Township or further south.

As the patrolman recognized Callen, he waved him down. "Mr. Red Eagle, Callen, do you mind having a look at the woman in the car up here? We don't know who she is, but she seems familiar with too many things not to have spent some time in our area. She's about your age, so thought," the man shrugged. "Your family knows just about everyone."

"Sure, Tom. I'll look."

His gut clenched in his fear that it was someone he knew intimately, and if that was the case, could it be one of the girls? That thought almost devastated him before he saw who it was. The policeman waved Callen through and indicated with his flashlight where he should pull over. It wasn't dark, but out on an otherwise deserted parcel of land, dusk gave things an eerie quality. Callen jumped out of his oversized pickup and slammed the door shut. As he followed the cop, he tried to see clearly, but it was difficult. He wanted to tell them all to turn down their blinding lights, but he decided not to waste his breath.

As he approached, the car that seemed to have run off the road into a ditch was alone. A woman running into the ditch got this much attention? He shook his head. It didn't make sense. A stiff wind caught the space between Callen's partially zipped jacket and his shirt, seemingly aimed at freezing him in recognition of being a good Samaritan.

Trudging through the newly fallen snow of a frigid March, he arrived at the car. The SUV did look familiar, but he couldn't place it, so not one of the ranch's women. However, everyone drove trucks or SUVs in this part of the world. Not much more of a clue there. He squatted down at the open doorway.

He had a bad feeling as he looked inside. He audibly caught his breath when he realized who it was. Bella. His brain instantly flashed back to yesterday when they had vowed to start again. His family questioned him about the speed that he made that decision, but he knew it was right. His heart pounded as he looked at Parker, who shrugged.

"Damn, baby. Are you okay? Did you hurt yourself? What happened?"

Bella stared at him in a daze, as though she didn't realize what was going on around her, but she looked scared like she understood enough to know she was in a real bind.

"Bella? Hey sweetheart. Can you hear me? It's Callen."

He called to her gently. Just saying her name reminded him of past longings. She turned to look at him with an expression of consternation as though she was trying to figure out who he was, but no true recognition. He took a quick glance in the front seat and saw the fuzzy pink bear he'd won her at the county fair all those years ago. It looked a bit worse for the wear, but obviously loved. He'd given that to her while they played with the Daddy/baby girl dynamic.

What he knew then was laughable, but now? No, now, he was all in with that dynamic and enjoyed it the most. Could they do that again? They hadn't covered that conversation yet. His overactive brain jumped to the question of why she was on this road headed out of town? He was only on it because he'd promised to look at a mare he was thinking of getting for Bella. He'd been too busy earlier in the day and now he was thanking God for that busy day.

All of his protective instincts that had awakened since seeing her again yesterday were ramming his gut and overrunning his thoughts. His brain came back online. He needed to take care of her now and worry about the rest of his shit later.

"Bella, baby girl, it's Callen. You hurting in there?" Her response was to stare at him blankly. "It's okay, honey. I'm going to make sure nothing happens to you. Are you hurt?" She shook her head very slightly and hissed. Her hand going to her head. That's when he saw the blood on the back of her head, matting her hair.

He placed his hand on hers and turned to Parker. "Hey, she's bleeding from her head."

"Yeah, and possibly more, but she won't let us take her in to see."

Something was off. "Honey, you're hurt. Do you know who I am?"

"No," she whispered. "But I think I should."

"Yeah, you should, but it's likely the shock and your brain got a little more jostled than you know. You'll be fine. Let me get you out and into the ambulance."

She whispered again. "Don't make me. I can't get in one."

"Why?" He remembered there was something about ambulances, but his mind was refusing to shake from the fact that she needed a doctor. Why didn't he listen harder back then?

"I don't know, but I know I can't."

The EMT said, "Callen, she needs to go. She hit her head and things don't seem right. Her car was mostly just in the ditch, but it was a drop. She doesn't remember what happened and she can't tell us her name. She doesn't know you, but she thinks she should. We can't leave her. What's her name?"

"Bella Thompson."

Callen dragged his hand through his longer than typical hair. Bella had always liked it that way. It was long enough to tie back again. It felt like coming home after a long absence. Well, he guessed it was for them. He went through phases where he kept it short, usually summer, then longer in the winters, mostly because he liked to remember when she drew her fingers through it, but now... fuck, he was a mess.

His caveman instincts, civilized though he thought he was, came to the forefront with the woman he had secretly never let go. They were trying to make this work again and that meant she was his and time to act like it.

"She doesn't like ambulances. Where will you take her?"

"Doc said bring her to his clinic and he'll give her the once over and decide if we need to take her to a hospital."

"Can I take her there myself?"

"No, man. It doesn't work like that, but you can ride with her if that will get her inside the rig."

Callen nodded. Once upon a time, he'd had a lot of conversations with Bella over her fears and once again he began envisioning a life together, just like he'd thought they'd be in high school. Life was different. This new chance with Bella demanded that things would be more defined, settled, committed. Seeing her in a vulnerable state pushed his *mine* instincts into overdrive. His chest burned with worry.

His heart pounded with the what ifs, and his knees wanted to give way when he saw her face tonight. He was glad she had come to the ranch before now. Questions that had gone unanswered for so long were no longer questions. It put them on more even footing and that mattered to them both. He didn't blame her, he just hated she was left to do it on her own. But no more. She'd agreed to try again.

He had committed to be the man she wanted and maybe, in light of the baby bear she had in her car, the daddy she needed. And all that fucking thrilled him. She was his, and he took care of those he claimed. He took a deep breath and steeled himself to be the man she needed as he squatted back down between the driver's door and the seat.

"Bella baby, it's time to go."

He firmed his voice just enough to get her attention and declare he was the boss without scaring her. He fell into the role he had always loved with her. Her protector, defender, her leader and now, the daddy role felt right, too.

She sniffled and pinned him with her tearful gaze. "I don't want to go anywhere, Daddy. I want to go home. Can you take me home?" Her whispered words damn near ripped out his heart. Her soul knew his soul, and that was all he needed.

He gave her a gentle smile. "I know, but that isn't a choice, baby. Not yet. Let's grab Pinky Polar Bear."

"Mmm... okay."

He reached over and grabbed the polar bear with the ratty pink ribbon around his neck that used to be a smart-looking bow and handed the cuddly to her. "Daddy, my head hurts."

He worriedly looked at the c-collar the medic had put around her neck before Callen had arrived. "Pounding hurt or headache hurt?"

"Isn't that the same thing?" she asked with that same cute, confused look she would give him in high school when he tried to help her with geometry. Her voice was still diminished in quality. Her Little was peeking out pretty strongly.

"You're probably right, baby."

Callen leaned down to help her get out of the car, passing her over to Parker, the EMT, who placed her on the stretcher. "Up you go, baby. I'll be right there. Don't leave without me."

He smiled, but she just nodded absently, tears rolling silently down her cheeks. His brave baby. He grabbed her backpack and found another cuddly on the floorboard. Pinky had been buckled in, but it looked like the panda bear flew from his likely perch next to Pinky. Scooping up the panda, he left her car for the tow truck before heading out of the ditch. He stopped and told the driver to bring her car to the ranch.

"I'll come square it with you after I take care of Bella. It will probably be tomorrow. Or one of the guys at the ranch will take care of you if you need it tonight."

Callen jogged to his vehicle and rounded up someone to drive it to the clinic. Then he flagged Tom down, gave him a quick update before walking with purpose as he advanced to the back of the ambulance, climbed in with Parker, and sat beside Bella as she lay perfectly still, her tears still streaming.

"It's okay, baby. I'm right here."

She nodded but didn't answer him. He wiggled the panda in front of her and she grabbed for him.

"How're you doing?" He continued when she didn't respond. He wanted to take care of everything and not involve her sister Tracy or her mom. But it wouldn't be right. "Bella, who do you want me to call for you? Your sister, Tracy? Your mom?"

"I don't know," she whispered. "I can't think. It hurts to think."

"It's okay, baby. Tracy is in Germany, so yeah, too far. How about your mom?"

"Can't you help me, Daddy?" Yeah, her mom was pretty ill with a bad liver, compliments of drinking over her depression most of her adult life. Callen remembered people trying to help the widow later in life, but she'd been too far into the bottle for far too long by the time many took much notice.

"Oh, I plan on taking care of everything. Daddy will take care of you, baby. Don't worry."

The EMT kept his head averted, but when he took her vitals again, Callen gave Parker a look that swore him to secrecy about what he was hearing, and Parker just nodded.

He told himself he would call Tracy if she wanted him to, but he liked being the one Bella relied on to keep her safe. Even if she didn't know what it was Callen was helping to do right now. His gut was still churning from his initial fear and multi-level shock when he discovered Bella behind the wheel and blood on her head and hand.

They took ten minutes to arrive at the clinic. Doctor Taron Marshall, Doc for short, was a man in his early forties with a kind, confident smile who ran a much-appreciated medical clinic. Bella turned toward Callen when they stopped. Their eyes met, and he gave her the silent reassurance he thought she was asking for. He rubbed her arm and squeezed her hand.

What was she thinking? Likely, so many questions that he was unable to decipher, but for now, Callen understood that his presence was enough to settle her. He tapped her hand, signaling his exit before jumping out of the back and started talking to calm her fears as they set her up to bring her out of the ambulance.

"I'm here, sweetheart. I'm going to be here with you." When she didn't reply, he continued. "I called Stryker to update him on things. He and Avery will be here soon."

"I don't know any of these people. I'm not sure I know you, but there is something about you, familiar, that quiets my anxieties. I want to know you. You seem nice. Just don't leave me."

"I'll put Pinky in your backpack, along with his panda friend."

"Ping-Pong."

"What baby?"

"Ping-Pong Panda is his official name."

"So, you know the cuddle toy's names, but not people's names?"

"Shh. He's my roommate, and it's easy to hurt his feelings."

"So, they don't like to be cuddle toys, but roommates? Got it. How many roommates do you have?"

"Don't know exactly. I think. But some. You can't have too many because guys don't understand."

"Ridiculous. Real men love cuddly toys for their girls. I think you should have all the cuddle toys you need or want."

"I...they comfort me when I'm lonely or sad."

"I get it baby. I'm going to be there now but cuddles are great when you need that extra snuggle."

Bella nodded her head and leaned into him. His gut felt like it had been kicked by the ranch's only mule. This was no time to walk down that illogical road of how much she was falling into the place he had tried to get her to before. Getting her to give into him and let go of her worries and concerns when she needed to. Even in high school, he had broad shoulders both figuratively and physically and she had fought him while holding tight.

But he'd heard her yesterday when she said she was independent. She'd been independent because there was no other way to survive but to take control of things. However, being his girl was another thing all together. She could be her own woman and give over to her man when she needed it.

When they were together before, she had never been able to do what she was doing now. Not completely. No matter how hard she had tried, and he had pushed, she was a stubborn little thing even then. And here she was, letting her baby girl out without prompting. Probably because she was hurt and disoriented that her inhibitions were removed along with some of her memory. He prayed one returned, but the other stayed gone.

When the clinic technician came to get a picture of her head, Callen started to walk in with Bella, determined she would not experience anything alone.

"Sorry, but this is something you can't be in there for. I promise to take care of her and bring her back promptly. Have a seat. We'll be back before you know it."

Bella reached for Callen's hand. He grabbed for hers. "Baby, it's okay. Just let him get a picture of your insides and he'll bring you right back. Daddy is staying right here, so you can find me when he returns you to me. Okay?"

"Yes." As soon as she had agreed, she was whisked into the scanner room and soon wheeled out again. A few moments later, Doc walked into the room.

"Bella Thompson, as I live and breathe. You are a sight for sore eyes. We've missed you."

Doc had done his residency with his father, the older Doc Marshall, so he knew most people for the majority of his life. He kept talking as he carefully examined her. He interspersed his conversation with medical questions and finally took a step back.

Bella knew some things and some things she didn't. Seemed like the people in her life and the last week or so were mostly a mystery to her, but everything else was fairly intact. Her heavy sighs announced how frustrating the whole situation was to her, but Doc didn't seem worried at all. His manner appeared to ease Bella. Callen knew it helped him not lose his control.

"How're things looking?" asked Callen when Bella didn't.

"As I suspected and hoped. You're fine, Bella, other than that knock on your head and a jostled brain. Your muscles will be achy for a few days, and the jolt you had likely tried to rearrange what the good Lord gave you. Everything is back in place, so after the shock has worn off, your memories will start returning."

"What do we need to do for her now, watch for? Why doesn't she know who people are?"

Doc put his hand up to stop the stream of questions. "Her head got a knock and a rough ride. Likely her holes in her memory are just a result of that. Let's give her a week and if she isn't better by then, bring her back and I'll re-evaluate. No restrictions after tomorrow. Bella, go slow. Don't push yourself because then it will take longer to heal. Patty will give you paperwork to go home with." Doc answered a few more questions before he turned to go.

"Why don't I remember who I am? Who anyone is?" It was as though she didn't hear him or remember what he said.

"Shock. Your brain was banged around a bit. Not sure precisely, but don't push it too hard. Being in familiar places may be the extra boost you need to start remembering." Doc looked over at Callen. "And she needs someone to watch her. I'm assuming that will be you, Callen."

"Yes. I'll take her to the ranch and let the ladies keep an eye on her when I can't."

"I'll send the aide over more often to Mrs. Thompson's house. You bring her back next week. Call tomorrow for an appointment." Doc waved as Nurse Patty came in to finish up.

"That's it for now," said Patty, who had cleaned up the cut on the back of Bella's head before giving the paperwork to Callen. "Tad dropped off your keys."

Callen smiled his thanks and turned to Bella. "Let's grab your things and go home."

"With you?"

"Yep." He produced Pinky and Ping-Pong from her bag.

The squeal she produced was subdued and cut off quickly, but it was enough to give Callen confidence that Bella would remember everything quickly. She might not remember that he had told her about the cuddle toys in her pack or about people right now, but emotions spoke to her. He could use that. It also helped to know he would be the one to take care of her. He could capitalize on the dynamic they had dabbled in because it obviously still interested her. It interested him, too. They would have that conversation soon.

Chapter 5

Back at the Ranch

It was late when Callen and Bella pulled into the entrance of Red Eagle Ranch. He'd called Stryker right after they had gotten to the clinic and told them not to come. Thankfully, they wouldn't be going to the hospital. The closest one in an emergency required a flight. Medi-flights were a way of life out here, which is why ranchers often took advanced first aid courses and everyone was respectful of their doctor. Knowing things weren't as bad as they thought didn't mean his family wasn't going to wait up for them. The front screen door was thrown open as Callen's big truck stopped in front of the large three-story house.

Callen spoke first. "Don't get out, Bella. I'll come around and help you. It can be a long first step."

"I can open my door."

"But you won't because Daddy said no."

She didn't, but the defiant look she shared with him was impressive for a woman who didn't have her full memory back. Callen hid a smile as he helped Bella down. She zinged his heart. It might have been a few years since they had spent any real time together, excluding her surprise entry back into his life yesterday, but she was still adorable when she pouted. Seamus walked out onto the porch and smiled warmly at Bella.

"We're glad to see you, Bella. I'm Seamus, Callen's brother. We've known each other a good long time and I'm relieved to hear you aren't more hurt. I've gotten your things from your vehicle, and I'll grab your things from the truck."

"Thanks. It's just her backpack," said Callen as he gathered her cuddle toys. Callen continued through the door that Stryker held open and waved Callen into the family room. "Glad it wasn't too bad Bella, and Doc could take care of things here. Avery has bedrooms fixed up. I'm assuming you are staying in the house at least tonight, Cal?"

"Yep. Until she gets her memory back."

Declan walked in. "The girls are warming up some soup and making coffee. Damn, it's cold out tonight."

Seamus walked in with Carson. "Might want to give Bella juice or herbal tea. Maybe something else besides regular coffee. Caffeine might not be the best way to go after a knock on the head," said Carson.

Kai walked in and Seamus dropped a kiss on the top of her head. "He might be right. Bella, I'm Kai. I'm with this big guy. Do you want herbal tea or juice?"

"I think I don't like herbal tea. I don't know why I feel that is true, but maybe some juice or just plain water?"

"That's right. I'd forgotten she doesn't even like iced tea. Mam was so sad she couldn't share a cup of tea with Bella, but what could she do? Bella had coffee and Mam had tea."

Kai nodded. "Okay, juice it is."

Callen settled Bella into the corner of the sectional sofa and sat next to her. "When the girls get in here, I'll introduce you. It's okay if you don't remember things or names. We are quite a brood to learn all in one go. And the likelihood is that you won't need help soon. Your memory will return and you will know us all."

Bella nodded. "I know this room. It gives me a comforting feeling."

Avery brought in the soup and juice on a tray. "Here Bella. It's extra warm, but not too hot."

"Thank you," she said. "I didn't want to put anyone out. Maybe I can go to a hotel."

The room went noticeably quiet. Callen leaned over and patted her hand resting on her thigh. "No hotel, but you're right about knowing this area. You grew up in a town not far from here and spent many summer days and weekends here. We have a room set up for you and you are always welcome to stay here."

"I remember I like to paint. Is that why I'm here? Do I still have family around here?"

"Your sister lives in Germany working for an American company. Your mom has a house in town but, honestly, it's difficult for you to live there. When you get your memory back, you'll understand, but until then, you're staying here. I'll call and get your things from the hotel."

"I'll get that taken care of tomorrow," said Stryker.

Bella opened her mouth to speak but was cut off by Callen. "And that's final. I have to keep an eye on you until you get your memory back. I promised Doc."

"Okay."

Teagan walked into the room and smiled at Bella. "Hi. I don't think we've met because I was teaching yesterday."

Renee said, "Teagan Manz, meet Bella Thompson."

"Bella? Callen's Bella? I didn't know you'd be here tonight. Are you hurt?" After a quick look around, she added, "Are you and Callen back together?"

Declan snaked his arm around her waist. "Teagan, Bella has been in an accident, and she's a little foggy. Her brain is healing from the trauma, and her memory isn't working right now. We weren't sure if she was coming back tonight or not."

Teagan looked stricken. "Oh, I didn't know." She turned her irritation and embarrassment toward Declan. She smacked his chest.

Declan's voice darkened, and his eyebrow raised pointedly. "You want to reel yourself in, baby, before someone gets a sore bottom. I didn't tell you because you weren't home yet." He turned to the group sitting on every available piece of furniture and drew her onto his lap at the end of the sectional. Teagan laid her head on his chest and kept quiet.

Stryker asked, "Is there anything special we need to do for Bella while she recovers?"

"Not really. She shouldn't push the memory recovery, but being in familiar surroundings should help cue her memories and once they start, I think they will just tumble into place. Doc feels it was a combination of the knock on her head and the shock of everything that caused her brain to shy away from some memories. She is under house arrest tomorrow so she can rest, but after that, she can do what she feels able to do without making things worse."

"That's reasonable," said Carson.

"Because I expect things to resolve in the next day or so, I'm not going through the stress of introducing everyone. But Bella, everyone here will answer any question you have and help you with anything you need. I don't expect to spend too much time away from you, but I'll have to do a little prep work for next week. I'll leave you in someone else's good hands when I do."

Bella looked a little overwhelmed and tired. So tired.

Avery patted Bella's hand. "When your memory returns, you will know everyone. But don't worry about all of that right now. You need to eat, clean up, and rest."

"Can you show me where to sleep?" she asked Avery.

"Of course, but I think Callen has that covered."

"I do. If you're ready to head up, I can help you get there and clean up some."

"But I didn't hear about what happened," said Teagan.

"I'll fill you in when we go to bed, Teague," said Declan.

"Why can't you just tell me now?" she asked with the faintest of pouts.

"Because Bella is tired and she can't participate because she doesn't remember, so I think it's kinder to do it in our room."

"On your own," grumbled Renee.

"Someone's about to start her period," replied Teagan.

Bella was shocked to hear that subject brought up in mixed company. The chuckles she heard around her told her it wasn't as out of the norm with these people as she had thought. Loose boundaries. Good to know.

"You're a woman. You can't believe that every woman is less than pleasant when they are about to start their period. That's crazy."

Teagan shook her head. "It's not when you factor in that two of us have already started. It means you have or are about to. Women in the same household and all that. But more than anything, I know you well enough and as a woman, understand intimately how it can affect us."

"What the hell is wrong with you? Have you been into the hard liquor?" Renee was red- faced.

Kai shook her head. "Okay, it's obviously gone too far."

Seamus chuckled. "Naughty, Renee. It's late, and time to put Miss Bella and the rest of you to bed. Looks as though we have overwhelmed Bella and triggered some moodiness in some of the rest of us."

Callen nodded. "More like the adventure and medicine have gotten to Bella. The rest?" He shrugged. "I can only handle one ailing girl at a time. Come on, baby."

EARLIER, WHEN SHE WAS too tired to eat, Callen kept reaching for the spoon, then stopping himself. He probably would have fed her if she hadn't been able to feed herself or given him the inclination she was willing that he do so. That thought brought a flush to her cheeks and a twinge deep down in her lower regions.

For some reason, that definitely excited her. She had called him daddy, and he had referred to himself the same way. Bella knew deep down in the depths of her soul that she wanted a man, a daddy who would put her first. Who held expectations and who praised her hard work and took her to task when she lounged through life too much. Both were hallmarks of her life. Her instincts told her Callen was her daddy.

Bella had worried she couldn't find a daddy that loved her the way she had learned she needed love. She wasn't someone who played with dolls, but she loved her cuddle. She didn't color in toddler pages but she loved intricate mosaics. She smiled. Bella was an artist, after all. Praise was a real kink for her and she needed a benevolent daddy.

Bella was under no illusions. Her life had not been easy. She was exacting sometimes and could be difficult to live with, but when she loved, she knew it would be complete devotion. She wanted that in return. She needed someone who loved her for her crazy hours of painting and her wild sense of what was proper eating. The man who loved her would find it his job to watch over Bella's physical upkeep when she was deep into a project.

This Callen might be a good fit. She tried to remember who he was to her, but nothing but a pounding head materialized. It was more than disturbing that she remembered so much about her life, but a few vital bits were elusive. No one acted as though she was a stranger, but she felt like one and yet she didn't. They all knew her and talked to her like she was an established but absent friend.

She was at a disadvantage and vulnerable. So vulnerable. And her head hurt. Not as bad as earlier, but it did. Sleep sounded so good. She desperately needed a shower, but she didn't think she could do that right now. She wanted to be taken care of. She wished she had her Daddy now.

Bits and pieces of her life began slipping into place. Callen Red Eagle. She saw smatterings of him like pictures reflected on shards of broken glass. Big enough to see parts of, but not whole enough to be able to glue back together. Time would fix that. Sleep would help. She wanted that.

"It's not safe for a shower right now, baby. I'll clean you up some and then you can shower in the morning."

"But, but..." She yawned. "Okay, Daddy."

Darn. Her rambling thoughts were coming out in her speech, and that was never good. She had no idea where that word had come from earlier in the evening, but thankfully, Callen didn't even bat an eye once when she'd used it here. She instinctively knew she was the type of Baby Girl that didn't become younger but liked her daddy to take over when she needed it. Right now, she wanted it so hard.

He proceeded to wipe down the areas where the blood had dried, but she didn't really pay attention. Her head was pounding, her stomach was rocky, and she was so damn tired. Laying her head down on the firm yet cozy pillow, she snuggled down into the bedding and drifted off to sleep to the knowledge that this man was going to watch over her and she was safe.

Chapter 6

Memories

Bella awoke to the sounds of horses neighing, dogs barking, and men's voices at a distance outside her window. She blinked, momentarily disoriented, as she took in the rustic homeness of the bedroom and sighed a strange contentment. She looked around and recognized the bedroom as Callen's. She smiled. She remembered more things. Her name, thank goodness, and a few more things. She would be fine in another day, she was sure.

Her thoughts returned to Callen. Last night, he'd given her a chaste sponge bath, for which she thought she was asleep for the majority of his efforts.

"This will be okay for now," he had said when showing her to the room last night.

Warm feelings flooded her as she thought of how well he took care of her. She wasn't quite sure why, but she would soon. Her memories were full of slowly untangling bits of her past. His words, "for now," echoed in her mind, hinting at the possibility of something more permanent in their future.

She remembered the ranch fondly, but particular memories of Callen were still vague. It felt as though they had so much more that she couldn't put her finger on. Doc has said not to force herself, so she would do her best to follow his advice, but it was so frustrating.

Bella inhaled deeply, the scent of fresh air and bacon frying filling her senses. She rose from the bed and peered out the window at the vast expanse of the ranch. The early morning sunshine bathed the land in a warm, golden glow. Winter wasn't much longer, and today was one of those beautiful false spring days that drew a person outside.

Memories flooded Bella's mind as she gazed at the familiar surroundings. She and Callen had ridden horses across the open fields, laughing together without a care in the world. The two of them sitting on the porch step late into the night, talking for hours under a canopy of stars until his father threatened to list Bella as a dependent on his taxes.

A smile touched Bella's lips, soon replaced by a furrowed brow. Those had been happier, simpler times. Painful memories began flooding in and she knew everything would come back soon. She was glad for the clearing of her mind, but she hated that the painful misunderstandings and heartbreak that eventually tore them apart was included in the unblocking of her thoughts. That was too many years ago to mourn them now. She knew she had grieved for them for too long. Could things be different now? Bella wasn't sure, but a flicker of hope burned inside her. Something told her things had been mended.

She showered and dressed quickly, carefully avoiding doing more than delicately washing her hair to avoid making her headache worse. She slipped past the kitchen carefully, determined to capture the beauty of the ranch through her art. Thankfully, Callen had grabbed her pack that held a sketchpad and pencils. Supplies in hand, she wandered toward the stables in search of inspiration. Her body was achy, but the beauty just couldn't be ignored. She'd take a pain reliever later.

Bella paused as she approached the stables, catching a glimpse of Callen brushing down one of the horses inside. He looked like he had just ridden the beautiful chestnut beast. Her breath caught at the sight of the man he'd become. His muscular frame bathed in the morning light streaming through the open doors. He looked up, meeting her gaze, and Bella's heart skipped a beat. A broad smile swept across his face, followed by a furrowed brow.

She quickly looked away, pretending to be engrossed in a sketch of the stable exterior. But it was a lie. She couldn't sketch while Callen's eyes were on her. Something told her he would remember she was instructed to lie low today and wouldn't be happy she was outside right now.

Bella let out a shaky breath, her pencil strokes becoming more erratic. Being this close to Callen brought equal parts joy and apprehension. She wanted nothing more than to run into his arms, to feel them wrapped tightly around her like they used to. But there was fear attached to that desire. And a feeling she'd recently been in his arms. She looked down and saw she'd gone from drawing just the barn and had subconsciously put Callen in the picture. She quickly opened to a new page.

"What are you doing out here, baby?"

"I'm sketching." Callen looked over at her pad and scrunched up his brow in confusion.

"Hmm, I guess I'll wait until you actually put your pencil on the paper to look."

"Rude. I'm settling in my mind what I am going to sketch. It isn't just a copy of what you see. You have to feel it. Wrap yourself in its essence before you can do any sketch or painting justice."

"Which is why I'm the rancher and you're the artist. How's your headache and memory?"

"Things are becoming clearer. I can't know how much I still don't remember, but I remember you, just not everything. I feel there are still missing bits, but I'm sure that will come."

"Do you remember us?" he asked hopefully.

"Some. Like I said, I don't remember everything. But I think I remember why we broke up, or the gist of it. I get the sense it was a long time ago, though, and yet," Bella shrugged. "I'm worried that there is a lot I don't yet recall, and it bothers me. Maybe when the last of the headache goes, I'll remember everything."

And the scars of the past that she did remember held her back from freeing her emotions. She couldn't risk having her heart broken again. She had a feeling she'd never recover from a repeat performance, but she was encouraged by the impression that she felt they were past that now. It was all so confusing and her impatience waiting for her mind to unravel things was making her even crazier.

"Care to fill in the gaps?"

Callen contemplated Bella for a moment. "I want to talk about that but I'd rather allow your memory to fill in as much as possible before we tackle that again. Right now, though, it's breakfast, and this cowboy is starving. You don't look like you've been eating properly. You're much too thin."

"I thought men liked thin." All the men she'd dated had. Huh, she remembered that.

"Not real men. They want their women to be healthy and eat when they're hungry, not limit their intake because it might add an ounce to their body weight. If you were naturally thin, that would be another story, but you have always been beautifully lush. A perfect weight. Have you lived these last years that way? Worried about gaining?"

Had she? She didn't think she had until this last boyfriend. She'd complied with plenty of things he'd said that she didn't actually believe until his words were her words. Loneliness will do that to a person. It did it to her and now she felt shame that she'd allowed him, or anyone, to influence who she became. Already being back home was challenging her ideals, and Bella wasn't sure she liked what that said about her. And there were more of her memories.

And looking at her friendly, neighborhood cowboy brought to her mind some heavy petting, recently. Mmm, regaining all her memories might be more deliciously entertaining than she had first thought. Bella was even more eager to get back to normal.

Bella's cell rang. Callen looked over her suddenly tense shoulders. Her sister was calling.

"Hello?" Callen reached over and put the phone on speaker.

"Bella? Thank God. Are you alright?"

"Hi Tracy. I'm fine. I just hit my head when the car slid off the road. Wow, news travels fast." She tried to laugh, and then Bella looked at Callen. "Yes, I think that's what happened. I hydroplaned and skidded in the rain."

He smiled and kissed the top of her head. "Makes sense," he said.

"What makes sense? Where are you, and who is that man?"

"I'm at the Red Eagle with Callen."

"What? Why the ranch? And Callen?"

"Callen came upon the scene last night. I was foggy and disoriented. I didn't know who I was or anything."

Tracy sounded stressed again. "But you had your driver's license, right?"

Callen spoke over Bella. "Hello Tracy, it's Callen. Bella didn't really remember anything right then. They didn't know who she was because she was sitting on her license and credit card in her back pocket and couldn't tell them."

"Oh. Bella, are you going to be okay?"

"Of course. It might take me another day for all of my memories to return and to feel strong enough to go back to mom's house, but I will do it and take care of things."

"But your work?"

"Tracy, I'm here. You are in Germany and can't possibly leave to come here. I'll let you know." Bella rubbed her temple.

Tracy sounded relieved. "Thanks, sis. I really said my goodbyes before I left for Germany. This job is for another year and I'm not sure I even want to come back home after this is over."

Bella sighed. Vanna's alcohol use, which started so she could cover her grief at losing her husband so early in their marriage, turned into alcoholism and its hold had never released her. Tracy said the last time she'd seen their mom, her skin was slightly yellow and the whites of her eyes, too. That had been a few months ago. Bella understood Tracy's sentiments, but she couldn't leave her mom to die alone.

"I get it. I'll keep you informed as things change."

"What about your own work?"

Callen leaned over her shoulder. "Tracy? Callen again. Bella still has a headache and body aches, and Doc says she needs someone with her for a day or two. We are keeping her here at the ranch and will support her with anything she needs to do when she's ready to do it."

Bella didn't want to tell her sister about the disaster her life had become in New York. She'd save that for a later conversation. Come to think of it, she wasn't ready to tell Callen her memory was coming back in leaps and bounds at every passing moment, either. She wanted to wait for some reason.

"It's alright. I can produce art almost anywhere."

It wasn't strictly true, but the sentiment was there. Tracy ended the call soon after, and Bella looked up to see that Callen had taken a few steps away and was leaning on the corral fence. She imagined he was giving her space to talk to her sister—after talking to her himself.

Bella looked at Callen before turning away and wondered why she felt like there was a loss she couldn't put her finger on. She did know one thing. She remembered her worry when Callen pulled out Pinky and Ping-Pong. And her relief. The crazy thing was, in her mind, she was sure he didn't care.

"Bella."

She gathered her pad and pencils as she stood to walk away.

"Bella Kaye." That firm voice triggered a chain reaction of tingles and aches in intimate places.

"Yes?" Damn him for striking in her deepest regions a yearning for the man.

"Baby girl, I can tell that you're getting your memory back." It was a statement that verified he had picked up on all the things she knew to say to Tracy. "You are going to find yourself in some deep trouble if you and I don't come to an agreement of how things stand between us and the expected behaviors associated with that agreement. You doing okay right now? Headache manageable?"

"I'm better than last night. I'm sure all my memories will come back soon. If you'd just take me to mom's house, everything will figure itself out."

"Until you are well enough, you're staying here. Doc called early this morning and said he had someone check-in a few extra times today and will again tomorrow to make sure your mom is okay."

"But she needs me."

"She is okay. You need to heal up before you can help her properly. Besides, once you're good with her care, then you have agreed to come back here and stay with me. It's only fifteen miles and you can help her whenever she needs it. I've already arranged to have the old studio cleaned up for you. You agreed to put in the best effort to make this relationship work. That includes the Daddy/baby girl dynamic."

"I know, and I want to try, but she needs me. And I'm not Little."

"No, you're my Baby Girl and that is different. You determine the parameters of play. You always have. As far as your mother is concerned, I've said it, but you might not remember, so I'll say it again. We will help you."

"Mom's health is why I'm here."

"Is it, or is it just one of the reasons you came home?"

Bella shrugged. "I can't remember."

"Oh baby, lying to Daddy will get you a hot bottom."

Bella's eyes widened, and she had to remind herself to breathe. Yes, she did remember right about last night, which brought back the memory of hearing his tone to her a long time ago, and her core twinged and tingled. Hard. She wiggled. This could fall into dangerous territory fast. Maybe is already had.

"Callen, we aren't those people any longer. We were kids. And last night, the Daddy thing was a mistake. I can't have everyone knowing private things about me. I'm not sure I'm ready to deal with some of those issues."

She hoped he dropped it because as much as calling him daddy and being called baby girl by him were the things her dreams were made of, she was not going to open that door. His brothers and their girlfriends would flip and she would lose their respect and if it got around, then there wouldn't be any way she could stay in town.

"I'm glad to know you can remember who we were then. Means you remember how it felt to be taken care of, given boundaries and that everything you did or said was important to someone. Me. We will absolutely explore that dynamic more because you loved it last night. I loved it too. By the way, where are Pinky and Ping-Pong?"

Mr. Red Eagle was playing dirty. He couldn't possibly want that, and neither did she. Right? She shook her head and a frown of sadness was followed by a soulful sigh.

"Callen, I wish we could be those carefree kids again, just for a day, but we can't. That was us playing house. It's been too long."

"Bella, if you want it as much as I do, it isn't child's play, or out of our reach, and I'm going to prove it. Breakfast, then talk. It will be alright."

Callen was pretty forceful and confident when he swept her in his arms and dropped a soul sizzling kiss on her lips before walking her inside. She wished she could find her own conviction that she knew what to do and that things would be okay. She entered the dining room with him, where Callen was respectful of her information, keeping things between them which she was grateful for. The conversation went from discussing her health, to the accident, to daily tasks and future events. But nothing about their dynamic, her cuddle companions, or anything else.

After breakfast, Bella slowly packed up her belongings in the guest room, her mind swirling with emotion. He would be back soon to talk, so she had to hurry. There was just her backpack and a small duffle bag that Callen must have pulled from the car. Her car! How was she going to get back into town and how damaged was it? She'd have to talk to Callen and find out the details, then bum a ride back into Buffalo Township. She didn't have time to take a day off to recover. No matter what her pseudo daddy wanted.

She folded her clothes meticulously, delaying the inevitable goodbye. The headache she'd had yesterday faded a little this morning, but it was back full force again. She thought back to what Callen said. She now could remember that they were trying again, but he wasn't pushing that agenda right now and she appreciated it. She just wanted a day or two without responsibilities and people who relied on her. Including herself.

Maybe what Callen had said might work, but she couldn't ever relax enough to let go around others. Well, except once upon a time with Callen. With Tracy taking the easy way out and washing her hands of the entire Vanna situation, Bella wanted him to take over even more desperately. But she couldn't do that.

Bella answered her cell. When she hung up, she sat hard on the bed.

A soft knock came at the door. "Come in," Bella said, her voice barely above a whisper.

Callen entered, his brows furrowed with concern. "I heard you on the phone again. Is everything okay with your mom?"

Bella blinked back tears, willing herself to stay composed. "It was the nurse. Mom's taken a turn for the worse. She had her admitted to the hospital for a few days, but I have to go back home today to take care of things so we can get support set up for her."

Callen crossed the room in two long strides, engulfing Bella in his strong arms. She melted against him, all her resolve to keep herself to herself crumbling away.

"I'm so sorry," he murmured into her hair. "When does she get out of the hospital?"

"I don't know. I forgot to ask."

"Let's call them back and find out. Tell them you had an accident and you aren't going to be home until tomorrow afternoon at the earliest, so they can't discharge her before the day after tomorrow. Besides, you can't drive comfortably right now and certainly not that far, so I'll take you when it's time. Until then, you can make the necessary arrangements from here."

"I don't want to drive. I can remember the hydroplaning now and I don't think I'm ready to get behind the wheel yet. I'm sure I will be able to tomorrow." Bella pulled back, looking up at him with watery eyes. "I do appreciate knowing you care. It helps. But this is something I need to do on my own, but thanks for the ride. I don't know about my car situation yet. Do you think I can drive it tomorrow?"

"Bella Kaye, listen to Daddy. You aren't doing this on your own. And before you say it, it is not an option. I know more of your memory has returned and probably most of it, so I bet you know we are trying to make us work again. Also, you were likely on that road last night because you were coming to the ranch for the night. Eventually."

"Well, yes. I was, but I had an errand to do first."

"What errand would take you out on that road at that time of evening?"

"I was there for a little while before someone found me. And before you ask, I don't know how long. I was going to meet a prospective caregiver. There are only a few around here that have free hours."

"Your car is here. Carson is going to have a look at it before turning you loose in it. I'm driving you tomorrow if you are better and your headache is gone. If not, it will be an additional day. We will go grab your mom when she is ready."

"Callen, I can do this on my own."

"Possibly. But do you want to?" Bella slowly shook her head. "You are my girl, Bella and if you don't remember what that entails, I'll remind you. It means that if I can help or any of us can help you, we do. You will help us if you can. It is the way Red Eagles do family and you are family."

"I wish it were that simple."

"Simple? Hell, baby, simple doesn't mean easy. Don't get the two confused. Being with me will be easy most of the time, but sometimes, it will challenge you. You may even wonder why you're with me, but plow through. The other side is always sweeter."

"Fine, I'll tease that out later, but the bottom line is I still have to take care of things on my own. I can't leave her to fend for herself, nor can I expect you to do more than support from a distance."

He stepped up to Bella, wrapping his hand around the back of her neck and pulled her in close. She snuggled even closer and breathed in his scent that was all warm man and pine forest in a rain shower. Earthy. It was one of the many things that drew her to this man. What was she going to do if Callen ever stepped away again? She knew she'd shrivel up. For now, she wouldn't entertain that fear and just soak him in, because the reward would be worth the chance.

Callen nodded, though his jaw was tight. "I understand. Your mom needs you and you aren't that far from the ranch, but thinking about not having you here with me is hard. It will be on most days and every night I can't wrap myself around you. So, we will compromise. The days you have some help you spend here. On the days your mom would be alone, you can be there."

He leaned down and kissed her softly, drawing out her response without demanding it. Bella moaned and he took the kiss deeper. When he released her, they were both short of breath. This man had upped his kissing game. She wondered if she could orgasm on one of his kisses. She could give it a try someday soon. She tried to tighten her core muscles in her lower region and wiggle a little rubbing on his thigh slightly without dry humping, but it wasn't enough. He kissed her temple and cheek.

"You are so naughty sometimes, baby."

Bella blushed. He seemed to read her thoughts. "Callen."

"I know, baby. It's all good. I'll work on figuring out the car situation. We have a few extra ranch vehicles. I could commandeer one if we need to."

"My mom has an older one. I don't know when she last drove it, but I'll find out if it works or I'll figure something else out."

"I'll work it out. Just let me deal with things."

Bella's fists landed on her hips in a show of defiance. "Callen, I can figure out my own transportation. Hell, if you'd stop rescuing me, I'd handle everything."

"You could, but Daddy said he'd handle the car situation and he will. You have too many other things to take care of. We'll swing by the machinery barn and see if Carson or Garret, our resident machinist, have figured things out yet. Once we know the damage and what it will take to fix it, we can go from there. If your mom's car doesn't work, I'll bring you one of the work trucks until yours is fixed. And that's one."

"Oh, you can't do that. Just let me call a tow truck. You have enough on your plate to add my life to it, too."

"And that's two. I'm throwing out options here, but right now, you need to simply say thank you."

"Thank you, but..." she shrugged in defeat. "Thank you."

"You are always welcome, sweet girl. But since I know you are still into being my baby girl, I'm going out on a limb and say it will be better for your backside if you learn to say yes, Daddy quicker. You are already on two when three is as high as this Daddy intends to go before addressing the issue."

"Callen, I'm sorry about that. I wasn't well last night and obviously not in my right mind."

"Or you were in your right mind, just less inhibited because you felt the connection we had and the daddy in me calling to the baby girl in you. Whichever it is, we'll tease it out, but I'd love to be your daddy again."

Bella knew she looked confused because she was. "You would?"

"It would be an honor."

"I'll think about it."

"You do that, but until you tell me no, you are my Baby Bella. Have you changed your safe word?"

"Zucchini? No. Do you know you are the only one who has ever asked me? Even when we played around with things, no one ever asked. I never needed to use it," she shrugged, "but it would have been nice to be asked."

"It's all about safety between us. Zucchini it is. Use it if you need it, but it won't stop any punishment. It just might change the way you receive it or the mode."

"I'll think about it."

"You do that, baby. You do that. Now, remember you are going nowhere until your mom is released. We'll call and get you set up for picking up your mom and we'll check on your car. Then you are taking a nap."

"No, I've got more things to do."

"I'm thinking you are going to want a nap to build your energy for tonight. Unless you are too achy or something. Yeah, we had better see how you are tonight before we make any plans."

"What? No, I mean, I'm going to be fine. I'll take a nap for insurance. It'll be fine. Honest."

"I hope so."

He dropped another gold medal kiss before grabbing her hand and dragging her along behind him toward the barns, a grin engulfing his whole face. Being with Callen would be exciting and life changing. She wanted to be ready for it. For him. The stakes were never higher and her worry about everything didn't seem as overwhelming as it had been before she decided to let Callen be who he wanted to be with her. Damn. He was everything she wanted in a man. If she could hold on to him, it would be worth it.

Chapter 7

New Normal

It was two more days before Bella was ready to go and pick up her mother from the hospital, located a couple of hours from the ranch. It was a smooth discharge and Vanna Thompson, who had been restless in the hospital, slept peacefully after seeing Bella and being assured she was going home.

Callen stood outside after helping to settle Vanna in her favorite recliner. "I guess this is goodbye, for now at least," she said.

Callen tilted her chin up. "It's not goodbye. More like see you later. I'm thinking of stopping by tomorrow."

She shook her head. "You're busy and coming here is not 'stopping by,' it's making a special trip. I have things to do, too. Maybe we can shoot for the weekend?"

"Now I'm thinking I need to make sure I come tomorrow."

She smiled at him. "No, mom's memory isn't that great anymore, and she gets anxious around people she doesn't think she knows. She still knows me, but the doctor has said it is likely that will come to an end any time now."

"Okay, but Bella, if I even get a hint that you need help, I'm coming. And if you need help and you keep it to yourself, that will get you a session over my knee, or the nearest table, sofa back, counter ..."

Bella laughed. "Okay, I get it. You won't be happy."

"And neither will you."

He drew her close once more, his lips finding hers in a kiss filled with longing. He made love to her mouth like she wanted him to make love to her entire body. Callen was clear that he had held off claiming her because he didn't want to hurt her. She loved that about him, but hated it, too.

He was meticulous about starting his kisses off softly, then becoming intense with his tongue invading every part of her mouth before softening again. He had ravaged her lips before the accident and she longed for that again.

"When the time comes, believe me when I promise to take you completely."

His tongue was magic, and his skill thrilled and intimidated her. He could excite her body like none other, but that brought on another fear. Did he expect she was equally experienced and confident with her lovemaking? Because she certainly was not. Her experience wasn't absent, but minimal.

She felt plundered and claimed by the time they came up for air. It settled something inside that she hadn't been able to do with her own reasoning. He wanted her, all of her, and that was something she had only experienced with Callen.

Everyone in her life, thus far, had an agenda that she was part of, but once that task or event was over, they moved on. She got it, but sometimes it would be nice to be wanted for who you were, not what you could bring to the table. Callen was that person for her. He always had been. She didn't have to pay her admission fee to be part of him. He got her.

Callen wanted her for more than sex, or what she could do for him, or who she could introduce him to. Artists were the worst, in her opinion. It was easy for them to say the right words because those were the same words they desperately wanted to hear from others. The more needy the artist, the better his act. But not Callen.

She didn't bring anything to the exchange but herself, and it was enough for him. She had always been insecure about her value to others, that she was not quite enough, so she worked extra hard in everything: class projects, grades, sketching, artistic works, friendship, lovers and relationships. But Callen wouldn't accept that thinking. He never had. In high school, he spent long hours showing and telling her she was strong and intelligent. Important.

Even if people around them seemed to be hesitant about their relationship, suspicious or jealous of her, Callen would not allow that thinking between them. He was so good for her in countless ways. Bella fought the urge to be more for him. Rejecting his help was one of those ways she tried to be less needy. He wasn't allowing that, either. She would have to learn how to be vulnerable with him. A hard ask.

"What has you in your head when I've been working hard to knock your socks off?" teased Callen.

"Why, looking for my socks, of course." Bella smiled as Callen squinted his eyes while he tried to figure out what her game was. It was nice to know she could keep him guessing while she figured out the game on her end. "Sometimes I'm intimidated by you," she risked saying.

"Baby, I have been told I have a large personality. But I promise, you are at the core of my everything. I want you so much, there are times I have to find something to take my mind off of you."

"And that scares me. It puts so much pressure on me to meet your needs that I worry you will find me wanting somehow."

"Don't allow me to do that to you. Push back. Because everything I do, now that you are a part of me, is with you in mind."

"Good to know I have untapped power. It will come in handy later."

Bella memorized the feel of his arms around her, the scent of his skin, the taste of his kiss. Then, with a heavy heart, she pulled away and walked him to the door. Once again, it seemed like the wrong time for them. They had waited this long; she hoped with all her being that he could wait a little longer.

Bella settled into a routine at her mother's house that she kept telling herself was temporary. She was waiting on either an assisted home placement or a more consistent worker to take care of her mom. In the meantime, she continued attending to Vanna's needs while also trying to find a sense of normalcy. Art was out of the question right now, and it made her antsy.

The nostalgia of being back home mingled with a persistent sadness over her mom's declining health and the revived memories of the loss of her carefree childhood years too early challenge Bella. Anger would try to rear its ugly head, then she would remind herself that her mother had lost her whole life to grief. She would typically reach for a paintbrush but contented herself with pen, pencil and paper.

It was too late for regrets or going back. Bella had to be able to sleep at night and even though her mother's choices were devastating to Bella as a child and young adult, her mother was her mother. Vanna didn't drink now. In the last year, Doc had scaled her back until she didn't require any alcohol, however she was just a shell of the woman she was early in Bella's life. Bella and Vanna had a few decent conversations, but the many lost opportunities in years gone by were just that—lost.

Callen swung by and took Bella to her follow up with Doc forcing her to go.

"I don't have to go, Callen. I'm fine. Besides, I've been several times already with mom."

"No ma'am. Doc deals with your mom's issues the other times you are in there. This is the time he pays attention to only you. Besides, I need to get a test to show I'm clean and so do you. Then, I want to go skin to skin if you're all in. I don't want anything separating us. Not latex, not people, not insecurities, nothing between you and me."

Bella rolled her eyes but didn't let him see her. Sure, she knew it could be interpreted as disrespectful, but it was automatic sometimes. She would try to change that habit, but not today. Since she seemed to have recovered from the accident, Doc was satisfied. The screening tests were completed, so Callen was extra pleased.

"Now the birth control conversation, Miss Bella."

"The what? Um, Doc, I don't think I need the birds and bees talk. That ship has sailed." Bella said with a laugh.

"Alright, young lady, that's enough of that. What I meant was, what are you using?"

"Oh. Well, until now, barrier protection and off and on birth control pills. Oh, right, that won't work now. Okay, so I guess I'll need a prescription for the pill but to be honest, I'm not always good at remembering. I get caught up in my work and that puts paid to remembering anything else."

Doc got on his computer and began typing. "These are to be taken religiously."

"I'm not a teenager, Doc. I know how to take them. I'm just being honest."

Doc stopped typing and spun back to face Bella. "Then what about and implant or injection every 3 months?"

"This is fine. I'll try to remember."

"Right. Just want to make sure you will. There are these other methods."

"No. I don't want any of the other methods, so this will be fine."

"Callen, this okay with you too?"

She loved his response. "This is all about Bella. I just want her protected. Her chosen method is all her."

"I expect you to ask Bella if she has been consistent and Bella you be honest. Callen will glove up if it keeps you two from coming up pregnant before you are ready."

"Yes sir. I absolutely want all of this on Bella's terms."

Doc turned back and finished typing on his computer and pushed back on the roller stool. "Okay, then. The script is on its way to the druggist. You're done here."

Bella was a little angry that she had to meet both men's expectations, but only a little. Callen had responded the way she wanted him to, but it was one of those areas that she wanted them to agree. Knowing he cared for and respected her, and what she wanted, made her smile. He had indeed grown up. Whether he knew it or not, it was something that said she mattered to him.

Several days later, Bella had missed her visit to the ranch because her mom was having a bad day. The new caretaker was coming Monday morning and would stay all week until Friday dinner. Bella agreed to cover Friday through Monday morning when she was relieved. It was the best solution and Bella was relieved. She still had the rest of this week to finish out, though.

She was preparing dinner, cleaning house, keeping an eye on her mom and more, instead of spending time with Callen and the rest at the ranch. Bella was feeling put out that her plans were blocked, but she was trying to get over it. Callen called when he could, but often his days were long and it wasn't until she was ready for bed before he called her. She hadn't painted this week and only sketched, which put her in a sour mood as well. She missed what she now craved. Callen.

The doorbell rang. She opened it to find the object of her thoughts standing there, a bouquet of wildflowers in hand. She had called him early and left a message, telling him her day's plan had changed. Instead of getting Friday off, she would have to stay to orient the new caretaker.

"Callen!" she exclaimed. "What are you doing here?"

"Is that any way to welcome your man?" he asked with mock dismay. When she didn't answer, his demeanor changed. "I had to see you," he said with rough with emotion. "I missed you too damn much. It was busy today, so this is the earliest I could get here."

Bella's eyes welled up as she took the flowers. No one had ever romanced her the way Callen did. Yeah, it was only just over fifteen miles, but workloads made it seem so much further. She'd turned away Kai's offer of help, who was already busy helping with the breeding. Seamus had him a true cowgirl. Avery had offered to come over an hour later, and she turned her down too. This was her job, not theirs.

"Thank you," she whispered. "Come in. I thought you were busy with breeding."

"I am. And we have another Duder group coming in at the end of the week to start helping us move the cattle out further, but I took this opportunity to sneak away. And because you have turned down offers of help, so I decided I needed to show up and see for myself how you were doing."

"Duder. I don't really think that is a word."

He shrugged as he took her into his arms. "What else do you call a person who comes to a dude ranch to do the dude ranch thing? A Duder works."

"Um, you could call them guests."

"Nah, since we have the lodge now, it doesn't work as well. Now stop talking and let me kiss my girl."

They sat at the kitchen table, the scent of home-cooked food and flowers filling the air.

"How've you been holding up?" Callen asked gently, taking her hand in his.

Bella sighed. "Some days are harder than others, like today. Sorry I couldn't come over. It was just too much for mom to be alone. And you sicced your brother's girlfriends on me."

"Nope. All their own idea but I hear you turned them down. What did we say about family taking care of family?"

"They had things they were doing."

"They did, but Kai had discussed things with Seamus and he agreed she should come and be with you today. Then Avery called when she heard you turned down Kai. She was hoping some familiarity would go further, but you shut her down too. Baby, you have to let them in."

"It's hard. And even though we talk on the phone most days, having you here with me helps more than you know. When I'm away from everyone, from you, it's easier to draw into myself and convince myself it's just me."

Callen rubbed his thumb over her knuckles. "I'm here for you, always. I'm sorry it's such a busy time of year on the ranch, but soon things will settle down. We'll get through this together. I have that group next week, but do you want the girls to come over and keep you company?"

"Oh, no. I wouldn't ask them to do that."

"You aren't. They asked me to make the offer. I'd take them up on it. They would each spend a couple of hours with you for relief and company."

"Well, then, I wouldn't turn them away if someone wants to visit. I think I have someone for the week days."

"That's great. What if we brought your mom to stay at the ranch on the weekends? Would that help?"

"I wish, but no. She has trouble with her memory and now that things are more of a challenge, I need to have her in town so extra help can be here. It will be fine once I get the work week off."

"Okay, then I'll come to you on the nights I can, and the girls will put coming into town on a rotation basis. You will come to us on a schedule, too."

Bella sighed. "Another set of schedules? I'm not sure I can do more. I've got doctors, medicine, physical and occupational therapies, nurse schedule, caregiver schedule, bathing. Another one is not in my bandwidth."

He dropped a kiss on her lips and headed toward her table. "No problem, because I can do the schedule. I just need your existing schedules and calendar to recreate a new one."

"Callen, no. I'll figure it out."

"Bella, Daddy said he would do it. What is your answer supposed to be?"

"Callen."

"Baby, I'd change your direction right now if you intend on sitting in that chair for dinner." His voice and his chastisement were going to send her into an embarrassing orgasm. Why she pushed, she would never know.

"I'm too tired and too busy to play."

"That is when it works the best. Give over, baby. Let me do this scheduling and tell Daddy yes, before it's too late to save your backside."

"I don't want you doing my responsibilities."

"I don't think I'm getting through to you. Lean over the table, baby."

"Callen, playing can't be part of my life right now. You... Ow! Cal—Ow!"

"You need to let go. Relax. The world won't end if you give over to me for a bit."

His hand landed on her pert butt. "Okay, okay."

"Too late. You need this, and I always try to give you what you need. Nice you have a dress on. No dropping your pants for me." He pushed her to lay over the table. "I just lift this skirt."

His hand came crashing down on Bella's backside. Several heavy swats, then a few not as hard. Callen continued covering her butt with swats without a word.

"I'm not crying Callen."

He landed a hard two slaps on her bottom. "Daddy." His hand came crashing down again. "Let go baby. You need this."

The slaps on her backside were fast and furious. A real spanking, and Bella melted into it. Her words came out in a rush. "Daddy, I'm sorry. Really, I get it. Stop."

"Are you saying zucchini, baby?" he paused and asked.

Her heavy breathing made words difficult. Finally, she pushed out a sigh. "No, Daddy."

He leaned down and kissed her neck. His whispered response next to her cheek brought a strong shiver of anticipation and arousal. "Thank you for being honest. Just a few more."

She squealed as the next rush of swats painted her ass scalding, and she expected a glowing red. "I'm sorry, Daddy. Really, *really* sorry."

The spanking ended, and Callen leaned over her to kiss her glistening neck. "Are you wet after your spanking, baby?"

"What? No. of course not." His hand landed sharply on her tenderized cheeks, causing her to rise up on her toes. "Yes, yes, I am."

"Yes, you are, and do you know why? It's because I know my baby and she loves being her daddy's good little girl. Now take care of your mom and then we can sit and have dinner ourselves while we work on this schedule together."

"You can't think to leave me like this."

"Oh, but I do. It might help you remember I don't play around when it concerns my girl. I say what I mean and I expect you to do the same."

"You mean, so long as I agree with what you say."

"Not at all. Just be respectful and careful about how you present your opinion and objections. Everything you do and say is important to me. Do you doubt that?"

Bella walked into his arms. "No. I know you're looking out for me."

After feeding Vanna her meal which consisted of soft foods easy to eat and helping her to set up a movie to watch in bed that she rarely paid attention to these days, they left her to eat their dinner. Callen had brought dessert, fudge brownies, and ice cream. One of Bella's favorites.

"So, I can publicly claim you as mine in case anyone has an idea to come sniffing around?"

Bella laughed. "Silly man, I don't have anyone that even remembers me. Mom's mail person is even different."

"Just the same, are you giving me permission to share about us? You're mine, so whether we make it official now or in a few days from now, the facts are the facts. You. Are. Mine."

Bella could feel the heat in her face. "Marking your territory, huh?" She smiled, then grew serious. "You're sure? I can't do that all in game again and find out you don't trust me or believe me or—"

He covered her hand with his big, warm ones. "I'm in it for the long haul. Forever. I've always known I messed up when I let you leave, but I promise I'm a better man now than my eighteen-year-old self, and letting you go would devastate me."

She smiled and put her other hand on top of his and squeezed. "I know you are. I wanted this too, for so long, but I pushed the possibility out of my mind because it was too much to hope for, so don't break my heart, Callen. Please."

"I promise to take care of you and handle you with kid gloves. Except when I'm ravaging you." He wiggled his eyebrows in anticipation. "Or spanking your hot as hell ass."

"You are not doing that. You snuck today in when I was tired and vulnerable."

"Hide and watch me. Defy me when I am looking out for you to keep you safe, happy and healthy and I will rain all over your parade again. I mean it when I say I'm taking care of you."

Bella was happy that Callen seemed to be her best ally, but there was a background question that highlighted her fears, even though she said out loud that this was real. The question popped into her mind at the worst times. *For how long*? He was interested, attentive, but for how long?

Chapter 8

Struggles

In the following weeks, Callen and the other family members visited whenever any of them came to town or thought they should check-in on Bella. She came to the ranch Monday afternoon to Wednesday and checked in on her mom and the caregiver, returning to the ranch to stay until Friday afternoon when she went to stay the weekend with Vanna.

Callen was everything he promised and more. Bella was afraid it wouldn't last and no matter how hard she tried to correct her thinking, it kept coming back to his past behavior. With each shared moment, their bond grew stronger, helping Bella believe in them a little more each day.

Though caring for her mother took priority, Bella cherished the stolen moments she shared with Callen. A tender embrace in the hallway as they passed when he was working on a leaking bathroom fixture at Vanna's house, or bringing dinner in from the main house so Bella didn't have to cook at his place. Fingers intertwined at the dinner table or a long, passionate kiss in the moonlit garden. As their love grew stronger, Vanna grew more confused and weaker by the day.

With each touch, their physical connection reignited. Every touch of his hand or kiss on her neck from behind, every caress, rekindled the desire that had always simmered between them. And Callen wasn't shy about displays of affection. He was open and generous with his smiles, touches, and kisses. Bella savored these intimate encounters, brief respites from the strain of illness and obligation.

These stolen bits of passion would be just enough to keep her need at a slow simmer while releasing the worst of the sexual pressure to help her get through another day. Callen seemed to be in the same boat, and that was nice. No one liked to suffer alone. On the nights Callen was able to make it into the little town, she forgot the world in his arms. Their passion provided an escape, however fleeting. When skin to skin, they forget their barriers and frustrations, if only for a moment.

"I never stopped loving you," Callen whispered, his body entwined with hers. "Thoughts of you consume my mind and body." He showed her the proof of his statement, bringing her hand to his erection. Bella rubbed him until he stopped her. "I'm going to embarrass myself if you keep this up."

She smiled sadly. Gazing steadily into his eyes, she said, "I feel the same way, but things are different. Maybe too different. Too complicated."

"Why do you think that?"

She cocked her head. "The question is, why don't you?"

Callen leaned back on the sofa and played with her hair, curling the soft strands around his finger. "I am choosing to see this as our second chance, and if I throw roadblocks like negative or disbelieving thoughts and doubts in the mix, I'm sabotaging things. I don't want to do that."

"I see it as acknowledging that I don't feel like I did in high school. My understanding of the world is vastly different and honestly, I'm more jaded and more understanding. I want you now, not for who you are with me and the family I could gain with you, which is still true to some extent but I want you because I feel good when I'm with you. I'm an artist that is gaining in recognition and I make my own money. But I still choose to try with you because of who we are together."

"And I agree. I'm missing something when you aren't close. I hate you aren't safe on the ranch every day of the week. But I tell myself it won't be forever. We will figure this thing out."

"On the one hand, I want to spend every possible moment providing care and comfort in Vanna's last days. On the other hand, I'm desperate to be with you, rebuilding what we lost. Creating new art."

"I know, but patience is a virtue and it's better to do what you feel you should, so you have no regrets. Doc has begun to prepare you for the end. Just do what you feel is right."

"I know you're right." But it was hard.

When she couldn't keep things together and she lost control, it usually ended with Callen showing up at her door. He would remind her of a few home truths. Today, Callen gave her a look that expressed his irritation at her words.

"I know this is difficult for both of us, but you do not get to send me the kind of text you sent me today."

"You didn't even respond."

"For good reason. This is the third such messages you have sent me in a weekend and that is all I'm going to put up with. You can be sad, angry, frustrated all you want, and you can call me and use those words and some like them, but when you message me and use the words you used today, there are going to be consequences."

"Okay, so you've said what you meant to say. Go home, Callen. I'm going to bed."

Callen stared at Bella for a moment before speaking. "Is the aide coming tomorrow morning?"

"Yes."

"Is your mom asleep?"

"Yes."

He took a step closer and pulled her even closer. His lips descended and with slow deliberation, he took her breath away. His tongue pressed insistently against her lips as Bella opened to him. The kiss became all-consuming. Her hands lifted to his hair, and he held her close, his right hand sliding under her hair and fisting. With a tug, he left her mouth and kissed down her exposed neck, sending chills tingling through to her core. He wasn't playing fair, and she hoped to God he didn't stop.

Her tears splashed on his face. "Baby, what's wrong?"

"Between you working, my art, coming here... I just...I miss you so much and I'm tired. I want what we could be and I'm afraid you will get tired of waiting."

"Baby, I've waited so long, I can wait longer. I'm going to be honest; I don't want to miss another moment with you, either. I'm happy to stay here at night, it if will help."

"I would love that, but you can't. You have the Duders to work with."

"Nope. This week I'm pawning them off to Carter, or Seamus, or Jacob or whoever the hell will take them. This week I'm with you. All day, every day."

"Really?"

"Yep."

"But you have responsibilities."

"I do. And this week it's you. You're right. We need more undisturbed time and we are taking it."

"I did get a call that there is a bed in a skilled nursing home attached to one of the hospitals that she qualifies for and I accepted for her. Mom didn't care. She said she liked the last place she was in, meaning the hospital."

"Is that going to work for you?"

"If mom is happy, then I'm happy. So, yes."

"Okay, when are we bringing her in?"

"Callen, you don't have to do that. I take her tomorrow afternoon."

"Perfect. I happen to be free since I'm taking the week off. Besides, Jacob hasn't played cowboy in a while. He's rusty and time he brushed up on his skills. I'll go grab my change of clothes from the truck."

"My boy scout."

Callen laughed. "More like your Red Eagle. Go to the bathroom and let me make a couple of calls. I'll hop in the shower after you. Then I want you in the middle of the bed, spread for your Red Eagle. I'll do the rest." When she hesitated, he continued. "If you are finding it difficult to follow Daddy's orders, your menagerie of cuddle toys will be the audience when I roast your bared backside and then you will find yourself laid out, spread eagle, for your Daddy. What will it be?"

"I'm going."

"Daddy."

"Yes, I'm going Daddy."

"Daddy's good girl." Bella smiled as she headed to the bathroom. The shiver of arousal at his words warmed her. She didn't even become irritated at herself when she preened in his praise. She was learning that praise could be a kink.

Callen stopped in the doorway of the bedroom as he exited the bathroom. The sight of Bella in the middle of the bed was something he would never take for granted. Her smooth tanned skin was warming his belly. Her body was so mouthwateringly tempting that Callen wasn't sure he could hold himself back long enough to make this good for his girl before he shot his load. Just watching her breath speed up for him, her eyes sharing his longing, her body arching toward him. It was so much.

Callen slid his body alongside hers on the bed and she stiffened slightly. He leaned over her so his lips kissed her temple, cheek, her ear. "Give over to me, Bella. Let me take care of you."

He smiled as his whispered words had the desired effect. Bella lifted her eyes to his and raised to lick his lips. "Yes, sir."

He turned into her mouth and consumed her lips, plundering her inner warmth as he took what he needed from her. Bella's hands slid down his arms to his hands, intertwining her fingers with him. He tightened the hold as he kissed down to her breasts, licking, nipping and sucking her nipples in his eager mouth. Her little cries of surprise and wantonness were making it hard for Callen to take his time.

He raised to cover her, his mouth descending on hers again in a sigh of possession. Bella was all he had ever wanted. Even while she was gone those years, he never found a woman that could compare to the teenage Bella, until now. Today, the adult Bella, the womanly Bella was more than enough for him. Forever. She was it for him.

His tongue made one final sweep and tangle with hers before he withdrew his mouth just enough to drag his tongue down her throat, pausing to kiss and suck gently. He continued his loving assault on her skin until he again landed on her eager breasts. Taking first one and then the other reddened, rigid tipped globes in his hand as he bathed her nipples with his tongue, nipping at them when she raised to meet him, to push her breast into his mouth.

"Naughty, baby girl. My pace." He held her breast with its rosy nipple to his lips and brought a portion of it into his mouth to add to the suction as she moaned and writhed beneath him. He did the same to her other globe and admired the perky tits and the way they presented so deeply pink and yearning for more.

"Please Daddy, I need more."

"Do you, now? More as in this?" His fingers tweaked her nipples. "Or this?" He kissed her belly, putting his tongue in her adorable belly button. She raised up. "Uh-uh. Lay still or Daddy stops."

"Daddy, Daddy, please." Bella immediately stopped, but then she whined, and that brought a smile to his face.

"So damned adorable. Daddy is in charge, baby. You are going to get what you need. I promise. Have you been careful to take your pill every day, sweetheart?"

"Yes."

"Good girl. Then your man is going to help you feel so good."

His hand slid down her soft belly, between her lower lips, and into her sweet, wet channel. He played with her clit for a moment before moving back to her opening. He smiled as she whimpered her dissatisfaction with his choice of delivery.

"Too slow." Bella wiggled and tried to put his hand where she wanted it.

His hand left her sexy bits, bringing them down in an arousal wet smack on her inner thigh. She screeched. "I said my pace, my choice, and you are not being a good girl. Do you need a reminder spanking, little girl?"

Bella's voice was irritated when she replied. "No, but I do need you to make me come. And I need you inside of me. Patience is not a virtue in all areas of life."

Callen laughed. "Understood baby. Now roll over so I can spank this beautiful ass for trying to control the play, and then I will give you what you want."

Bella rolled without hesitation and the spanking he gave was pure sexy foreplay. His fingers touched her clit as he spanked her bottom, her thigh, her puffy lower lips. It hurt so damn good that her orgasm was upon her before she could respond and tell him. He kept spanking her glistening bits and clamped down on her pelvis as she bucked against him, almost making him come as he watched her. God, he loved this woman. But she was definitely naughty.

Pulling her up on her knees, he slid his naked cock into her drenched chamber. It felt like home. A warm, inviting, comforting, excitement-filled adventure with the woman he couldn't envision loving more. His parents told him that would only grow and intensify, but damn if he could imagine that. She was his, and he was the luckiest man alive.

Chapter 9

Nothing is Simple

Bella's fingers danced across the phone keypad with a sense of urgency, her heart torn between concern for her ailing mother, the call of responsibilities that awaited her in her career and Callen. Some of those concerns included the bigger decisions about where she wanted to go from here and building a life with Callen at the ranch. She wasn't sure she could do it all, but she was going to try.

Callen watched her from the kitchen for a moment before walking over and kissing her neck. "Are you okay, baby?"

Bella rolled her eyes. "I've been relegated to the holding music of death."

"Do you need your daddy?" He spoke low and quiet and moved his lips further down the line of her throat, trailing little kisses as he went.

"Yes, I'd love to hand this off, but you can't do this because I have to."

"I can give you a little play after that if you want?" He started trailing kisses on the other side of her neck.

"Cal, stop," she whispered in an irritated voice that didn't fool Callen. "That tickles."

"Is that what you call me?" he asked brusquely.

"Honey, I can't play right now. I have responsibilities."

"Look at me, baby girl."

95

Bella turned to stare into the dark pools of bottomless blue eyes shining with his love and chastisement. Her belly clinched and the telltale tingles in her nether regions were making her wiggle. He grinned. The bastard. He knew exactly what he was doing to her. She licked her lips and heard him groan. Fair play and all that.

"When you've done with what you have to do, I want you to text me and then strip naked and wait for me on the bed."

She frowned and shook her head, holding her hand up to stop his words. After another connection and a few more rings, a warm, professional voice on the other end greeted her. Bella turned away from Callen to speak and had to pause her sentence when a big rancher hand smacked her backside as the owner of that hand left the room.

"Good morning, Nurse Anders speaking."

"Hel-hello, this is Bella Grego—Thompson," she began, her voice steady despite Callen's swat, the name stumble and the storm of emotions brewing inside her, not betraying her. "I'm calling to arrange care for my mother. She has been discharged from the hospital, but we don't want her returning. The hospital social worker suggested I try to arrange for a return to her care facility or in home care by someone who can be there when I can't."

"Of course, Ms. Thompson. Her name?"

"Vanna Thompson."

"Oh, yes. I have her referral from the doctor right here and we will make sure your mother receives the best care possible. Our nurses are highly skilled and compassionate. Let me get you in contact with a home health aide that will be a companion helper for your mom. I understand she needs twenty-four-hour care, so given your rural location, going back to her facility will be necessary but we will come alongside her until she doesn't need us any longer. And luckily, we have a bed for her."

"Thank you," Bella said, relief washing over her as the nurse detailed the arrangements. The conversation ended with a promise—a lifeline to services and some daily care that allowed Bella to breathe easier knowing her mother would not be alone. It would allow Bella to return to painting and time with Callen without guilt.

With her mother's care settled, Bella stepped out of Callen's office at the other end of the common ranching complex into the sweeping expanse of the property, the earthy scent of freshly mowed hay mingling with the crisp air. She made her way toward the main house where Callen's family gathered, the sounds of laughter and clinking dishes spilling out from the open windows.

She couldn't believe how happy she was. It was almost an overwhelming feeling when she was with Callen and now his family. She missed this for so long that it felt like a pipe dream instead of her life. She wanted to paint so badly her whole body ached for the need. Callen greeted her at the door with a nod, his tall frame filling the entryway. His eyes, mirroring the Mediterranean's own deep blues, held a softness she knew was reserved just for her.

"Come on, baby. Your trip to the bedroom to pay for your naughtiness will have to wait. I was coming to drag you from the office because we're just about to start lunch," he said, guiding her back inside with a gentle touch to the small of her back.

He leaned in close and kissed under her ear. It tickled. She pulled her shoulder up to block his access and giggled. "Daddy loves it when you giggle. You only do it when you're happy."

She turned to look him in the face. "I love you so much it hurts. It's scary."

His kiss was gently confident. "I know, but life is scary sometimes. We will always tackle things together."

"Promise?"

"Promise."

The dining room was alive with the vibrant energy of Callen's siblings and their fiancées. They welcomed her with smiles and a space at the table, treating her as one of their own. Plates piled high with hearty fare passed from hand to hand as conversations ebbed and flowed.

"Did you know our ancestors lived on this land for generations?" Declan asked, passing Bella a dish of steaming vegetables.

"I did. How far is your tribe from here?" Bella queried, scooping the food onto her plate as she settled into the rich tapestry of stories being woven around her. She loved hearing these from Callen's family because it fueled her imagination, which flowed from her fingers into art.

"A little bit away," said Renee.

"I try to envision what it was like all through the ages as I paint or sketch. Research and experiencing it now sparks my imagination."

"Perhaps that's why your art captures the essence of the landscape and this ranch so vividly," Callen added, pride evident in his voice, "because you are part of this place as much as any of us."

"My family has lived here for generations. Not as long as your family has, but French Canadian, Irish and British settlers were part of my ancestors. They aren't as exciting as your history but I'm content to know about them. This land has always felt a part of me." Bella replied, her cheeks coloring slightly at the compliment. But she knew it was more than heritage—it was love, for the land, for her art, and for the alpha male cowboy who had become her protector, her challenge, and her muse.

Stryker made a noise. "Don't let Mam hear you say that. She'll give you an Irish history lesson for days." The room burst into laughter.

Seamus smiled warmly. "Mam said she was so excited to see you again on the last video call. Besides, there will be so much going on when they first arrive. I think you'll be safe enough from any chiding for a few weeks, anyway."

Callen nodded. "Yep, because it will be the children that will be getting the third degree first. She'll focus on the imports after that." He grinned and looked at the room full of girlfriends and fiancées.

"But Jacob here," said Declan, "is going to be in the hot seat first. He and Sage already got married."

Stryker grinned. "Without Mam and Até. Thanks for making the rest of us look like angel children."

"Ah, but I'm a cousin."

Renee laughed. "Tell Mam that and see what you get as her answer. If I were you, Jake, my boy, I'd come clean, apologize and think of a good replacement, like a reception at the ranch. Otherwise, Mam will be saying, 'What must have gotten into ya mind, boy? Did you lose all the sense the good Lord gave ya?'"

Jacob looked at Sage and she shrugged, then grinned. "I could do with a reception. I'll set it up for Mam to start thinking about it and we will be well on our way back into her good graces before she comes home. But you owe me."

"Me?" asked Jacob.

"Yep, because Mam has always wanted more girls and we," she waved her hand between the other women at the table, "are the more. You boys are a dime a dozen in this family."

"And?" encouraged Jacob.

"And therefore, she will be happy with my offering of making it up to her, but if you offer it and work on it, it might not be enough. Easier to forgive you if she knows I accept my new daughter's status and give her due respect. See, you forget that I know your mother."

Bella nodded. "And I don't know about the rest of you, but Até is gentler with girls, or he used to be with me. He always required much less of me when it came to ranch work."

Renee nodded. "Yes but when you wanted to work further out on the ranch, it was sometimes a pretty hard sell."

Avery said, "That's good to know. I don't think I'll be able to do much outdoor ranch work when they get home. I'll be showing by then."

The room got very quiet then burst into questions and congratulations. Everyone was talking at once. Carson broke in with, "If you have told us, that means you have already told the grandparents, right?"

Stryker looked horrified. "You bet your ass we already told them. I know where the line is in this family and keeping Mam out of something like this is a suicide move."

Bella loved listening to the room talk and laugh. Teagan and Kai were quieter than usual, and Bella would try to snag them to explain before she went back with Callen to his cabin. While some of it was true, their soon-to-be-in-laws would be their best allies and would love them completely, their men would never allow anyone to be anything but kind to them. That was the Red Eagle way.

The sun shone brightly through the window as Bella wiped the remnants of cerulean blue from her fingers. She slowly stepped away from the canvas that had consumed her morning, observing it with a critical eye. The sun was already high in the sky, casting a golden glow over the sprawling land that stretched out beyond the windows of the designated studio space in one of the ranch's outbuildings. Her fingers weren't as cold as they might have been because Callen had rigged a small heater in the section Bella occupied.

She could hear the distant sound of horses, their hooves pounding against the ground in a rhythmic beat that called to her restless spirit. She had always loved horses and the companionship and bonding were unique to the stately equids. Now she could ride them whenever they were not scheduled for a guest and the freedom was exhilarating.

"Come on, Bella," Callen's deep voice rolled toward her from the doorway, his silhouette framed by the sunlight. "Let the paint dry. The last Duders have checked out and are on their way home. Seamus doesn't need me to help with the last of the stabling before the storm tonight, so we have some free time that I'm not going to waste. With you painting again and me dealing with ranching duties, I know we haven't had as much time since your mom went into the assisted living. You will be going back tomorrow to see her."

"You won't be able to go with me?"

"I can't this time, honey. Do you want me to send someone else with you? In fact, I should have thought of that sooner. Let me see who I can grab."

"No. I can do it alone. I'll just miss you."

"I'll miss you more, but you shouldn't go alone."

"Callen, I can do it."

He watched her for a few moments and then nodded. "We can try it this time and see how things go."

"They will go fine. Now show me where you want to go this afternoon."

With a last glance at her work, Bella allowed herself to be drawn away, swapping the scent of oil paints for the earthier aroma of leather and hay as they made their way to the stables. Her boots crunched on the gravel path, and she felt the subtle vibrations of the earth beneath her feet. Here, she was part of a greater existence. It was something she tried to share in her art.

The stable doors swung open, and the rich smell of horse and saddle soap mingled in the air, laced with the scent of manure. Callen led a chestnut mare towards her, its coat gleaming in the daylight, and she was already tacked up.

"Smells like the stalls haven't been mucked out," said Callen. "After this storm, we should be able to begin letting them out longer." He nodded toward the beauty he was leading. "Her name is Daisy."

Bella reached out, letting her hand glide along the horse's neck, then flank and quarter, feeling the warmth and power of the animal under her touch. "Hello Daisy. You're a sweetheart."

With Callen's steady hand at her backside, she mounted the horse, gripping the reins with a familiarity that belied her city living these last years.

"Ready?" Callen asked, flashing her a smile that was both challenging and encouraging.

"Always," Bella replied. Then she grinned. "Oh, you meant to trail ride. Yes, I'm ready for that, too."

He dropped his voice. "Good to know you'll be ready for other things later tonight, baby girl. I wonder if you are ready for everything I have in store for you?"

She shivered with anticipation at the implied activities. Yes, she would be. "It is too cold for any hanky-panky outside Callen Red Eagle."

"Ah, so now you put stipulations on always being ready. It's warming up some but guess I better get you moving or neither of us will get what we want tonight and I aim to please my girl before she sleeps."

"I'm holding you to it."

They rode until the horizon threatened to swallow the sun and the shadows grew long. Returning to the ranch, Bella dismounted, her legs wobbly but her soul steadied by the ride.

"Thanks for that," she said, her gratitude evident in the softness of her eyes as she looked up at Callen. "Good thing you brought lunch or I would have died of starvation. I'm starving again. Think I'll grab a snack before dinner."

"Riding will do that to a person. Right now, I have a few things I need to finish before I end the day. I'll be back in about an hour," he said.

He drew her into his arms like he had done countless times over the last few hours. Bella watched his head descend and hide the late afternoon sun only to set off fireworks in her lower region. He was a man who could kiss at twenty paces and give her an orgasm with nothing more than a look. He was that sensual. That passionate. That loving. She could feel her body flush as he ran his finger down her cheek. "Later baby girl."

Back in her room, after envisioning all kinds of ways that Callen might take her, claim her body tonight, she sighed in anticipated bliss. Bella's hands were still trembling from the day with Callen and the night to come when her phone rang. It was a Rapid City area number, at first worrisome but it was unfamiliar, so not the facility that housed her mother. She answered with a cautious curiosity.

"Is this Bella Gregoria?" a cheerful voice inquired from the other end.

"Yes, speaking," Bella responded, her grip tightening on the phone.

"Hi, Bella! I'm Jennika, the owner of Dakota Brewed. I've seen your work at the gallery downtown, and it's just stunning. We're looking for a local artist to feature in our coffee shop, and your landscapes would be perfect."

Bella's pulse quickened. Another commission, another chance to share her vision outside of New York City. "I'd be honored, Jennika. Thank you!"

"Great! We can discuss the details whenever you're ready. I think your paintings will add so much character to the place." Jennika's enthusiasm was infectious.

"Let's set up a meeting, then. I have some new pieces that might fit right in," Bella said, the edges of her mouth curving upward in anticipation. She was so glad her muse had returned and he had encouraged her to paint. She'd left all her gallery pieces in the galleries and they had sold very well. They were requesting more. She had a nice nest egg, but if she wanted to stay here, she would have to keep that up. She'd given up her eclectic apartment and her cost of living had almost dropped to nothing, but still, she wanted enough in the bank to take the financial worry off of her, and that required a fairly large bank account. Her growing up experiences had trained her and Tracy to work to make money so you can be independent and still have fun.

"Looking forward to it," Jennika replied before they exchanged goodbyes.

Bella placed the phone down, her thoughts swirling with new questions and dreaming of things that could happen because of this new exposure. She didn't think she'd be able to connect with the local population and was going to see about putting up some paintings in the Red Eagle Lodge and possibly have an introductory glossy sheet to show some of her area art in the welcome packets and possibly to the website for the ranch. Doing a show in the largest city on this side of the state was going to do as much or more to getting the word out than her local efforts.

Callen knocked on her door after showering, and Bella realized she hadn't showered yet. She shared her good news and then quickly stepped under the warm flow of water, her mind refusing to stop its running commentary. Maybe she really could stay here with Callen. Maybe she wouldn't need to leave when she didn't need to watch over her mom anymore. She was distracted by a big, already showered man slipping into a shower that suddenly seem much smaller than it had when she'd entered.

"You need me to wash your back?" Callen's eyebrows wiggled suggestively.

"How did you know?"

"I'm perceptive like that."

In a few moments, the only things heard were running water, skin slapping against skin and subdued moans of ecstasy, followed by grunts of satisfaction. Finally, with the water turned off, heavy panting filled the room. Then a heavy, melodic beat filled the room.

"Is that your phone, Callen?"

"Damn, that's Stryker's ring." He strode over and snatched up his phone. "Shit timing, man." He tweaked her sensitive nipple as he walked out of the bathroom talking to his brother.

She brushed her teeth and combed out her dripping hair, putting in a leave-in conditioner due to the long time under the water spray, and finally slipped into the bedroom. She was only partially surprised that he was still in the room and not just in the room; he was still naked.

"Mister, my boyfriend will not be happy if you are found in my room without your clothes on."

"Will he? I say we test your theory out."

Bella laughed. "You're insatiable. I think I should leave you like this and take these dirty clothes to the laundry." She bent to scoop up his discarded items of clothing.

Callen lounged back further on the bed. "Go ahead. I'll just wait for you to come back."

Bella, wrapped only in a towel, realized he had the upper hand. She wouldn't be caught in the rest of the house nearly naked. Then she grinned and threw her robe on and reached to open the door. Callen flew off the bed, landing next to her, his body leaning across her to hold the door closed.

"You will pay for that, my girl." Bella shrieked as he scooped her up and tossed her onto the bed.

He pounced and began to tickle her. "Callen. Cal, stop, I beg you."

He kissed her hard, softening his lips as he pushed his tongue against her teeth, begging entrance. She opened to him, kissing him back, her tongue dueling with his in a dance of passion. He released her to take in more air as she inhaled shallow breaths.

"Shh, baby. You have to keep it down. We might be at the end of the hall, but we are still in the house."

He shifted his fingers from her ribs to her breasts, massaging and lightly pinching her nipples. Giggles turned to moans as he paid close attention to her firm, rounded breasts that had always seemed just enough for him. "Gorgeous, baby. Just a little more than a handful, but not too much to handle."

Her muffled giggle brought a smile to his face. She raised her hand to his face and stroked his jawline. "So handsome. You know, I hated you for a long time. I thought if you weren't so handsome, then I wouldn't worry about some gorgeous girl taking you from me."

"Sweetheart, after I discovered you, there was not one that could hold a candle to you. No one. I'm so thankful you came home."

"We can thank Tracy for not agreeing to come home to take care of mom and for not letting me forget that what happened between us was a terrible mistake not an intentional act. She said I needed to clear the air with you. And then there was Stryker."

"I'm going to have to buy that sister of yours a dozen roses and my brother a beer."

Bella smiled. "Nah. We'll send her jerky from the Smoke House. That will say thanks the way she hears it. You'll still owe your brother a beer."

Callen nodded. "Done. Now, can I get back to the kissing and sucking and making you come apart?"

"Yes, please."

Callen pushed her back and climbed between her legs, sliding down to the end of the bed, swiping his tongue from one bundle of nerves at her clit to the back bundle of nerves, his tongue dancing at both points. Bella groaned quietly, remembering where they were.

The pounding on the door got a disgruntled "go away" from Callen. He looked down to return to his feast when Stryker spoke through the heavy wooden door.

"Fire!"

Chapter 10

Choices and Decisions

"**D**amn." Callen kissed her inner thigh as he jumped up. "Sorry, baby, but that is one of the words that no one on a ranch can ignore. Get dressed."

He dressed in a few seconds, walking into his boots as he took off downstairs. Bella followed as quickly as she could, but the guys were all outside by the time she made it to the first floor. She looked over and exchanged a look with Kai.

"What's going on?"

Kai shrugged, "I don't know. We were in the kitchen so I know it isn't in the house, but when Libby went to look, Stryker told her to stay put and for the women to all stay inside. Gotta say, I hate it when they do that. We can help, you know."

"I do know, but I also understand these men protect what is theirs and they are not going to change anytime soon. Unfortunately." Bella said as she walked toward a window.

Kai said, "Bad timing, huh?"

Bella smiled wryly. "The worst."

"There will be more chances later tonight."

Bella nodded with a frown. "I know, but Callen was... I was... yeah, bad timing. What's taking them so long? I don't see any smoke."

Renee walked in the kitchen door with Avery. Teagan was at the college teaching class. "There's a fire at the Tillotson homestead. No one has lived there for a while, but it was still a good place. The guys were looking at it just the other day to see if they wanted to purchase it. It has good pastureland."

"How could it just start burning?" asked Kai.

Renee shrugged. "A few reasons. Aged electrical, lightning strike, heat concentration, malfunctioning heater, tree falling on part of building and creating a spark, lots of things."

Kai squinted her eyes. "I don't know. It sounds a little fishy to me."

"Carson is going to be pissed off because he thought they could put a cattle manager over there with a couple of guys to take care of the livestock they relocate there."

Bella nodded. "Yep, sounds fishy. Was there electricity running into that house that no one was living in for a while? Seems unlikely. We haven't had a storm in the last week. No heat to concentrate this time of year. Malfunctioning anything wouldn't be the case with no electricity and unless there was a gas generator or heater, no ignition source. Now, a tree falling might work but my science says, unlikely."

Avery shook her head. "It's a shame. Stryker and Jacob were really working a sweet deal for the place. Now the owners can sell it as land with a few outbuildings."

"Seems to me that the price would be less without the house," said Kai.

"Nope. Now, the new owners won't have to tear it down to use the whole property as grazing land."

It was a few hours later, when the guys came back home, dirty, tired, and irritated about the situation, that the rest of the story was revealed.

"Well, it's out," said Seamus. "It was an old house, but a damn shame we lost it."

"How did it start?"

"Not sure. Probably some kids were playing around and got the fire started on accident. Maybe used the fireplace and didn't pay attention. The fire department will see what they find out."

Stryker ran his dirty hand through his equally dirty hair. "Well, we can build something on it for our guys to stay in while over there."

"Did you already buy it?" asked Renee.

"First thing this morning," said Seamus.

Carson shook his head. "Bet that scorched Parker Green's ass. He wanted that piece to build a golf course on. A freaking golf course in ranching country. Idiot."

"He already called me soon after and said he'd make me regret it. But I mean, what could he do?"

The room was noticeably silent for a full minute. Callen asked, "You don't think he'd... no, none of us would do that. We're ranchers and cattlemen first."

"Who knows?" asked Renee. "How can you be so sure he wouldn't?"

The response was another silence except for boots pulled from tired feet and dropped, hitting the floor in loud thuds.

"Well, go get cleaned up and you can worry about all that later," said Libby from the kitchen door. "Dinner in thirty minutes."

Dinner was full of conversation about the fire, the purchase, the rearranged plans, everything.

"Seems to me that the best thing to do would be to clear away the debris, check the electrical pole, the septic field and tanks, plumbing piping, and so on. Then, if it works, rebuild on the same plot," said Carson.

"Maybe," said Stryker, "but sometimes it's just cheaper to build new from the ground up."

"I'd at least have a look at things first. Luckily, we have cousins," said Declan as he pulled out a chair for Teague and one for himself as they joined those at the dinner table. Before he sat, he filled Teagan's plate. "Here baby, now eat well. You haven't been eating enough healthy food these days."

"Declan, I cannot eat this much food."

"Okay, but you will do the best you can. We talked about this."

Renee shook her head. "I think they are all on a health kick. It's like someone tells them something ludicrous, like sugar is bad for your health and they try to eliminate all sugar from your diet. It just can't happen."

Carson laughed. "Renee, hate to tell you, but it is bad for your health."

Renee stuck her fingers in her ears. "Nope, not listening. La-la-la."

The tension was broken, and Bella relaxed. They still had a problem, but suddenly it seemed fixable.

Days later, Bella found herself amidst the buzz of conversation and clinking glasses at the art exhibition. Her paintings adorned the walls, each one a testament to her journey and diversity. Attendees circled the room, their eyes lingering on the bold colors and emotive landscapes that spoke of open skies and wild hearts.

"Your use of light is exceptional," an older gentleman commented, his eyes locked onto the painting of the recent sunset. "It's as if I can feel the heat of the day cooling into night."

"Thank you," Bella replied, the compliment warming. "I want people to not just see the landscape but to feel it, to be there with me."

"Mission accomplished," a woman chimed in, her attention caught by a different piece. "You have a unique touch, Ms. Gregoria."

Bella's cheeks flushed with a mixture of pride and humility. "I'm always learning through nature and experimenting as I go. But I'm glad it speaks to you."

The evening continued with more praise for her technique and subject matter. There were a few discussions about inspiration. Several attendees expressed interest in purchasing her work, their admiration boosting Bella's confidence in her craft selling outside of New York City. It wasn't just about selling paintings; it was validation, acknowledgment that her passion could resonate with others, could stir something deep within them.

"Here's to many more sunsets," Callen said, appearing beside her with two glasses of champagne.

"Yes," murmured those few admirers close enough to hear the toast.

Bella smiled, her heart full and for a few moments, she could forget her other responsibilities to her mother, her sister, Callen and herself and simply bask in the glory of a job well done. She clinked her glass against his. Yes, things were going to be fine.

"Ms. Gregoria? This is Marlene from the Green Willow Gallery," said the voice on the other end, crisp, and all business. "I'm calling with fantastic news. Your piece, 'Whispers of the Prairie', has been sold to a private collector."

Bella's heart leaped in her chest. "Really?" The word came out as a breath, a whisper of disbelief.

"Indeed," Marlene continued. "And not just sold—the collector was absolutely enamored. They said it spoke to them on a spiritual level."

A wave of exhilaration washed over Bella, her cheeks warming with the flush of success. "Thank you, Marlene. This... this means so much to me."

"Your work deserves this recognition, Bella. We're all thrilled for you here at the gallery. I know you have sold in New York, but our buyers have seen this landscape and it takes a lot to impress them about their everyday experiences. You have done it."

Ending the call, Bella let out a joyous laugh that echoed off the rafters of the high ceiling. Her gaze drifted through the window, where the vast expanse of the ranch called to her. When she stepped out of the converted building, she found the stable beckoning her to celebrate on horseback.

She stepped outside, the door closing with a satisfying click behind her. Callen's prized stallion, Thunder, galloped across the pasture, his mane flowing like dark silk in the wind. Bella watched, mesmerized by the raw power and grace of the animal. She reached into her pocket and pulled out a small sketch pad and pencil, her hand moving deftly to capture the horse's fluid movements.

"Hey, beautiful," she murmured to a mare Callen had called Pansy as she ambled over, nuzzling Bella's hand with a velvety nose. Bella pulled a bit of apple from her pocket and shared with Pansy. She was mesmerized by the softness in Pansy's eyes, the gentle slope of her back, and the protective stance she took around her foal. She added them to the background of the sketch.

As the afternoon wore on, Bella sketched furiously, her pad filling with the life of the ranch—horses grazing, cattle lowing in the distance, and the playful antics of a litter of puppies that belonged to the family's loyal border collie. Today it would be the animals, tomorrow, the mountains, the grasslands, the buildings. The rustic cabins dotted along the mountain ridge. There was so much she could paint. Even the little town had old buildings to bring back some life into or take them as they were today, worn but proud. Her mind was racing with possibilities.

"Got quite the audience there," Callen's voice drawled from behind her.

"Oh. I didn't know you were here. I can't help it," Bella replied without turning, her eyes fixed on the page. "They're inspiring."

"Seems like everything on this land inspires you," he noted, leaning on the fence, his gaze following hers.

"Maybe," she said with a secretive smile. "Or maybe I'm just seeing it all clearly now."

"And maybe," said Callen, "you are ready for me to build us a house so you can see it every day."

"Thanks to my models," Bella said, closing the pad with a sense of satisfaction. She tucked the pencil behind her ear and turned to face him, her expression alight with the day's achievements. "They don't complain, they work for free, and they're quite the lookers."

"Sounds like you've got it all figured out," Callen teased, offering his arm. "So is that a yes on the house?"

Bella bit her lip, and he removed it again. "I'm not sure I'm ready yet."

"Okay but don't forget the question is on the table." He kissed her lips gently. "Come on, let's get you back before the light fades. I need to feed you before I make you work."

"Work?"

"Yep. You get to do all the work tonight. The artist rides the rancher."

Bella looped her arm through his. "I'll do my best to create a work of art."

"I have my full faith in you."

"You know, that will give me the control, right? I'll be in control of you."

"Yep, you will. Can you handle it?"

"Oh, I can handle it cowboy, the question is, can you?"

Callen laughed. "Let's find out."

For the next few days, Bella stayed near her mom in the assisted living home. The nurses had told her that Vanna's caregiver needed a few days off and it was a good time to visit if she wanted to see how her mom was doing. Bella could see her mother was getting weaker and less reactive to things around her. Late afternoons and evenings were the worst for her. Her breathing had settled down again, but the nurse told Bella it was a matter of time before it would bother her again.

Vanna still talked to Bella sometimes, but they had very little in common and Vanna had begun to ask to talk to Tracy. Tracy was often unavailable. Bella spoke to her sister and laid down the law.

"Look, I respect that you don't want to come back and help with mom but you have to take her calls if you are able. It puts her into a blue funk and can make her go down faster."

"Bella, you are not blaming me for mom's bad liver, her heart, or anything else."

"I'm not, but I do want you to be her daughter enough to at least take her calls. It means so much to her and she did give you life."

"Fine, I'll talk to her when I can. Now turn off the guilt trip. It's not fair."

"If you feel guilty, it isn't me doing that, but I'll try not to set you off."

That was yesterday, and now Bella stood at the threshold of her converted barn studio. She was in her element, surrounded by brushes, her canvases, and sketched the pictures in her mind when the shrill ring of her cell pierced the quiet. She had just gotten back to the ranch a few hours ago and Callen had Duders this week. She figured someone must have told him she was back.

"Hello?" Bella answered, wiping her hands on a rag.

"Ms. Gregoria? This is Jane from the gallery," the voice on the other end was brisk but warm. "We have a client who's absolutely enamored with your work. They're requesting a commissioned portrait."

Bella felt her heartbeat quicken at the prospect of more exposure. A portrait commission was new territory for her, an exhilarating challenge since the majority of her recent works were nature based.

"I'd be honored to accept if I can," she responded, her mind already whirling with ideas. "Tell me about the subject."

As Jane relayed the details, Bella's imagination took flight. She envisioned the person's features, the quirks of their expression, the story their eyes would tell. "I'll send you a still shot and set up a video call. You and the prospective client can take it from there."

"Thanks! That sounds perfect."

By the time she hung up, Bella was eager to begin, her artistic instincts buzzing.

"Who is this person?" asked Callen that night when she told him about the commission.

"I don't know yet, but I will after I contact him."

"Give his name to Jacob or Renee before you go out to meet up with him."

"You are not checking into this person's background."

"Oh, so you decided you aren't going to take the commission?"

"I am, but without you riffling through his background. It isn't a crime."

"No," agreed Callen, "it certainly isn't. But it also isn't safe and you will be safe. So give the name to Renee or Jacob. They'll know what to do."

Within a couple of days, Bella had set up a schedule and offered to meet the client in the place he was most comfortable so she could take a few pictures, do a few sketches and then go back for the painting. Callen was working and kept the Duders out for a couple of days to camp on the "trail." He didn't mention the portrait again.

Days passed, and the portrait began to take shape, a life emerging from the fabric of the canvas. Bella poured herself into the painting, capturing not just a likeness, but a soul. You seem to be discovering the essence of your subject.

"Feels more like a dance than a wrestle," Bella replied, her eyes narrowing critically before a smile broke through. "But I think I'm leading."

"Can't wait to see it finished," Callen said, and left her to her solitude.

When the portrait was complete, Bella felt a deep sense of satisfaction. It was more than just a painting; it was a piece of her, a testament to her growth as an artist.

"Glad you were able to do what your buyer wanted. It was a beautiful work, baby," said Callen as he led her to a chair which he sat in. "But you didn't ask anyone to run a background on your subject like I asked you to do. That will cost you a sore bottom."

"Oh, no. You are not spanking me."

Callen cocked his head to the side. "Aren't I? I was keeping you safe by asking you to get a background on this guy. You didn't, and now you want to bail on this consequence too? I thought better of you, little girl. Are you saying zucchini?"

"I am not consenting."

Callen sat quietly for a moment and then pulled her onto his lap. "Do you trust me, Bella?"

"Yes. You know I do."

"Am I your daddy?" She closed her eyes for a moment and then dropped her head. "Yes."

"Then I am charged with keeping you safe and happy. I make sure you are doing what you need to be healthy and not put yourself in danger. What you did was not safe. You could have endangered yourself and that will never do. The penalty for disobeying Daddy when he is trying to keep you safe is a punishment. Today, that punishment is a spanking. Who knows what the next punishment will be?"

"Callen, I was in pubic at all times."

"Is that what you call me when you are in trouble?"

Bella could feel her core grow tingly and wet. God, she loved this play and yet, Callen wasn't playing in the truest sense. He was serious, and she wanted that right now. How did he know when to take things to another level? And yet...

"No. I've just been so stressed that I didn't want another layer of hoops to jump through."

He nodded. "I get it, but this was not negotiable. Your safety is never negotiable. I haven't pushed this part of the dynamic because you have been under so much stress and responsibility, but I believe it's time."

Bella sighed. She agreed and disagreed. Was it worth the conversation? Probably not because the result was always the same. She consented, and he spanked. "Fine. Okay."

"Okay-y-y?"

"Okay, Daddy."

Callen nodded, stood her on her feet and helped her drag her yoga pants down her legs to pool at her feet, along with her underwear. "Wait. I thought we were going to talk about it."

"What is there to say? You disobeyed Daddy when he was trying to keep you safe."

When he put it that way, she didn't know what difference talking would make. "What if someone comes in?"

"Baby, this place knows what a spanking sounds like and they wouldn't dare open the door. Over you go."

The second after she was settled over his lap, Callen's hand bounced off her backside in a two smack per cheek rotation. The first few were not bad, but when Bella sighed, Callen spanked hard, his hand bouncing off her perfect bottom. He didn't lecture, just smacked her trembling ass and soon she was wiggling to avoid his hand connecting on her skin. The heat rose.

"Callen, I mean Daddy, please, I get it."

He had the audacity to laugh! "Not yet, but you will."

He never rubbed her bottom like those in her books had said happened. He never lectured, which she was glad of, but he never took a break, either. "Please, please. I can't do this any longer."

Callen hesitated and then continued until she felt as though her bottom was scorched and swollen and the tight hold on her tears was released. Just when she was about to open her mouth to yell the 'Z' word, he stopped and miraculously the gentle soothing came couched in nonsensical words. Callen cooed and rubbed her back until her tears subsided. He brought her up towards him and hugged and kissed her.

"Bella, baby, you did so well. Daddy wasn't gentle, and you took everything I gave you. You are so special. Daddy is so proud of you."

"Thank you. But can I go to the bathroom now?"

"Need to rush?"

"No, but..."

He slid his finger with audacious intent through her wet silkiness and tweaking her clit before introducing it into her heated entrance. He sighed, and she moaned. His finger was large, but she needed more. More of everything.

"Callen, I need you. Please, I need you now."

"See what the prospect of taking you with a red-hot ass does to me?" He brought her hand to the bulge in the front of his jeans.

"Aren't you worried someone might come in?" She heard the amusement in her voice.

"Listen, if they didn't come to investigate the spanking, then they won't come to investigate the pleasure sounds you will be making."

He punctuated his statement with a repositioning of Bella on his lap, legs spread wide and her sex open to his slow tracing of her pink slickness. He pulled out his phone and adjusted the screen so she could see her clit swell, her pink flesh turn slicker and redder. As she grew closer to her climax, one hand reached up and tweaked her nipples, first one and then the other.

She cried out when the first wave of ecstasy rolled over her. He kissed and whispered in her ear as she continued to come. He unzipped and settled her over his erection quickly, pumping into her as though it were his last opportunity and even when she thought she was done, a third wave overtook her. Without a word of warning, he let go. As they both relaxed, Callen flipped her around to lay her head onto his shoulder. He continued to kiss her and whisper words of love as she calmed her breathing and went limp in his embrace.

"I love you so damn much, Bella. I don't know how I did without you for so long but I'm determined never to do without you again."

Not long after the showing, Bella's success was magnified when she discovered her work both from the gallery and the portrait splashed across the pages of the Rapid City newspaper. The article was complementary, and her name was printed boldly alongside images of her paintings.

"Look at this, Bella! You're the talk of the town!" Callen waved the paper with pride as he approached her near the stables.

"Not to toot my own horn, but I'm thrilled." Bella laughed, accepting the newspaper.

"Nothing wrong with a little pride," Callen grinned, wrapping an arm around her shoulders. "Especially when it's well-deserved."

"Thank you," she murmured, leaning into his embrace, the paper crinkling between them.

"Here's to making more memories," Callen said, squeezing her hand.

"And painting them," Bella added, a playful gleam in her eye.

"Exactly." Callen laughed. "Bella, I love you more every day and I know you have to check on your mom, but I want you to move in. Permanently."

"Callen, I don't know. I mean, I love to be here and it seems to excite my imagination and desire to do better art more often, but live here? I'm not sure. Are you ready to commit that much?"

"Yes, I'm more than ready to commit. And since your mom is in a facility that can meet her needs better than if she stayed here in the backwoods, I think it's more than time to do this."

"It's true. I've been able to go several days without needing to be there. But that commitment is hard to swallow."

Callen leaned in closer. "Why, baby? What are you afraid of?"

"I'm not..." Callen's eyes bore into hers and she knew it was not going to work to try to hide herself. "I'm afraid of things not working and my heart breaking again. I'm not sure how well I'll survive that."

"I don't intend for you ever to need to survive me...us. But loving you? Keeping you safe, happy and healthy? Yes ma'am. I intend to make sure those things are in place." He kissed her lips and savored the experience. Bella could kiss. "I also intend to keep you satisfied. Ready to go to the house? We'll have an early night."

"Mmm, I like early nights."

"Me too."

Chapter 11

The Offer

Bella's hand trembled slightly as she unfolded the heavy parchment letter, her name elegantly scrawled across the front. As she perused the contents, her eyebrows arched in surprise. Anthony Shaffer, her most recent art client and a fairly new patron of her art, was offering her an apartment on his sprawling estate and a studio to do a series of paintings depicting western South Dakota through the ages. The offer was generous, almost too good to be true, with the promise of safety, luxury and what she feared was much less freedom due to the security measures described.

Bella paced the length of the cramped living room in her mother's home; the letter dangling from her fingertips. Why it hadn't been delivered to the ranch, but her mother's home didn't raise alarms at first. But when the question did arise, she wondered at how the sender knew she would go to her mother's place since Vanna was gone and she only check on it whenever she went to town.

What should she do? According to the directions to his estate, Anthony Shaffer lived outside of Rapid City so she wouldn't be able to stay at the ranch during the main project work, but she would be able to visit her mom more often. She wondered what Callen would say about the arrangements. Bella knew what he would say, but would he try to stop her from taking this opportunity? Did she even want it? Yes, she did. But fear from an unexplored source rippled through her.

She checked in with the care home every day telephonically and she came into town every week to see her mom and to stay the day. That wasn't the problem. Daily access to Callen was the real problem. He was more dominant when it came to her safety. The estate would provide a sanctuary for her creative spirit, but at what price? If she stayed away from the ranch, Callen would want to visit her often and she would want to go to the ranch.

Bella had just returned from visiting Vanna and meeting Mr. Shaffer for lunch. They discussed his ideas for the series he hoped she would paint. He insisted she paint it. Maybe she could do the inspirational sketching and the first round of canvas prepping and painting on the ranch. Then transfer the work in progress to the city for the bulk of painting work. She thought she could sell that compromise to Callen, and she hoped Mr. Shaffer would be equally agreeable.

"Ms. Gregoria," said Anthony Shaffer. She did not use her birth name in business, and this was purely business. He had addressed the offer to discuss the project to Bella Thompson. She was glad he defaulted to her pseudonym.

"Please, call me Bella."

"Thank you. I am Anthony." The conversation went well until Bella tried to steer Anthony to her compromise. "Bella, I think staying at the estate will enable you to paint freely without interruptions. Your safety will not be compromised with your own personal bodyguard."

"I don't think that will be necessary. I have a close friend in town, my mom is in town, and I don't want to be away from the inspiration that I get from the ranch. I can rent a small apartment and once the sketches are agreed upon and the background created, I can come to work in the studio you provide during the day, returning to the apartment at night."

"I am a very influential man with many business interests. It would be imprudent of me to not ensure your safety while associated with me."

"I'll find an apartment close to the estate but still in the city."

"I'll have to take that into consideration. You are a determined lady, Bella Gregoria."

She cringed at her first discussion with Callen on the subject. "No. That isn't going to happen. I understand this is your career, your livelihood, but you are not living on someone's estate to paint for him. We will figure something else out."

The conversation went down from there. He didn't even hear anything after that. He dropped a possessive kiss on her unsuspecting lips and left the room.

The second discussion happened at Anthony Shaffer's home during her next trip to visit her mother. The estate was beyond words glamorous, well protected, with lots of men around. Too many. She didn't have to wonder what her Callen would say about that. Anthony seemed to have no female employees except house cleaners and a cook. He must be a very important man indeed, to need so much. She smiled to herself. It made her think of the mafia and Bella intended to research him more. But not turn his name over to Renee or Jacob, even if she wanted to, which she kind of did.

"So, you will accept my offer of housing and the studio, no?"

"I'll have to think about the apartment, but I would be happy to work in a studio so long as it has natural light and enough space for several easels."

"It will be arranged. You can give your specifications to Jarl, my second, and he will make sure you have all you need. I apologize, Bella, but I have another meeting soon. Please let Jarl know of any needs you have while you are working on the paintings."

Anthony Shaffer was charming, but in a dominant, *no one says no to me* scary kind of way. It felt like it was an awkward, even fake, demeanor. As though he didn't play nice with many people. But he was willing to play the game with her. Why?

Her attempt at researching Anthony Shaffer came up with little more than a business owner with multiple branches from pawn shop to pet store to mining. He must be very busy running the diverse businesses and showing his face at big name charity events. It seemed like a crazy dream and yet, as she peered out of the small bedroom window that offered a limited view of the neighborhood surrounding her mother's home, hesitation gnawed at her. The ranch was wide open and free. The Shaffer estate was anything but that.

Accepting Anthony's offer meant wrapping herself in a cocoon of comfort but at the direction of others. Possibly expected to perform at their whim almost, and Bella's independence bristled at the thought. She had difficulty with the Red Eagle men taking care of things she would have dealt with alone while living in New York. How was she going to let someone she didn't know take care of those same things?

She didn't even agree that Callen should build a house yet, so how was she going to handle a stranger with power and control, dictating what she was doing? She envisioned having to meet schedules from mealtimes, to possibly when she left the estate and when she painted and sketched. No, that would never work. She was having trouble thinking of creating at a studio that wasn't hers. How was she going to figure this out?

"Pros and cons," she muttered to herself as she pushed past the thought that she was in her mom's house to clean. The pros were clear: security, space, and the kind of opulence she'd only seen in glossy magazines. But the cons... they were deeply rooted in who she was. Bella had fought tooth and nail for her autonomy and being seen as a capable, talented woman. She had built her life on the belief that she could handle any curveball thrown her way, and her upbringing had offered her many of those.

And there was Callen, whose love and possession she cherished but whose desire to protect often felt like a gilded cage. This would be even more than that. It would be without the love Callen offered, but with Callen's worry about her in a strange place with strange people. He wouldn't see another person's security staff as a good choice. She didn't know if she agreed with that thinking, but she wasn't sure about living there for the time she created the series. It could take a while. Several months.

And the thing that seemed to seal the answer was Callen wouldn't be able to stay with her when he visited. Correction, *wouldn't* stay with her there because he wouldn't allow it to happen. A deep sigh escaped her lips as she sat down, the well-used chair creaking under her petite frame, long legs stretched out in front. She ran determined fingers through unbrushed hair, snagging on the tangled strands. Her mind suddenly raced with images of her first winter in New York and Allie Day's warm smile and open arms, ready to show her the ropes.

Allie was a few years older than Bella and had landed in the Big Apple from the mid-west for the same reason as Bella, to grow her presence in the art world. She became Bella's anchor in New York's less desirable neighborhoods. It was among those same streets that Allie said she found the raw, unfiltered inspiration for her art; it was there where her soul felt most alive. And yet, she'd moved for the love of a man.

When Bella was dealing with everything surrounding her ex, Allie had offered to take Bella in. She had joined an art community in Rapid City and invited Bella to join them. That is when Bella decided to first go home and deal with her mom's health issues and the plan was to join Allie who was deep into sharing the sharp darkness of parts of the inner cities of the mid-west. Bella's inspiration was found in the country, the mountains, Black Hills and ranches laid amongst the grasslands and valleys. And she could join Allie for a while.

She went back to the ranch studio, even though Callen was still with the Duders for a little longer, for a sense of security when she called Mr. Shaffer to tell him her decision. It if killed the deal, so be it, but she hoped it didn't. With the scent of oil paint lingering in the air, Bella wrote her whole thought process down that brought her to this decision. She'd need it for both Shaffer and Callen. She picked up the phone, her voice steady as she dialed Anthony's number.

"Mr. Shaffer, I can't tell you how much I appreciate your kind offer to stay at your home during the creation of your series," Bella began, her heart thumping against her chest. "But I have to decline. I have friends in Rapid City, and I'll stay there or in a short term rental when I'm not using your studio."

The silence on the other end spoke volumes. She imagined Anthony's surprise, frown lines would be etching themselves deeper into his forehead. She'd seen them when she had discussed roadblocks to him in person. But this was about more than comfortable living; it was about proving to herself, and to Callen, that her strength was not just a façade. And that she knew what she needed to create the emotive pieces she was becoming known for.

"But you will have everything you could want while you are my guest."

"And I appreciate that. I do. But I need to make my own choices, live in a place that I'm comfortable in, even if it's not wrapped in luxury. I'm afraid that won't happen if I live on your property."

"Is this about Callen Red Eagle?" Anthony's voice finally broke the quiet, concern threaded through his words. "Because if it is—"

"No, it's about me," Bella replied with surprise. How did he know about Callen? She firmed up her tone. "And the life I want to build on my terms. I will work in your studio as agreed, but I must be out and absorbing the world around me. That includes spending time at the ranch to find my inspiration."

"And you feel you cannot do that while residing on the estate."

Bella sighed. "I can keep odd hours sometimes and that would be disruptive to your home. I much prefer my own space."

"But Callen is a part of your reasoning. He could come with you." It was a statement, a decision, not a question, as though the solution was within his reach.

Bella laughed. "I might have been a hard sell, but Callen is a no sale. Even I couldn't convince him to stay away from the ranch so I could work. Something I wouldn't try to do. He has a job to do and a business to run, which requires his presence during certain times. Sorry, but the answer has to be no."

"As you wish, but you are free to change your mind at any time."

"Thank you."

It was a week later that Bella twisted the key in the stubborn lock of her new rent-by-the-month apartment. Her small frame leaned hard into the weathered door until it gave way with a groan. The space that greeted her was cramped and dim, the single window scarcely offering any respite from the oppressive walls. She stepped further inside, her artist's eyes immediately taking in the peeling wallpaper and the linoleum floor that had seen better days.

The one the landlord had shown her was "representative" of the other apartments. It might have had the same footprint, but nothing else. This efficiency was musty and smelled of neglect and mold, which mingled with the faint odor of cleaning solutions used in an attempt to make the place presentable. It was almost enough for Bella to pick up the phone and call Anthony to take him up on his offer. What a dismal alternative. Her resolve for independence was quickly fading.

"Charming," Bella murmured to herself, a wry smile tugging at the corners of her lips.

Her eyes danced with a mix of challenge and resolve as she surveyed her new domain. It was a far cry from the luxury Anthony's estate would have provided, but it would be fine and she could clean it well enough to stay here for the time needed. Besides, her friend Allie would show her the best places for things around here. And her actual time here would be negligible.

She unpacked a few essentials, the old pipes clanging loudly as she twisted the knob on the faucet for a glass of water, which was not clear enough to risk drinking after all. The kitchenette boasted a stove that looked like it belonged in another century, and cupboards seemed to hang onto their hinges with sheer willpower. But Bella wasn't deterred; she had always been resourceful, turning the simplest of materials into works of art.

She called Callen to check-in. "You didn't tell me you were leaving."

"Callen, you knew I was going today, and I knew you had guests. So, I just left when I was ready. I called you when I got here."

"You know better, baby girl. We are going to talk about this when I get there."

"When you get where? You're coming here? Callen, I'm just setting things up and I'll be home in a couple of days. You don't need to come right now."

"Yep. On my way first thing in the morning."

"I'm in trouble, aren't I?"

"Oh, yeah."

Bella next called Allie and filled her in on things. Allie giggled when she heard Bella had left without telling Callen. "Well, if your Callen is anything like my Randy, that is going to be some discussion when he gets there."

Bella groaned. "Don't remind me."

The following day, Bella stood outside as a battered pickup truck pulled up, a few pieces of essential furniture sent over by Allie, arrived stacked haphazardly in the back. The driver, a friend of Allie's who owed her a favor, tipped his hat and set about helping Bella unload.

"Thanks, Jed," she said, handing him a cold bottle of soda. She was glad she'd run out and picked up some groceries. "I owe you one."

"Anytime, little lady. We creative types need to stick together," he drawled, wiping his brow before driving off.

As she arranged an old easel by the window, the best source of light she could muster, Bella felt a surge of nostalgia mixed with excitement. The threadbare couch that had likely served as a bed for many a study night was replaced by a sofa bed of slightly better quality and state. She knew who owned this couch, so her worry wasn't as heavy when she eventually crashed on it. It now claimed its spot under the window, while a bookshelf, slightly askew, became a makeshift divider between living and painting areas.

She draped a vibrant throw, a relic from her bohemian phase in New York that she had grabbed from her bedroom at the ranch, over the back of the couch, instantly injecting life into the space. She would have to bring a recent painting or two from the storage at the ranch to perk up the depressing walls. She placed Pinky and Ping-Pong on the sofa and stood back.

"*I sure miss the ranch, but it looks like we're going to be just fine,*" she whispered to the room and her cuddle bears, feeling the space respond with silent affirmation. Bella rolled up her sleeves, ready to tackle the last of her unpacking, ready to face the challenges ahead, her spirit undaunted by the humble beginnings of her new temporary home.

Callen's boots echoed against the linoleum as he stepped into Bella's unlocked apartment, his eyes taking in every corner of the cramped space with a furrowed brow. The scent of fresh paint mingled with the mustiness that clung to the air, an odor that no number of scented candles and disinfectant could mask. His gaze lingered on the peeling wallpaper and the worn-out couch beneath the window.

"Damn it, Bella," he muttered, turning to face her, the set of his jaw conveying his disapproval more clearly than words ever could. "You can't stay here. It's too small, too rundown, too unsafe, even if you deigned to lock the damn door."

Bella stiffened, feeling as though the walls were closing in around them—not from the size of the room, but from the weight of Callen's concern and irritation pressing down on her. She watched him prowl the limited square footage, his tall frame seeming out of place among her borrowed used furniture.

"Callen, I know it isn't much but I have to live here while I do this commission and it is a big one," she said, her voice steady despite the fluttering in her chest. "I will be at the ranch at the beginning of each piece. Then I'll come here to do the bulk of the painting and then back to the ranch to prep the next one. I need to do this even if it is in a less than ideal situation. I have a lock on my door." She indicated the single dead bolt.

"Baby, that isn't going to keep a gnat out if he wants in."

"Well sure. He could probably slip in anywhere," answered Bella, being deliberately obtuse.

He stopped and faced her, his piercing blue eyes softening slightly. "Bella, let me rent you a place somewhere nicer. Somewhere safer. You deserve better than this. And I need to sleep at night."

Her heart swelled at his offer, touched by the sincerity she read in his eyes. But alongside her similar apprehension was a fierce surge of independence. Bella had fought hard for her autonomy, and she wasn't about to relinquish it—not even to the man whose protective instincts were as much a part of him as the cowboy hat perpetually shading his eyes. But she loved the hell out of the fact that he was horrified.

"Callen, I know you mean well," she started, gathering her resolve like armor. "And I'd almost let you do it, but it will be for just a few months and nicer places want you to stay 6 months to a year. I want to go back home when I'm done. Besides, I can't have you fixing everything for me."

"Why not? And tell me again why you are in this apartment, anyway? I thought you had a friend you could stay with. In fact, I'm sure there was someone named Allie that you had arranged to stay with. Another artist."

"We discussed this. I'm here because I have to work at the estate in the studio they created for me. I also declined Anthony's offer to stay on his estate which leaves me here in the evenings."

"Yeah, that wouldn't have set well with you or me if you'd taken him up on that offer. But why not stay at Allie's place?"

"She lives quite a distance from the estate. Nearly an hour in traffic and actual miles are nearly 45. I guess she has a fiancé now. He's a nice guy in the Air Force and so they live near the base. Anthony lives outside the opposite side of town." Bella shrugged. "It was a no brainer. Please be okay with this. I don't have a choice, and I really want to be near enough to drive home if I work late. If I am too tired, I won't want to drive and we are back to staying on the estate."

He took a step closer, the frustration evident in the rigid line of his shoulders. Yet when he spoke, his voice was laced with the warmth that always seemed to reach past her defenses. "All right, baby. If that's what you want, I won't push. But just know that I'm here for you—always. And I want this Allie's full name and phone number. Her fiancé's too, if you have it."

Bella reached out, her hand finding the firmness of his muscled arm, grounding her. "I know, Callen. And I love you for it. Just trust that I know what I'm doing. I'll get you everything you need to feel better about me being here."

His fingers brushed over hers, a silent vow passing between them. In that touch, she felt not just his love, but his respect for her choices—a gift more precious than any comfortable apartment he could offer.

"Oh, and we are making this place as reinforced as possible."

As Callen left, he vowed to be back in a couple of hours to upgrade her security. Bella turned back to her apartment, its imperfections suddenly less daunting. But it wouldn't be a lie when she also acknowledged her desire to finish as soon as she could and still do a good job.

"Can you believe it? An apartment on Anthony's estate. The place is dauntingly enormous and so extravagant." Bella murmured into her cell phone, a storm of emotions swirling within her as she recounted Callen's offer of another apartment to Allie. Bella sat perched on the edge of her sagging couch. Allie's voice, filled with an understanding that only a true friend could offer, met Bella's trembling tones with unwavering support.

"Sounds fancy, but it isn't you, Bells," Allie said, her voice carrying the weight of wisdom earned with experience. Only Allie called her Bells and the only person she'd ever allowed to do so. "You've always been about carving out your own path, not walking down someone else's, no matter how well-paved. And in this case, it sounds like the pavement is money."

"I know. I can work there, but I needed my own space, too."

Bella nodded, a smile tugging at the corners of her lips. Allie knew her too well. "It would suffocate you and you'd be so uptight, afraid you weren't doing as he wanted, even when you weren't painting."

"Exactly." Bella replied, her gaze drifting to the window where the city sprawled beyond.

"Then that settles it," Allie declared. "Follow your heart, girl. It's never led you astray before. Well, except for Garrison Gold." She laughed.

"Thanks for that reminder." Bella rolled her eyes. "Callen seemed to accept my choice as well. I just hope he keeps in that mindset until I'm done."

Later that afternoon, Bella found herself facing Callen, his silhouette framed by the doorway. His presence was a comforting force, yet she steeled herself for what he might say once he'd talked it over with his brothers. And there was no doubt he'd done just that.

"Hi," she said brightly and accepted his toe-curling kiss. "You're back."

"Yep, and I've brought reinforcements." In walked Kai and Sage along with Jacob.

Jacob rounded the corner and touched his hat when he saw Bella, his frown evident. "Callen, you said she would be fine. No way is this a place she can stay in. A stiff wind could knock this place down."

"Bella won't be here long. She gave me good reasons why she chose this place. I might have wanted her in a different situation all together, but she lived in New York City, remember. I doubt there aren't many tricks she doesn't know by now. So, let's get her door fitted with extra deadbolts." The girls followed Callen inside and soon began stripping the dingy wallpaper with Bella.

"I brought you two choices of cover up paint. A dark blue and a pale yellow," said Sage.

"Um, I don't know what the landlord might say."

"I asked," said Callen. "He said no problem so long as we leave everything when you move out. I agreed."

It didn't take long before the steamer had the wallpaper down the best it was going to be without scrapping, and the girls had roughly painted over the walls. It was immediately brighter and much better than the wallpaper. They ordered in food before Jacob and the girls left, leaving Callen.

"I hate you being here, but at least I feel a little better about your safety. The cameras are only allowed inside here but that should be enough."

"Let me pay for your work, Sir."

"Oh, yeah? Just what kind of payment did you have in mind?" he asked as Bella unzipped his pants.

"How about a massage?"

"Well, if you insist. I wouldn't say no to a little hand manipulation."

Bella laughed and kneeled in front of him, taking him from his pants. She took him inside her waiting mouth and sucked hard. Callen's intake of breath was harsh.

"Bella baby, you have to back off a little unless you want me to blow in two minutes. I think we can both take our time and enjoy ourselves."

Her answer was to run her tongue up and down his penis while sucking softly then energetically, followed by gentle again. She was doing what he did to her, tease. And she decided it was great fun on the giving side. After a deep throat tongue massage of the sexiest kind, Bella enjoyed not one but two orgasms as she held onto the kitchen counter. Callen was gone now, leaving her languid and satisfied after her orgasm and his warning ringing in her ear.

"I expect you home in a couple of days. Then once you come back here to work, every other weekend. You call me every night and no touching that sweet pussy until Daddy does. Understand?"

His use of the name Daddy was a surprise. She thought they'd let that go for now, but she was so happy he hadn't. It was hard for her to submit sometimes, but Callen seemed to know just when to introduce the dynamic. It gave her a warm, cared for feeling she needed to carry her through the next few days and then weeks between visits.

"Yes, sir, I understand. But it isn't fair."

"Don't care. You want this adventure, and I have agreed for now. Those are the terms."

"So, you aren't touching yourself either?"

"Nope. Only with you."

"Fine."

"Is that how you answer me?"

"No, Daddy. I understand Daddy."

"Good." He kissed her hard. "See you soon, baby."

A couple of days later, after getting familiar in her apartment life, hanging out with Allie and spending time with her mom, Bella returned home to create the final sketches for her commissioned series. She then prepped the canvases and let them cure a little. Finally, it was time to go back and start the real work.

Callen Red Eagle watched from the porch as Bella wrapped her delicate brushes with a tenderness that spoke volumes about her passion. The sun was setting on the horizon, casting a warm glow over the ranch that had been their sanctuary. He leaned against the wooden railing, the worn surface familiar under his touch—a stark contrast to the opulence of the Shaffer estate.

"Be careful with these," she murmured to herself, placing each brush into a sturdy leather roll.

Her fingers lingered on the recent canvas she was painting little by little for a present to Callen's parents, tracing the edge where paint met fabric. It was more than just material; it was a part of her, a silent testament to the hours spent in the embrace of her art done for love, not money.

"Always," Callen responded, his voice rough like the terrain he tended and the cattle he worked. His eyes betrayed the tumult within—pride for her talent, concern for her well-being, and an undercurrent of fear that whispered of empty spaces she would leave behind.

"Callen," she said softly, turning to face him. "I know you're worried, but this is a chance I can't pass up. I'm making good progress on the first painting."

"I know, sweetheart," he replied, pushing away from the railing to close the distance between them. "I won't stand in the way of your dreams. Just promise me you will stay safe." The shadows lengthened around them as they stood embraced in their love, stretching across the land that was as much a part of Callen as his own flesh and blood. It had become just as precious to Bella.

She nodded, reaching up to trace the line of his jaw with a fingertip. "I promise to be careful."

He enveloped her in an embrace, the kind that spoke of deep roots, shared history and abiding love. "You've got a gift, Bella. And that fella, Shaffer, sees it too. But don't let that world change you."

"It won't," she assured him, pulling back just enough to look into his eyes. "If New York City didn't do it, Shaffer's world wouldn't either. I'll be back before you know it."

As night began to fall, she continued her preparations, rolling her spare canvases with care and packing the pigments that were her weapons against the blankness that awaited her. Each item was a piece of the life she was temporarily leaving, and though the prospect of creating new work thrilled her, the ache of departure hung heavy in the air.

"Remember to call your sister," Callen reminded her. "She'd want to hear about this."

Bella smiled, grateful for the reminder of family, no matter how far. "I will."

Finally, she was ready, and she stood at the threshold, her bag slung over one shoulder. She took a moment to breathe in the scent of home—the earth, the cattle, the faintest hint of sagebrush carried on the breeze. It was a fragrance no perfume could replicate, a sensory anchor to the life she and Callen had built. She wondered how something so sustaining went unnoticed until it was absent.

"Always come back to me soon, sweet Bella," Callen said.

"Always," Bella echoed, stepping off the porch and into the twilight that signaled both an ending and a beginning.

She'd waited to leave until the final moment, and she hated that she had to leave at all. In that moment, she vowed this would be the one and only time she would agree to leave her home to do art for more than a few days. With one last glance back, she saw Callen framed in the doorway, a solitary cowboy whose strength was matched only by the love he held for the sassy, independent woman who captured his heart.

He stepped closer and drew her to him for one last embrace. One last kiss. He whispered in her ear, bringing tears to her eyes and hesitation to her heart. His kiss was deep and all-consuming. His tongue gently waltzed with hers. His hands caressed tenderly, leaving her even more aroused than if he had ravaged her. Tonight was for sweetness and careful caresses. Callen read the situation correctly, his insight impeccable.

"Go create something beautiful, just like you."

She received his love as he was offering it: without fanfare and without vigorous lovemaking. He offered it to her without strings or gratification to follow. It sealed his love in her heart and strengthened her return of loving adoration.

She stepped out of his embrace. "I will, and I'll be back as soon as I can... for more cuddles and orgasms." She smiled at her own sassiness.

Callen swatted her ass in response. "And to start building your own home."

And today, that sounded perfect.

Chapter 12

Arrival

The opulent gates of Anthony Shaffer's estate swung open, revealing a world of such wealth that it seemed plucked from a fairytale. She hadn't come in the front gate when she had discussed the details of her commission and now she was very glad she had not agreed to stay here. It was even more intimidating.

The sprawling grounds were meticulously landscaped, with topiaries sculpted to perfection and fountains that danced in the sunlight. As Bella's eyes traced the path up to the grand mansion, her breath hitched in awe. Marble statues lined the walkway, and the façade of the house itself was a masterpiece of classic architecture, its windows gleaming like eyes set with crystal.

Anthony Shaffer stood on the steps, every inch the wealthy businessman: impeccably dressed in a bespoke suit that spoke volumes of his status. His sharp gaze found Bella as she approached, and a practiced smile played on his lips. It all seemed like a front of beauty over a scary reality.

"Ms. Gregoria," he greeted, voice smooth as aged whiskey, "your art has captured my attention. I've acquired a couple more of your pieces. I will be honored to grace my walls with your work. Come see where I have decided to display the pieces you are going to paint for me."

"Bella, remember?" She smiled, excitement fluttered in her chest at his compliment. This commission could catapult her into the spotlight she had only dreamed of, providing recognition and exposure for her talent. She prayed the personal cost wasn't too high.

"Mr. Shaffer," she replied, "I appreciate the opportunity." She glanced around, the enormity of the estate making her feel small, yet her passion for art bolstered her resolve.

"If I am to call you Bella, you will call me Anthony."

"Of course."

"Good. Now, let us get to know each other a little more and I will show you to your studio. I must admit that I did worry about the possibility of you changing your mind and I'm relieved I didn't misread you." The man attending the door stepped aside. "Thank you, Macon."

Anthony turned back to Bella and slipped his hand to lie gently at the small of her back, guiding her inside. Bella tried not to stiffen her muscles, but the only one who touched her like that was Callen. He dropped his hand.

"I trust everything you have asked for has been delivered. I will leave you to decide how to arrange things." Anthony continued, stepping aside to welcome her into the inner sanctum of his home. "You'll have complete freedom to create. Consider this as your home away from home." He gestured expansively, encompassing the luxuriousness of his domain.

As they walked through the halls, Bella took in the grandeur—the walls adorned with priceless artwork that they lingered and discussed. It was a far cry from the rustic charm of the ranch, the simplicity where her heart found solace.

"Your vision on the theme," Anthony said, watching her closely, "I trust it implicitly." Bella nodded, feeling the weight of expectation settle upon her shoulders.

"Thank you, Anthony," she said. "I have done some sketches, and I'd love to share those with you to get your thoughts. I believe I see your vision, but it is important that we agree."

Still, a twinge of hesitation gnawed at her. Accepting meant stepping into a world unknown, one that glittered with promise but also shimmered with uncertainty. But the pull of her craft was undeniable, a siren call to which she had always answered without fail. The one thing she had confidence in was her art...and Callen, of course.

"Excellent." Anthony clapped his hands together, the sound echoing off the high ceilings. "Let us toast to new beginnings," he declared, leading her towards a room where the sunlight caught on crystal decanters filled with dark, light and amber liquids.

Raising her glass, Bella allowed herself to be swept away by the moment, envisioning this to be her exciting next step in sharing her visions with the world. Bella pulled her sketchbook from her bag and carefully showed the first sketches of what she had in mind for the series. When she was done, she leaned back and waited for Anthony's words. If he didn't like it, she would need to have a more in-depth discussion with him about what he wanted.

"Bella, it is more than I had hoped for. You really have an eye and even in these sketches, there is an emotion I can feel. Your insight and instincts are astonishing." His phone rang.

"Excuse me while I take this."

His return was quick. "Apologies. I must attend to this issue." He introduced the man he had previously identified as his second in command. "This is Jarl." She had spoken to him last week, and he was who she sent her list of supplies to for the studio.

"Nice to meet you in person," said Jarl.

"Nice for me to put a face to a name and voice." Bella immediately thought Jarl was as dangerous as Anthony, without much of the charming businessman act.

"Jarl, we must go. This is Roxie, my housekeeper, and she will show you where to park during the daytime and where the studio is." He turned to the older woman, "Roxi, give her the rundown of the meals and all that is needed for her to enjoy her time here while she creates." He turned to Bella again. "I shall see you soon, my dear."

Jarl stared at her for several long seconds before nodding in her direction and exiting behind Anthony. When the duo returned several days later, Bella began noticing Jarl crossing paths often. She wasn't sure how to take the attention, but being second to a powerful man like Anthony had to make you leave an impression. She just wasn't sure exactly what that impression was or why he was interested in making it.

After a week of working in the studio most days and visiting her mom in the late afternoon when she could, Bella decided she needed some of her old faithful items at the ranch. And she missed Callen. They spoke every night, but a quick weekend trip would be good for both of them. Besides, she needed some loving. But after that two-day break, she was back at the efficiency apartment and back at the estate to work.

Anthony's estate provided no shortage of inspiration, its opulent gardens and reflecting pools igniting the flames of creativity within her but she still needed to be in the country, in the Badlands, exploring canyons and rejuvenating in the Black Hills for the full historic affect. Her first painting was done. The second needed more finalizing.

She had decided to work forward, from the untouched world of the Native Americans and first immigrant settlers to present day. Each painting was a collage of period scenes depicting a distinctive era with its challenges, rewards, and many sacrifices. Bella got in her car, filled up with gas, checked her map, her snack and water supply and cash stash. Research was done. Now it was time to find her solace and inspiration.

The city faded away as the mountains and rawness of the wild emerged. Bella was lost in the grandeur of the world around her. She sketched, meditated, inhaled the scene she was creating in her mind and on paper. It was her happy place. Finally, she reluctantly gathered her things, loaded her car, and headed back to her temporary home, tired but ready to start on the next painting.

As she passed a small town, her cell phone rang. "Hello?"

"Bella?" came the rough voice.

"Who is this?"

"What the fuck do you mean, who is this? It's your security. Where are you?"

"I don't know who you are. I'm hanging up now." That was strange and unnerving. She tried to shake it off when another call came through and this one had the Shaffer Estate listed as the caller.

"Hello?"

"Bella. Are you okay?" asked a rather concerned voice that sounded familiar and yet not.

"Who is this?" she asked for a second time.

"Jarl."

"Oh. Was that you who just called a moment ago?"

"No, it was one of our security detail. The one who was assigned to you today. I have discussed with him the way to address a lady. He won't make a call like that again."

"Thank you. What can I do for you?"

"Bella, we have been looking for you and when you didn't come in this morning, we began to worry." She heard the censure in his voice.

"Sorry. I have to clear my mind sometimes and since I am in between paintings, this is the best time to get out into the untamed world and experience it. I didn't say I was coming in today. Sorry to have caused him distress. Did you need something?" This was what she was worried about if she stayed at the estate. Too much monitoring.

"Yes. You should let us know you are doing something like that or going outside of your typical routine. Better yet, allow one of our people to go with you for safety."

"Again, I am sorry and I will let you know when I am not coming into the studio during the week but I am vetoing any attempt for someone to come with me or follow me. This is part of my creating and I won't have it tampered with by other people encroaching on my time. I am fine and I will see you Monday morning sometime."

Bella hung up. Her unease over that conversation had her taking a detour and driving to the ranch. She wasn't sure if she would tell Callen, but she would definitely snuggle into him and breathe in his strength. She had time to decide how she would deal with the situation when she returned.

Bella always felt relaxed and happy to begin a new week after spending time with Callen and the Red Eagles. She didn't share the conversation she'd had with Jarl, but somehow Callen knew something was bothering her.

"You didn't call. I'm glad you're here, but I might have been off on the ranch overnight. We are getting more reservations now, and I don't want to miss your visits." His kiss belied his words of warning. "What's wrong, baby?"

"Nothing. Just homesick for you and the ranch."

Callen's smile was tinged with acceptance. "I'm skeptical that there isn't something else going on but I trust that you will tell me what I need to know. Promise me you are safe."

Bella struggled with her answer. "Honestly, why would you think that I'm not safe?"

"I've been there a few times, remember? The girls talked me off the ledge a few times over that neighborhood you are staying in."

"I'm careful and I haven't had any trouble at this place."

Callen watched Bella for a few more seconds before he released a heavy sigh. "Alright. Now, let me help with your homesickness."

She had relaxed in Callen's care and kept her thoughts to herself. The goodbye was easier this time, but still tugged at her heart. Their daily texts and calls became lifelines, small anchors in a sea of opulence that felt worlds away from the dusty trails and weathered fences of the ranch. And Callen.

"Morning, beautiful," Callen's voice crackled through the phone line, gritty as the gravel roads back home. Wednesdays were difficult for Bella and even though she was hard at work, burning through Monday and Tuesday, the middle of the week seemed to drag.

"Morning," Bella replied, her heart aching with the familiar timbre of his voice. "I miss you."

"Miss you more," he said, a statement woven with the simple truth of their love. "How's the paintings coming along?"

"Slower than I'd like," she confessed, eyes tracing the arc of her latest creation. "But I'm getting there. It feels good to be challenged. I'll finish number three in the next day or two."

"Never doubted it for a second," Callen encouraged, his confidence in her became a steady pulse that gave her strength. Especially on Wednesdays.

Bella's days unfurled in a rhythm of artistry and solitude. The commissioned series demanded more than mere talent; it required her to delve into uncharted depths, to confront the raw edges of her imagination. To research, explore, examine first-hand accounts of life during the era in history and then translate that to sketches that would help her create the next painting. She loved it when the vision was clear. This was hard work, but the rewards were turning into masterpieces of her imagination.

The challenges were many. The composition had to be exquisite, the historical background exact, and the execution flawless. And though Anthony Shaffer appreciated her work, his scrutinizing gaze often lingered longer than necessary, weighing on her like that wet army blanket when she was caught in a fall rain squall with Callen as a teen.

She painted for hours on end, losing track of time as she poured her essence into every piece. She was used to this, but Anthony's household was not. She often left late in the evening, returning early. Yesterday she fell asleep in the studio. Jarl and Anthony were appalled. Callen would have put in a bed, but these men were not stopping there.

"I have set aside a room for you upstairs. If you find you are here after ten at night, then I want you to use the room. I won't be happy if you are tired and driving yourself back to your apartment." Anthony's tone said he did not expect any argument. She didn't offer any but decided to set her phone alarm, so she was gone before ten each night.

When she told Callen that night what she had decided, he was upset as well. "Why would you work so late?"

"Hello... artist. I get inside my head and the work pours out sometimes. I don't stop the flow unless I'm too tired or it plays out."

"No more. I hate to say I agree with Shaffer, but this time, I do."

"So, you want me to stay in the room they have made up for me? Excuse me, the suite of rooms?"

"No, Bella, I want you to stop working past ten p.m."

"I'll try."

"I wish I could come this weekend, but I'm so close to finishing the next painting, I don't dare lose my muse."

"I thought I was your muse."

Bella laughed. "You are, but Pinky and Ping-Pong have decided to step in when needed."

"So long as they move over when Daddy is around."

"No worries there. I miss you so much. And I miss orgasms."

Callen laughed. "So, it's really what I can give you that you miss, not me."

Bella replied nonchalantly. "Potato, *Patato*."

"Brat. I'll remember that. Sounds like orgasms aren't the only thing you are missing. A good spanking might help you be sweeter."

Bella laughed again. "I doubt it."

When fatigue clawed at her resolve, Bella would close her eyes and imagine Callen's strong arms around her, his breath warm against her ear as he whispered words of encouragement. She longed for the rugged comfort of the ranch, the scent of leather and pine that seemed to embody their bond.

"Can't wait to have you back home," Callen texted one evening as the setting sun threw shadows across her apartment.

"Neither can I," she typed back, her fingers lingering over the keys. "I'm doing good work, though."

"I know you are," came his reply, swift and sure. "Just don't forget where you belong."

With each passing day, Bella's paintings neared completion—a testament to her dedication and the love that sustained her through the lonely nights. Her hands, stained with paint, ached with the effort, yet she pushed forward. For Callen, for herself, for the future they dared to envision together.

"Anthony told me how well you are doing," said Jarl, as he stood too close. "He is pleased, and he has high standards, so well done." Jarl continued, leading her past a series of imposing doors. "Your talent has caught more than just his eye."

Bella's heart fluttered uneasily. His words, meant to flatter, felt like a cage closing in—a golden one, perhaps, but a cage, nonetheless. She noticed the way his gaze lingered not on the paintings that adorned the walls, but on her, as if trying to discern secrets hidden within.

"His faith in my art is appreciated," she said carefully, her thoughts flying to Callen and the safety she felt in his presence—safety that now seemed so far away.

"Ah, here we are," Jarl announced, stopping before an elaborate door. "Your sanctuary should you need one some evening."

He swung it open, revealing a room bathed in sunlight, with a view that swept over the rolling hills of the estate. It was breathtaking and Bella realized with a sinking feeling, designed to be isolating. Just as she had feared.

"Thank you," she murmured, stepping into the room.

"You will dine with us tonight," Jarl stated, more an edict than an invitation. "Seven sharp. Anthony is eager to discuss your progress."

"Of course," Bella said, her voice steady despite the tremor she felt inside. "I look forward to it."

"Do you know your way back to the studio?"

"Yes, thank you."

With a long appreciative look and a nod that barely disguised his interest, Jarl left her to the silence of the room. And somewhere beneath the layers of civility and grandeur, Bella sensed the stirrings of a story she hadn't been told, a danger wrapped in silk and smiles. She would have to tread carefully here, amidst the beauty that could so easily become a trap. Keeping her head low was how she would finish this series and complete the commission Anthony Shaffer had already paid dearly for.

Bella hesitated at the threshold of the grand dining room where Anthony Shaffer and Jarl Berg awaited her presence. The clinking of fine porcelain dinnerware and the low murmur of conversation seeped out from the opulent space. "Miss Thompson, how delightful of you to join us," Anthony greeted, his voice smooth like aged whiskey, an undercurrent of power rippling beneath each syllable.

Bella was startled at his use of Thompson rather than Gregoria. "Thank you for having me," she replied as she took a seat, her eyes not missing the way Jarl's gaze lingered a moment too long. Or how Anthony's manner was a touch too familiar. Though she hadn't eaten more than a few cookies, the heavy scent of roasted meat and rich sauces did little to ease the knot forming in her stomach.

Dinner progressed, with Anthony leading the discourse, sharing anecdotes of his travels and art acquisitions with a charm that belied the cutthroat businessman he was likely to be. Jarl interjected sparingly, his words sharp and calculated, often probing, as though seeking to unravel the layers of the woman before him. Bella did not like the feeling it left her with.

"Your sister must miss you terribly, all the way in Germany," Jarl mentioned casually, a statement that felt more like a test than genuine interest.

How did he know she had a sister and where she lived? That gave her something to worry about. "She does," Bella managed, her response curt as she steered the conversation away from personal territories. "But tonight, let's focus on the series' progress."

"Indeed," Anthony said, lifting his glass in agreement. "To your exceptional talent and the masterpieces you create. my dear."

The toast masked the underlying tension, a veneer of civility that couldn't quite hide the predatory glint in Jarl's eyes or the calculated scrutiny from Anthony. Bella sipped her wine, the notes of oak and berry offering no comfort. She could feel the threads of control being woven around her; a web disguised as approval.

Retreating to her studio later that evening to gather her items for the weekend, Bella shed the weight of the men's gazes as she stood alone before her canvas. Her unease was strong. Just one more touch on that rock turned into more touches. The colors blended and contrasted on the canvas. With every layer of paint, she poured her longing for the open skies of the ranch, her resolve to remain true to herself, and the strength to withstand the tempest she sensed brewing around her.

The hours slipped by unnoticed. The moon climbing higher as Bella worked tirelessly, her dedication to her craft a lifeline in a sea of uncertainty. She moved with a rhythm that was hers alone. Each brushstroke was an affirmation of her identity. Her prize of completion was within reach, spurring her to work on.

As the night deepened and the first light of dawn began to whisper through the curtains, Bella stepped back to survey her work. Painting number four was done. And she was triumphant and exhausted. She went to the kitchen to grab a roll and some coffee before going home to sleep.

Jarl stopped her before she left. "Mr. Shaffer would like to see you for a moment in his study."

"Of course," she replied, her voice steady despite the tremor of apprehension that quivered within her. She followed Jarl, noting the calculated precision in his steps—a predator confident in his territory.

As they approached the study, hushed voices seeped through the closed door. Bella's hand paused on the ornate handle, her artist's intuition sensing discordant tones in the murmurs beyond. With a deep breath, she pushed the door open and stepped inside.

Anthony sat behind a mahogany desk cluttered with papers, his expression one of annoyance as he cradled the phone to his ear. He waved dismissively at Bella, signaling her to wait. She took advantage of the moment to study him—the way his eyes darted about, the slight tremor in his hand. These were cues that spoke of secrets, lies, and deals best left unscrutinized.

"Thank you for waiting, Bella," Anthony said once he'd hung up, his smile failing to mask the tension in his jaw. "How progresses your latest masterpiece?"

"Progress is good," she answered, forcing a smile. "I just finished number four this morning."

"Excellent." Anthony leaned back, steepling his fingers. "I understand you stayed all night. That displeases me. I cannot have my artist exhausted. While I would love the series as soon as possible, and my clients are eager to meet you and experience your work, it will not be at the expense of your health."

"Understood," Bella affirmed, though a knot tightened in her stomach. After a few more words, Anthony dismissed her as though he had lost interest.

The word 'clients' echoed ominously. It wasn't just art that Anthony traded, and whatever else he dealt in was frightening to imagine. She turned to leave, only to find Jarl blocking her path, his gaze unsettlingly intense. "I trust you're finding everything to your liking?" he inquired, a hint of something darker lacing his words. "Do you need any assistance with anything?"

"Everything is fine," Bella replied, sidestepping him with practiced grace. "Thank you."

Once back in the safety of her car, Bella locked the doors and left the estate as calmly as she could. A calm that was the polar opposite of how she was feeling inside. She sighed in relief when Callen called.

"Hey Baby. Are you coming home today?"

"I can't. I haven't seen my mother this week, and I worked too late to drive. I'm sleeping and then relaxing for the rest of the weekend."

His tone sharpened. "Should I come to you? You sound weary."

"I am. And weepy because I'm tired. And seeing problems where there aren't any. I just need sleep."

"I wish I could come to you, but I'm tied here. I can send the girls or someone to check on you."

"No, I just need sleep. I'll be fine. I'll talk to you tonight."

"Okay, baby. Sleep well."

Eight hours later, after Bella had slept off her sleepless night hangover, she answered the door to Callen. Her heart jumped in relief. "How did you know?"

"I listen to my baby and when she says in her sighs and weary voice that she is stressed, I find someone else to cover my work and I take care of my girl. Always."

The weekend wasn't about sex or getting any other needs met, but comfort and bonding. And recharging their emotional battery.

The days passed, a blend of brushstrokes and watchful eyes. Bella sent ideas to Anthony, always keeping the true heart of her work obscured until she could unveil it on her terms. And though Jarl's advances grew bolder, Bella's resolve hardened.

"Careful not to push too hard, Bella," she cautioned herself after she had pushed back when Jarl wanted to watch her paint and she had denied him.

He was surly when he left her, but he said nothing as she sketched a particularly daring piece imbued with her silent warnings. It was her feelings she was expressing. Feelings and renditions that were not likely to find themselves in the actual painting she was working on.

Wars, invasions, inner battles, and outer conflicts represented more than history for her paintings. It was a risky game she played, but Bella Thompson was no stranger to risk. She had faced down her fears before—she would do so again. Callen wouldn't be happy, but she would put off going to the ranch one more weekend. It would make three weekends she was away, but he'd come last weekend so she could say she thought that counted. It didn't, and she knew it, but sometimes the saying that it was easier to ask forgiveness than permission rang true. Her butt might pay the price, but it would be worth it to finish the last painting.

Chapter 13

Jarl

Bella's studio, a sanctuary of solitude and creativity, hummed with the soft bristles of her brush dancing across the canvas. Each stroke was deliberate, an extension of her innermost thoughts, manifesting in vibrant colors and bold textures that told stories hopefully for many to enjoy. And she was jumpy.

Jarl had begun to show up everywhere. On her way to the kitchen, traveling in and out of the house, even once he was outside the bathroom door when she exited. It was beginning to get creepy and caused her a growing unease. She was going to leave in another hour or so to head to the ranch. She had finished the sketches for the fifth painting, and now she was through the preliminaries and had done the first preps for the fifth and final painting. She put the first layer of background on the canvas and stepped back. Yes, it was coming along nicely.

The tranquility of the moment shattered when the door creaked open, the unexpected sound jarring Bella from her reverie. Her heart stumbled over its rhythm, much like the wayward dollop of linen white that now marred the corner of her nearly finished first layer. She ignored the intruder and quickly blended the coloring in to add an element of depth. She turned toward the door.

Jarl Berg stood framed in the doorway, his imposing figure a stark contrast to the ethereal lightness of the studio. His eyes, sharp and calculating, found Bella immediately, tracking her every move with unsettling precision. A smile, if one could call it that, curled the edges of his lips—a predatory semblance of pleasure that unnerved her profoundly.

"You are quite an accomplished artist, and I understand you are largely self-taught. So this is true talent."

Jarl's voice cut through the silence, low and smooth, laced with a possessiveness that had no place amidst the scent of oil paints and turpentine. Bella didn't need to look up to feel the weight of his gaze, heavy and unrelenting, nor did she have to see his smile to know it held a darkness that belied any genuine affection. The word evil flashed in her mind's eye, bringing with it a shiver of apprehension.

Bella's grip on her brush tightened, a tremble betraying the calm she tried to portray. "Oh, I am just layering the background. The first layer is nothing but a neutral color." She was glad she had finished the paint wash over the canvas. It was time to dry, and it was her blessed cue to leave. She took a shallow breath, willing herself to focus on the array of colors in her beginning palate before her and not on the man who loomed in the doorway like an unwelcome shadow.

"Your hands," Jarl observed, his tone deceptively soft, "they move with such grace... much like the rest of you." His comment slithered into the room, wrapping around Bella's thoughts and squeezing tight.

"Thank you," she managed, her voice a whisper against the roaring discomfort in her ears. Her voice was shaky.

Bella shifted her stance ever so slightly, the muscles in her back bunching up as though preparing for flight. The air between them crackled with tension, the once sanctuary-like studio now feeling too confined, too intimate.

Jarl took one deliberate step forward, his boots scuffing softly against the wooden floor. "Not just talented, but beautiful, too. It's rare to find both qualities so... intertwined."

The implication of his words hung heavy in the air. Bella recoiled instinctively, creating a fragile buffer zone between them. Her eyes, wide and watchful, darted to the door then back to him, calculating the distance, the risk. With each second that ticked by, the sense of being cornered grew, a silent alarm ringing through her veins. *Keep things cool, Bella. You are going to the ranch this weekend. Get your things together while you wait him out.*

Bella's heart pounded like a drum in her chest, each beat echoing Jarl's footsteps as he prowled closer. She stepped away and began gathering her items. "I have to give this at least a day or two to dry before I add another layer." The smell of linseed oil and turpentine that once comforted her now seemed to suffocate. She decided right then to stop using linseed when she could because the faster her worked dried, the faster she would be done.

Her mind raced, thoughts tangling like brambles. This wasn't just Jarl being forward or overly familiar; there was something far more unsettling about his attention. It clung to her skin like a second shadow, dark and cold. Then he smiled ever so slightly and it gave her the feeling that he saw her as his next meal.

"Is everything alright, Bella?" Jarl asked, his voice low and smooth, but to Bella, it might as well have been laced with venom.

"Fine," she lied, the word tasting like ash on her tongue. She couldn't shake the creeping dread that Jarl's interest in her was an omen of something sinister lurking beneath his polished veneer. Whenever she was in the room with him, she couldn't shake the feeling she needed a shower.

"I'm going to check on my mom first thing in the morning. I may not come back until Monday. I'll let you know if I don't make it back Monday."

"Would you like to have dinner here? With me?"

"I'm sorry, I just can't."

"Ah, yes, Callen Red Eagle. Impressive boyfriend. But tame. You need a man with fire in their belly, Bella."

She feigned amusement. "I'm not sure I could handle more than Callen."

"It would be fun to see, though, wouldn't it?" Jarl abruptly turned and left the room, chased out by her sigh of relief. She didn't even want to think about what he meant by that statement.

Later, after Bella arrived back at the ranch, watching the setting sun cast long shadows over the land, Bella sought refuge in Callen's arms. They stood in a quiet corner, where the wooden fences met and the horses grazed just within sight.

"Bella, what's wrong? You have been jumpy and quiet. Usually, you are the first one to offer to do things, join the girls or me riding or sketching your heart out. You aren't doing any of those things."

"I'm just ready to be home. I've got this last one to finish. I've started it, but it's getting hard to be away from you." She spread her hands to encompass the surrounding ranch. "And all of this."

Bella couldn't tell him what she was really bothered about because he wouldn't let her go back. She needed to finish what she started, but it was becoming hard. When she did finally come clean about Jarl and Anthony, she knew her daddy would come unglued. So it would be better for everyone, especially her, if she kept things quiet.

Callen's jaw tightened, a muscle twitching as he listened. His hands, rough from work, rubbing her arms as he held her in his. The air between them grew heavy with unspoken words and shared worries.

"Are you going to stick with that reason?"

"Of course. It's the truth."

"Would you tell me if there was anything else that is causing you concern?" Callen probed, his voice steady but edged with a protective sharpness that belied his calm exterior.

"Yes, I would, and I will if I have more trouble."

"More trouble?"

"You know, anything more than I just told you."

Callen gave her a sternly assessing stare and seemed to wait extra-long before he agreed to let things go. "Alright," Callen said, nodding slowly. "We'll figure this out together. I'll come and see you more often.

"That sounds like a lot, and I'm just tired. I'm probably overthinking things."

"Baby, I can't imagine you are. Not to make you feel bad. You are the one who often misses things said or done around you. You are most often hyper-focused on things like the way a waterfall looks or identifying the exact color of a sky or tree bark, and the rest of the world fades away. If you feel uncomfortable, like you miss home or anything else, it's because they are real feelings."

"I guess."

"No one is inappropriate or bothering you, are they?"

Bella was startled at how close to the mark Callen was and she worried because he was staring intently at her. "No. I mean, it does feel odd sometimes with men everywhere, or when I pass an odd guy at the apartment entrance, but that's it."

"That Shaffer guy and his sidekick not giving you any trouble."

Bella knew she had to play this cool. Straight-up lying to Callen would get her a hot ass every day of the week. "Callen. I can take care of myself and nothing has happened."

"I hear a *yet*. I know you are able to handle things but don't forget that you're more important than anything to me. If I need to get coverage every day and stay with you until you are done and home for good, I will."

"Thank you, Callen," she whispered, her voice wavering with a cocktail of emotions. "You know just what I need to hear." Callen grounded her swirling thoughts. His embrace was firm yet tender, a fortress against the storm of her anxieties. But what was she going to do?

"You are starting on the fifth painting, right?"

"Yes, it gets harder, believe it or not, the closer to modern day it gets. But I've started."

"I won't ask you to paint faster because I know it doesn't work that way. No more working late or overnight stays. It's important that you get the painting time in, but let's not make you an easy target for becoming overwhelmed and I just don't like you near so many men after dark or alone at all. You leave before dark and call me when you do. Then call me when you get home. You forget and I don't get both of those calls, and you will have a hard time sitting because I will be driving to you."

"That sounds all good, but you aren't always within the cell service area."

"Then you text me. If you need to speak to Stryker, or Avery or Renee. Hell, call anyone and everyone. Leave messages and keep calling. Call Allie." Callen took a long few seconds to think. "Damn, now *I'm* overthinking things."

As they stood there, the world seemed to shrink until it was just the two of them, wrapped in the cocoon of their connection. Her head rested against the broad expanse of his chest, the steady rhythm of his heartbeat a comforting drum in her ear.

She felt him kiss the crown of her head, a silent promise to take care of her, that she was important to him. That nothing would happen without Callen and the Red Eagles knowing and taking care of things. His kisses moved to her cheek, her lips, the little crook in her neck. This was home and she would do whatever she could to get back soon.

Chapter 14

Times up

Bella was stressed. Her mother wasn't doing well and the pressure to finish her last piece was strong and yet, she needed to stay near to Vanna right now. It became much more difficult than she had ever expected. Her petite frame leaned close to the artwork, eyes narrowing as she executed each stroke with precision—a dance of light and shadow born from the bristles of her brush and other tools of the trade. Her resolve to not use linseed oil was not all together successful. It created longer drying times than synthetic additives, but sometimes it was the only option for the result she wanted. Bella was feeling overwhelmed and powerless to change things.

Outside, where the moon cast an eerie glow over the combination of manicured lawns and the rugged landscape background, Bella felt as though she was being watched. Jarl had not advanced his attentions, but he had not retreated either. He was fixating on Bella with an unsettling fervor. Thankfully, tonight he'd been called away. He and Anthony Shaffer would return tomorrow sometime, giving Bella some much needed time to stay in her studio and paint.

She'd called Callen at the right time and then had gone to snag dinner in the kitchen before calling him back and saying she was home safe. Bella could feel her buttocks tense as she lied about going home, but she needed to stick with this crucial part of the work. The fifth piece was difficult and demanded concentration.

Within the confines of her studio, not always aware of the watchful eyes on her, tonight she was able to relax and continue to pour her soul onto the canvas. This was where her heart sang and her identity sprang. It was also where she had discovered Jarl staring in the window from the garden yesterday.

Jarl had shifted slightly, his shadow haunting the perimeter of Bella's safe haven. When he realized he had been discovered, his jaw clenched, and for a moment, the dangerous edge of his intentions seemed to glint in the sunlight. Bella hadn't known how long Jarl had been watching her, but she had gone to Anthony and complained early, before the two had left.

"Jarl seems to be everywhere, and it's unnerving. I am nearing completion of the fifth painting, but I can't work in these conditions. I feel as though I must look over my shoulder and it takes my concentration away from the work."

"My dear, no one on this estate would lay a finger on you. They would protect you with their lives. You are my guest and are under my protection. Jarl is just making sure that you have all you need. Are you sure he isn't just curious about your paintings?"

Bella knew when to drop back. "Maybe. But it's difficult to stay focused, so could you ask him to stop?"

"Of course, my dear. How is this painting going?" His smooth change of subject did not go unnoticed, but she had made her point. Thankfully, for the rest of the week, Jarl left her alone.

Sighing with deep satisfaction, Bella stood back and looked at her creation. It had so much depth, it would take an admirer a while to see all there was displayed on the canvas, and that made her proud.

It was just Thursday but Bella needed the break. She visited Vanna who was sleeping a lot more. Allie was on a skiing trip, so Bella went home. She left a message on the studio door that she would be back Monday.

"Tell me about your painting this week. You look tired. I could have come to you." Callen finally broke the quiet, turning his gaze to Bella.

She glanced up at him, the corners of her mouth curving into a slight smile. "You've worked a long week, too. It's easier to relax here than where I am. The painting and the week are hard to describe," she began. "Every piece feels like I'm capturing a fragment of a dream and my interpretation of what is a foggy truth in history."

"Does it ever scare you? Putting so much of yourself out there for everyone to see?" His voice was low and filled with a genuine curiosity she loved about Callen. He was always honest and raw.

"Sometimes," she admitted, tucking a loose strand of hair behind her ear. "But it's also liberating. Each brushstroke is a word in a diary I didn't know I was keeping. It's a little scary, too. It's like giving voice to my thoughts, but in a gentler way."

He pulled her closer and kissed her with a fervor she longed for. "I miss you so much and I am not doing this ever again."

"Because all of this is exhausting," said Callen. "You look so very tired baby. Part of me wants to make you take a week off, but the other part of me wants you to be done with this commission. I'm not going to agree that you do something this intense away from the ranch again. I know we've talked about it, but I mean it."

"Yes, I *am* tired, but when I'm painting, I'm alive. It's when I stop for the night that I feel the strain. But I get some sleep and start again. I'll take commissions in the future, but I agree to discuss a better way to execute them. Remember, though, it's my career and therefore my choice." She snuggled close and sighed. "I miss you so much. It's painful. There is a better way and I'm going to find it. I did all my art in my apartment in the city. I want that again."

"So, do you think that you made a good choice here?" Callen's hand rubbed up and down Bella's arm. She felt the warmth of his hand in the chilly evening air.

Bella shrugged. "I don't think I made a bad one. We all live and learn how to do things better. That is what I choose to believe here. A chance to learn a better way to still enjoy creating my art."

Callen nodded, seemingly digesting her words. "It takes a special kind of courage to bare your soul like that," he said. "You always were a rebel." He smiled and leaned over to kiss her lips. "You're too far away. Come cuddle closer."

She definitely had a praise kink and her daddy was good at it. Bella sighed as though she'd been waiting for his invitation, she stood and climbed into his lap. She had wondered at first why the chairs, including porch rockers, on the ranch were all so big. She'd thought it was because the guys were big, tall men, but she soon decided it was because they had their women sit on their laps so often.

In the quiet comfort of the porch, with night settling around them, they continued to talk into the evening, sharing pieces of themselves and their week as naturally as the last vestiges of the sun left the sky and the night welcomed the stars. The one thing Bella didn't share was Jarl's interest in her. No need to rock the boat. She was getting closer to the finish line.

Dinner had been lively tonight. No different from any other night, and Bella longed to settle back into the routine of the ranch. The rest went to town to enjoy the local watering hole.

"I'm more inclined to stay home with you and show you how much I missed you but if you want to go out, I won't object to going with everyone else."

"Callen, you know I will pick being alone with you every time over any other entertainment."

Avery leaned in closer. "I get what you're saying now, because of the circumstances, but you won't always think that way. See, when you get them every night or most nights anyway, you can have your cake and eat it too."

"Good to know, but I think I'm going to sit this one out."

"Just remember what I said because it will come true for you, too."

Bella grinned. "But it's different for you. You're engaged."

Renee nodded. "And pregnant. Maybe you should stay home and get what you can before you are the size of a house."

Sage joined the conversation. "What... Callen? Slow off the mark? No engagement yet? He'll get around to sealing the deal soon." She leaned into Bella and spoke in a conspiratory tone. "The Red Eagles are notorious for being cautious, but they always come through."

"Time to go, girls. There is too much chit chat and not enough getting ready. You have thirty minutes. Then we are leaving with or without you," said Seamus.

"See what you aren't missing, Bella?" asked Teagan, as she followed the other women up the stairs.

Once everyone left, Callen began describing his own plans for the evening. "There is a lot in our program tonight, starting with discipline, because you aren't getting enough sleep. You aren't taking care of my baby the way she should be cared for."

Callen laughed when Bella eagerly went over his knee. "I was hoping you'd spank me. I need to relax so badly."

"You know I would have done it if you asked me." He arranged her as he wanted her.

"I haven't been able to break past the embarrassment of that."

"One step at a time, my sweet girl."

"Time to tell me what is really going on." Four semi-warm up swats landed on Bella's upturned backside.

"What? No, you are supposed to be relaxing me."

"I will but I want you to start talking or the relaxing will turn in to exhausting. I will give you what you want or what you need after I get what I need. The truth." Four more firm smacks landed on her perfectly round bottom. "Daddy isn't going to wait for long. The next spanks will count."

After his hand landed twice, Bella screeched her surrender. She wanted comfort, not discipline. "I'm just finding things hard with all these men at the estate. I think other things are happening there or Anthony and especially Jarl are spending too much energy checking one me or sending their men to check on me."

"Dammit." Callen rubbed her warm butt cheeks. "I'll figure this out. Give me a few days. Don't go back until I have a plan."

By the time Bella returned to the city, she had instructions to wait on

Chapter 15

Jarl/Callen visit

"**B**ella?" The voice sliced through the silence like a dissonant chord, and Bella's hand paused mid-air, pigment-laden bristles hovering just above her creation.

She turned as she sat her brush down, her keen hazel eyes falling upon Anthony, who leaned casually against the doorframe. *How odd. He had never been this casual in his manner.* His smile was all charm, but something in his demeanor - a shadow that flickered behind his gaze perhaps - unsettled Bella.

"Mr. Shaffer," she acknowledged, her voice even and controlled. She plastered on a courteous, yet noticeably forced, smile that didn't quite reach her eyes. "To what do I owe the pleasure?"

He sighed. "Bella, Bella. How many times must I remind you how you are to address me?"

"Sorry, Anthony."

He smiled, all charm. "I was in the neighborhood, so to speak," he said, stepping into the room with a confidence that seemed to claim the space as his own.

Technically, it was, but Bella had it on loan, so she bristled and felt a little uncomfortable. He glanced at the completed canvases on easels all covered with cloths, arranged around the room, nodding in appreciation. He looked at her painting.

"Your work continues to impress."

"Thank you," Bella replied, tilting her head slightly as if to regard him more closely, though she kept a polite distance. Her fingers tightened imperceptibly around her paintbrush, the only sign of her growing discomfort.

"Is there something specific you wanted to see?" she asked, hoping to keep the interaction brief.

"Simply checking in on the progress of my commission," Anthony replied smoothly, circling the room.

Bella watched him, noting how his steps seemed to measure the studio, how his eyes lingered not just on the sketches of the artwork but also on the hidden corners of her personal retreat in the attached room. Bella took breaks in there, called Callen in there, researched and took naps when she'd exhausted herself before going home to crash on her sofa bed. The bed upstairs was infinitely more comfortable, but she couldn't risk that any more. Not with Jarl hanging around.

"Of course," Bella responded, turning back to her canvas, letting the act of painting shield her from the unease that crept up her spine. "It's coming along."

"Excellent," Anthony murmured, though his tone suggested his mind was elsewhere. After a moment, he added, "I have great expectations for the unveiling event."

Bella nodded, her movements precise as she returned to her work. "What did you have in mind?" She hadn't thought there would be an unveiling to more than Anthony and maybe his close associates, but evidently, she was wrong.

"I'm working out the details, but it will be worthy of the art."

"I'm sure it will be. I'm positive you won't be disappointed in the finished works."

"Never thought I would be," Anthony said with a smile that hinted of darkness that belied his light words.

Anthony always seemed too busy, too intense, too secretive but polite to her. Jarl seemed too much of everything. Both men gave her the impression they would kill a man if they were in their way. He gave her one last lingering, assessing gaze before turning on his heel and departing as suddenly as he had arrived.

Once alone again, Bella exhaled slowly, allowing herself a moment to shake off the chill that had settled over her. She cast a glance at the empty doorway, a frown etching itself across her features. Something wasn't right. Intuition told her so. But for now, she pushed aside her suspicions and refocused on finishing this project. It was high time she finished this and go home.

A few hours following Anthony's visit, the studio door once again opened soundlessly. Bella noticed it out of the corner of her eye and wondered who it could be now. Her peripheral vision was quite good, so she waited until the person entered the room before she turned her head fully. Jarl Berg stepped through the threshold, his silhouette momentarily looming in the doorway before he moved into the natural light spilling from the tall windows. His eyes, sharp as a hawk's, immediately found Bella in the corner.

"Ms. Thompson," he intoned, each word laced with a knife sharp precision. "I am doing a check of the premises and thought I would check-in on you. Is all going well?"

"Mr. Berg, its Gregoria," she responded without turning, her voice steady despite the shiver that traced her spine.

Keeping the line of professionalism was suddenly very important. He inclined his head slighting in a small acknowledgement for her correction. She kept her attention on the canvas, where shades of indigo and crimson came together under her deft hand.

Bella continued. "Yes, all is well here. Just trying to finish a delicate segment before I lose the natural light." Bella was under no illusion that Jarl would actually be the one doing safety checks. As Anthony's second in command, it wasn't in his job description.

"You are a hard worker." Jarl remarked, taking a few steps closer.

"Staying focused keeps me immersed. The outcome is better quality in a timelier fashion," Bella quipped, her response clipped, hoping to convey her disinterest in prolonging their interaction. But Jarl was not dissuaded.

"Indeed, time is a precious commodity," he said, leaning against a nearby table laden with paint tubes and brushes. "One must seize opportunities as they arise."

"Opportunities?" Bella inquired, feigning ignorance. "I'm just a painter, Mr. Berg. My only opportunity lies within these canvases."

"Ah, but such talent can open many doors," Jarl pressed, his tone suggesting an intimacy that Bella had no intention of exploring.

"Perhaps," she conceded, her focus returning to her artwork. "I have experienced the large galleries and the amount of effort they take. I find I prefer the simplicity of my studio and my own timetable."

"Of course," Jarl murmured, though his eyes betrayed his reluctance to accept her indifference.

With a polite nod, he retreated, but Bella sensed this was far from the last she would see of him. In the days that followed, his visits became more frequent, his stays longer. No more lurking, but this was equally disturbing. Maybe even more so. She thought about discussing it again with Anthony but decided he didn't actually care enough to address things again with Jarl, if indeed he ever had. He hovered over her coming and goings like a storm cloud disguised as casual loitering.

Bella's strokes grew more guarded, her palette knife scraping with a tension mirrored in her tight shoulders. She took note of how Jarl would position himself near the exit or by the window, his posture casual but his eyes alert, tracking her movements with unsettling scrutiny. It was almost as though he were worried she would slip away without him knowing.

"How do your mother and sister feel about this once in a lifetime opportunity you are working on?"

"My mother is ill and my sister doesn't concern herself with my affairs."

"Family should always be a concern," Jarl countered, but Bella did not take the bait.

"Perhaps," she said, her tone dismissive, signaling the end of the discussion. She knew Callen would be furious to find out Jarl was bothering Bella, but she couldn't tell him and yet, she knew she should. The thing was, she didn't have anything but her gut feeling about this being a dangerous situation. Her fear was things could easily blow up if she didn't figure out a way to redirect Jarl.

Each hour that passed with Jarl's shadow casting over her studio chipped away at her sense of security. Bella became increasingly vigilant, aware of every creak of the floorboards, every flutter of the curtains. She was an artist trapped in a web woven by watchful eyes. Not just Jarl, but now she thought she was being followed to the apartment and once, she was positive she recognized one of Anthony's people outside her apartment building. Her once peaceful haven was transformed into that gilded cage that she had tried to avoid at the beginning of this adventure.

Callen announced that he was coming to see Bella. No guests on the ranch this week and he had been working on a solution. "I think I have the best solution."

Bella's heart sang. Callen was always thinking about her, even when she made it painfully understood that she wanted to be that independent woman people admired. But she wished, in this situation, Callen would stay.

"I would love it. I'll go visit mom and then grab something to cook."

Callen hesitated. "No, I'm going to order in food. No need to cook. Besides, not sure that stove is safe and I have cuddling that needs to happen as soon as I get there. No time to cook and wash up."

Bella laughed. "Whatever, but I'm game for whatever you want to grab."

Their moment of peace lingered, but shadows crept back into Bella's mind, casting doubts and fears as she saw another of Jarl's security team pulling down her road Friday evening as she parked near the apartment entrance. She had identified their vehicles. Not the estate ones they drove everywhere else, which would stand out in this neighborhood, but a late model sedan. It was something people noticed around here.

After they ate their fill of Bolognese, Calamari, and tortellini, and each had a glass of red wine, Bella figured Callen was as mellow as he was ever going to be outside of post-orgasm.

"Callen, there's something I need to tell you." Her voice quivered slightly as she stepped out of his embrace, the comfort replaced by urgency. "It's about Anthony... and Jarl."

Callen sat up, his manner on alert. "More than you have already told me?" She nodded. "I'm going to kill them."

"No listen. I just need to share how this week has gone." He listened intently, his jaw setting firm as she recounted the unnerving behavior of her studio's visitors, her discomfort growing with each word.

"Jarl watches me like a hawk," she confessed, the vulnerability in her gaze seeking reassurance. "And Anthony, there's darkness lurking behind his charm. I can feel it. And they follow me when I leave the estate."

"Fuck. Let's call them and say you are finishing the work at the ranch. I'll pack your place up and load it into the bed of the truck. We can be out of here tonight."

"What? No, I can't. Part of the agreement was that I created under his roof. The studio during the day is better than staying in his place in the suite he set up for me, all the time."

"Shh, Bella, look at me," Callen urged, his protective instincts flaring. He held her gaze, steadfast and unyielding. "I won't let anyone harm you and I'll check out the car outside. I'll figure something out. You focus on your paintings. Let me worry about those two."

"No, I can't let you do that, but I would love to hear your ideas on how to keep Jarl from bothering me. And what about them following me? And parking outside on the street?"

"Actually, because of this neighborhood, I'm good with security out on the street, so long as they don't come inside."

"Okay, I can see your point, but what if they do? And what about Jarl? What can I do about him? Or Anthony if he gets more involved. It just seems as though the closer I get to finishing, the wolves are closing in."

"Alright, let's think this through," he said, his voice steady and pragmatic. "We need a plan to keep you out of Jarl's reach while you're there painting. And Anthony's. I'm pretty sure I have a good one. But I'll call to make sure we are getting the help I asked for."

Bella nodded, casting her gaze downward as she toyed with the hem of her shirt—a nervous habit that betrayed her anxiety. As he expected, she began to pace and when she stopped for a few seconds, she'd shift on the balls of her feet.

"Who do you need to call? I have to agree, Callen."

"Nope, the rules have changed. You let me handle this and I'll let you stay. Veto my rule and you will be out of here in two shakes of a lamb's tail. If you don't believe me, try me."

"Look, I could change my routine, avoid places where Jarl usually goes in the house," she suggested, her thoughts racing. "If I stay out of sight, maybe he'll lose interest."

"From what I hear, he seeks you out, so Jarl's not the type to give up easily," Callen replied, running a hand through his thick hair. His eyes, sharp as the eagle he was named after, seemed to calculate their every option. "We might need to confront him directly. Let him know he can't intimidate you."

A shiver ran down Bella's spine at the thought of a face-to-face confrontation. "But what if that makes things worse? What if he retaliates?" Her words tumbled out, fear edging each one.

"Listen to me, Bella." Callen's hands found her shoulders, his grip firm yet reassuring. "I won't let Jarl lay a finger on you. I'm going to tell Stryker I'm going to stay with you. I promise we'll handle this quietly. There are ways to deal with men like him without causing a scene."

His confidence was a solid wall she could lean against, yet the flicker of doubt remained. Could they truly outmaneuver men as cunning as Jarl or Anthony in their own space? Was it a false hope?

"No. I don't think Anthony will allow me to be harmed or even approached while I am painting his series. Too many people know I am here. There is something about getting those paintings done that he is eager to do. That is the crucial point. I trust you. Now you have to trust me."

"Okay. Suppose I agree, it still doesn't set well with me to sit back and wait." He pulled her close again, his lips brushing her forehead with a protective seal. "The Red Eagles take care of their own."

"I'm trying not to put that statement to the test."

Bella paced, her hands wringing together as she contemplated their precarious situation. The thought that she might have underestimated the situation sent a shiver down her spine, not just of fear, but also of anticipation. Soon, she would be back on the ranch permanently. She would spend several days, when she was all finished, to see her mother. That would help with the reason she was leaving early during the day.

She would visit more artist events and find more things. She had tried to keep to a strict timetable, but she was a creative sort. They never kept schedules for long. It would mean they couldn't rely on her being in the studio at specific times.

Callen ran his hand through his hair. "I'm going to make my call."

"To?"

"Someone I know. Until we get a plan together, I'm going to need you to call me every time Jarl bothers you. Anthony, too, for that matter, hangs around or gives you the creeps. When you call me, I want you to refer to me as Uncle Kiernan."

"Why?"

"Because if I am correct, then it will make them pause and wonder who this uncle is since they have done a background on you and didn't turn up any uncle with that name."

"But what good will it do?"

"If they are into any of the things I suspect, they will know someone with that name."

"If they ask you about him, simply say you don't like to talk about that part of the family." Callen looked at his girl's confused face. "Trust me, baby girl."

Bella stared at Callen for a minute before nodding. "Okay. I'll trust you with this. I hope you aren't getting me deeper into trouble."

"Good girl, now, let Daddy show you how he de-stresses his girl."

"Mmm, yes, please."

The shrill ring of the phone shattered their tranquility. Bella tensed, an involuntary shiver coursing through her as she reached for the cell. Callen's grip tightened protectively.

"Bella," came the polished voice of Anthony Shaffer. "I trust your latest pieces are nearing completion. I am sorry to disturb you this evening. I trust you aren't in the middle of something important."

"As a matter of fact, I was. Is there something I can do for you, Anthony?"

He hesitated at the answer he obviously didn't expect to receive. "I apologize. I have to fly out tomorrow for a series of meetings that may take me the rest of the week. I am interested in the sketch on this final installment. I know you have shown it to me and we agreed but I like to keep them. Can you come to the estate?"

Bella hesitated, the knot in her stomach tightening. She exchanged a fleeting glance with Callen, finding a silent fortitude in his steady presence.

"I can send you photos."

There was a pause. "I would enjoy hearing you interpret the piece."

"Yes, alright, but I have a guest that I am bringing with me," she answered, her voice betraying exasperation but none of the apprehension that clawed at her insides. "I'll be on my way as soon as I'm done talking to my Uncle Kiernan. It's late where he is."

He hesitated, then responded overly brightly. "Excellent. I look forward to meeting your guest." The line went dead before she could muster a response.

She clicked off the cell and placed it in her back pocket slowly, feeling Callen's questioning gaze on her.

"I've been summoned," Bella echoed, the word tasting rancid on her tongue.

"Hey," Callen said, his thumb brushing away a stray lock of hair from her forehead. "Remember what I said? You're not facing him alone. I'll be right there with you."

"Let's do this then."

Bella stepped out of her car and onto the gravel driveway of Anthony Shaffer's expansive estate. The crunch beneath her shoes echoed against the grandeur of the looming mansion, a stark reminder of the world she was about to enter and had entered nearly every day for months. Her heart thudded in her chest as she took in the meticulous grounds. Not for the first time, she wondered if the statues were created on the property as well. She clutched her portfolio tighter to her side and Callen on her other side, holding her hand tightly.

"Ms. Thompson, welcome," greeted a servant at the door with a practiced smile that didn't quite reach his eyes. Bella nodded, offering a restrained smile of her own as she crossed the threshold with Callen.

"It's Gregoria," corrected Bella with a smile.

"My apologies."

"Thank you. Good evening, Macon,"

"Ah, Bella, you've arrived," Anthony's voice was smooth as silk, yet carrying an edge that sent a shiver down her spine. "And Mr. Red Eagle, I'm happy to meet you at last."

Callen shook hands with Anthony. "Thank you. Glad we are finally meeting as well."

He emerged from the shadows of the hallway. Jarl, his ever-present shadow, trailing behind him like a dark omen. Bella shivered, and Callen squeezed her hand. He seemed at ease. Could she have created a problem where there wasn't one?

"Anthony," Bella acknowledged, her professionalism a cloak she wrapped tightly around herself. "I have the sketches you wanted to see."

"Please, show us," Anthony gestured towards a private sitting room, his charm surface-level but convincing to the untrained ear. "But let me get you some refreshments."

"Really, we have more in our evening plan, so no thank you," said Callen.

Bella nodded as she pulled out her sketches, remaining steady despite the trembling in her hands. Anthony's eyes roamed over her work, a predator assessing his prey, while Jarl, who had slipped in behind them, watched her, his gaze unsettling in its intensity. She didn't dare cast a glance in Callen's direction, but she could feel his anger.

"Exquisite work, Bella," Anthony praised, though his eyes never left her face. "Your talent continues to impress." Anthony had seen these before. Not one of them were new. What was he up to?

"Thank you," Bella replied, keeping her tone even, her mind racing for any sign of their true intentions.

"Please, let us continue to the studio. I need just a glimpse of your current piece before I attend the meetings."

Jarl and Anthony were completely appropriate for the rest of the short time Callen and Bella were at the estate. Callen was fuming by the time they made it back to her car. "Who do they think they are?"

"I said they were obvious."

"Obvious? They were practically drooling."

"Good. That means I'm not imagining it."

"I still think you should finish your work at the ranch."

"Callen, I'd love to, but breaking the contract means I forfeit what I have painted and the money. I've earned every bit of that commission. I'm not bailing now."

"Dammit, Bella, I want to spank you so badly right now. You are not being very obedient."

Bella laughed. "So, what's new?"

"Nothing yet, but after I settle the naughty artist's debts that you are racking up, things will be very different. You can count on it."

"Yes, Daddy."

"Keep saying that, as I have my wicked way with you. It's the least you can do. And Uncle Kiernan is sending me someone to watch you while you are at the studio. They would have already been here but they were finishing up another job."

"Who?"

"You leave that to me. I'm in charge now. You just say, yes, Daddy."

"Yes, Daddy."

Bella was surprised when a woman knocked on her door Sunday morning, moments before Callen drove away. Bella looked outside as Callen was climbing into the pickup truck. They spoke through the window and then

"Hello?"

"Do you know who I am?"

Apprehension crowded Bella's mind. "Um, no. I don't think so."

"And yet you opened the door to me. Did you use your peep hole?"

"I thought you were my boyfriend's friend... hey, who are you exactly?"

"Your bodyguard, aka, your girlfriend, from New York."

"Oh, right, umm,.."

"I'm going to hang out with you while you finish your commission."

"But if you are a friend of mine, then you would have been an artist."

"Yes, that's true. Good thing I used to make money drawing caricatures of people in the parks in Chicago."

"But now you're a bodyguard?"

"Yes. I was bored so I changed careers and now I make a lot more money. Are you going to invite me in?"

Bella stepped back. The woman walked in. "I'm Maeve, by the way. And you are Bella."

"Yes,"

"Callen said you were trusting." Maeve looked around the room. "This is it? Kiernan didn't say you were renting a dump. I suggest you stay with me. I rented an apartment down the street and it's so much better than this. I'll take you there later. Ready for work?" Bella was stunned and stood staring at Maeve. "Oh, and in case you are worried that Callen is paying me, your Uncle Kiernan is picking up the tab. I was finishing up one job, and I offered to stay in the states for a little longer. Got any coffee?"

"Um..." Bella pointed to the pot. "I'm not sure I understand."

"Oh, right," said Maeve as she poured a cup of coffee for herself. "Kiernan assigned me to you. Kiernan, you know, Callen's uncle?"

"You mean he really has an Uncle Kiernan?"

"Callen's mom's older brother, but everyone calls him uncle, except me. Anyway, I work for Kiernan and he diverted me to this job since I was in the area and we needed a cover story. Your friend from college works great or a friend from New York, but it's easier to hide a college friend. You can have limitless college friends. I vote for that."

Bella scrunched up her face. "I'm not sure this is going to work. I mean. How am I supposed to paint with an audience?"

"I won't talk to you unless I have to. I'm a quiet person, really." Bella gave Maeve a look that clearly communicated her disbelief. "Really. I'll prove it to you once we get into your studio. Promise."

"That better be the truth, because I need quiet more than a bodyguard, so I'm expecting you to deliver."

"Done. Now can we go? This place is making me break out in hives."

Bella rolled her eyes. "What a wuss. Let's go."

BELLA SIGHED. SHE HAD hit a creative snag. Stress, probably. Glancing over at Maeve, she smiled. "Looks like your assignment will be over soon. You have done what we wanted you to do. Jarl and even Anthony have kept their distance. They haven't quit having me followed when away from the estate, but with you in the car, they haven't approached. I can handle that. And oddly enough, you make me feel safe."

"And you have to admit, my place is so much better than yours," added Maeve.

"So much better. Callen was almost more excited that I was staying here most of the time than he was that you're here."

"See, I tell you that I am under-appreciated."

Bella laughed. "And under-paid?"

Maeve shook her head. "No, never that. Your uncle Kiernan is very generous."

"Callen's uncle."

"Listen Bella. You are a Red Eagle for all intents and purposes. If Callen hasn't proposed, he will. You know why all these Red Eagle men aren't marrying yet, right?"

"Something about waiting for their parents?"

"Yep. Their mom and dad are staying with her father's brother."

"Uncle Kiernan?"

"No. Uncle Ewan. That is Kayleigh and Kiernan's uncle."

"Got it."

"It can be a lot."

"I think I am seeing things a little clearer. Where do you fit in?"

"I work for Kiernan sometimes."

"What do you do when you aren't working for him?"

"What place do we order from tonight? Thai? Or, how about Mexican? I haven't had good Mexican in a while."

"You are so obvious. Why don't you want to tell me what you do with the rest of your time?"

"If I told you, I'd have to kill you." Maeve gave Bella a deadpan expression.

"No, really." Bella put down the stack of takeout menus.

"I am serious. I do work for several business associates, each with their own agendas. You happen to be in the best position to meet criteria for one associate and you are Kiernan's family. Win-win for me and you."

"Fine. Does Callen or Stryker know about this?"

"Nope, and we aren't telling them. It's safer that way."

The next morning, Bella and Maeve drove to the estate to pick up her sketches of the last painting. Bella had been worried that Jarl or Anthony had some plan to get her alone. Both had begun to be testy whenever they spoke to her and she was hesitant to talk to them unless about the art she was creating. Evidently, Jarl and Anthony thought she was still in the studio. When Bella rounded the corner to tell Anthony that she was going to the ranch for a short break and would be back Monday or Tuesday, she overheard fragments of their hushed conversation. Instead of going on to Anthony's office, she lingered behind the half-closed solarium door and found her fears crystallized into a cold, hard reality.

"... after the unveiling, she'll be ours," Jarl's voice, laced with possessiveness, made her blood run cold. "Not much longer now. How do we get rid of that friend?"

"Patience, Jarl. We must not rush this. She's a rare find. I'll take care of Maeve. I might know of someone who would love the spitfire. Her auburn hair and slight accent turn many men on." Anthony's response was calculated, his words cloaked in darkness.

Jarl made a sneering sound that made Bella's belly churn. "I don't want to fight for my treats."

Bella's breath hitched in her throat. Her belly jumped in fear. They were speaking of her, she realized, not as an artist, but as an object to be claimed. Panic clawed at her insides, but she willed herself to remain calm. She couldn't let on that she'd heard their vile intentions, and she had to tell Maeve.

She knocked on the door and pushed it further open. "Is something the matter, Ms. Thompson?" Anthony called out, his voice suddenly too close.

Correcting Anthony was no use. She ignored his disregard for her desires. "Nothing at all," Bella forced a smile, though she felt it falter. "I must be getting back to the ranch for a few days. Breaks are necessary," she said with a wry smile. "But I'll be back Monday or Tuesday to start the final tweaking."

"Of course," Anthony agreed, though his eyes narrowed ever so slightly. "We wouldn't want to keep you from your break. I look forward to the last painting and the unveiling."

Jarl asked, "Any idea when that will be? There are several people Anthony would like to invite. They are some very intrigued art enthusiasts and they need to adjust their schedules."

Bella shrugged. "I'd like to say absolutely, but I honestly don't have a definitive timeframe. I'm having to visit my mother more often lately."

Anthony nodded. "Very well then. You will keep us informed."

It was not a question but an edict and Bella took it as he meant it. She had a few days to figure how she was going to finish and be ready to leave as soon as possible afterwards. Bella knew the unveiling wasn't something she would attend if she intended on staying safe.

Bella excused herself, her legs carrying her calmly but swiftly away from their sinister plotting. With every step, she felt the walls closing in; the air growing thinner. She had to get out, had to warn Callen, but first she would grab Maeve and go to the ranch. This was not turning into anything she had expected when she began this journey, and she was glad she had Maeve.

As the estate's grand façade faded into the distance, Bella's mind raced with the chilling knowledge of what awaited her after the unveiling. But she was not alone, and she would not make things easy for them. When she started talking to Maeve, she swore. Callen would have a fit when he found out.

Chapter 16

Change of plan

The afternoon sun cast a warm glow over the studio, where Bella stood before an easel, her delicate hand moving with precision. She'd waited until after the second weekend before returning this morning. She had all but removed most of her personal items from her apartment and put them in Maeve's second room in her suite. All Bella could think of was to finish and go home, but nothing seemed to be cooperating.

Her petite frame leaned in for some close work, her eyes narrowing as she focused on the smallest details—a cluster of wildflowers that needed more life, the hint of a shadow beneath the ancient oak tree that anchored the scene of western history and modern-day life. She had worked with Allie earlier today to capture that essence. Maeve sat quietly in the corner.

Life seemed more subdued these days. The world beyond her artwork faded away. Maeve had decided to appear to back off for a bit, only coming with Bella when Jarl was around, which was surprisingly little these days. Bella didn't want to speculate why that was.

Suddenly, a whisper sliced through the stillness, fracturing her bubble of solitude. Muffled voices that were obscured by the thick plaster walls of the adjoining room snagged her attention away from the painting's final touches. Bella's heart was more uneasy the closer to finishing she became. She strained to make sense of the indistinct murmurs. She waved at Maeve.

She set her brush down and took a tentative step toward the source of the secretive conversation, her ears tuning to the cadence of hushed tones. A frown etched itself upon her lips and she glanced over to see Maeve walking from the door she had presumably locked and then stand on a chair to the vent. Bella squinted her eyes as though that would help her hear better. Seeds of suspicion rooting deep within her gut.

Bella's pulse quickened as fragments of the hushed exchange began to crystalize into a menacing understanding. "After the unveiling," Bic's gravelly tone was unmistakable, even through the barrier separating them, "that's when we make our move." Bic was the man she had figured was following her or those under him. He was the head of Anthony's security, so it made sense. Maeve had seemed unconcerned with any of this until she finished her paintings. Things had now changed.

"Quiet, you fool," Jarl hissed, his voice a slimy whisper that sent a chill slithering down Bella's spine. "Walls have ears, and this plan is too important to risk."

The words struck Bella like a physical blow, her breath hitching in her throat. Kidnap? The thought was an icy shard in her heart, fear coiling tightly around her chest. She pressed her back against the wall, eyes wide with the terror of being hunted prey. Her mind raced, images of Jarl's cold, calculating eyes searing themselves into her thoughts.

She needed to tell Callen. Yet doubt clouded her resolve like a looming storm. Callen, with his fierce alpha presence and protective instincts, and his family would undoubtedly confront the danger head-on. But could she burden him with this knowledge? Callen would be angry if she didn't and with Maeve having heard some, if not all, of what was said, it was not something she could keep from him.

Bella's fingers twitched, longing for the comfort of her paint-brushes, the familiar caress of canvas—a solace now tainted by the dread of what lay beyond the art studio's sanctuary. Her thoughts were a battlefield where the desire to shield Callen clashed with the urgent need for his support. Every instinct screamed at her to run to him, to seek the safety of his embrace, to let his strength fortify her own. And yet, she hesitated, the weight of consequence heavy on her shoulders.

Maeve whispered in Bella's ear. "I'm going to unlock the door now. They have finished talking. We'll discuss this after we leave here. Keep painting if you can. Or clean the brushes or something so that we don't leave right after they talked. Give it at least fifteen minutes."

Bella nodded. Her mind returned to whether she should risk telling Callen or hope Maeve didn't tell him. In that moment of in-decision, Bella realized the depth of her feelings for the cowboy who had stolen her heart. It wasn't just the threat to her safety that tor-mented her; it was the thought of endangering him that frightened her most. She knew, without any semblance of doubt, that action was imperative.

Watching Maeve unlock her apartment door, Bella collapsed on the sofa. Maybe she had misheard or misinterpreted. It would be horrible if she did. The look on Maeve's face told her she didn't. Maeve placed a finger over her lips to indicate quiet. Bella watched her walk around the apartment with a bug detector and finally, she nodded at Bella.

"Well, I heard enough to say I need to work out an alternative ending."

"Are they thinking of kidnapping me?"

"Sounds like it. So, we must tell Callen, Kiernan, and my other client, who was worried about this same thing and has a stake in the process."

"Maybe I could sneak away right after the reveal. We don't have to tell Callen. I'll just show up. I can come up with some excuse to slip away and then disappear into the night."

"Sorry, but I don't think anyone will allow you to do the reveal. Jarl made it known he knew where your family lived, and I am sure Kiernan will send someone over to her soon."

"You don't think that he would do something to Tracy?" That thought hadn't really occurred to Bella. Her fear ramped up.

"I have no idea, but better safe than sorry."

Her plan would be to complete the commission as quickly as possible and still create well. She knew she could do nothing else, so she determined to keep her focus, create beauty and then go back to Callen and her new forever. All before Jarl knew she had left. She quietly began to formulate her plan without bringing in Callen or telling Maeve that there were now two people outside her building. He would be angry when he found out and there would be hell to pay, even from the other guys, but she had to take charge and keep the others safe.

Finally, this was the last day she would walk into this studio and the last day she would have to hide from Jarl. They called him the vice president of operations, but she knew by now that it was a cover for what he really was, and that was a crime boss' second in command. And Bic was Shaffer's enforcer and the man Jarl most often had to keep an eye on her. She had spotted him often in the last month and realized he had been doing it the whole time. Jarl and Anthony wanted her for some horrific reason, and they had gotten sloppy with hiding that fact.

Callen called Bella after Maeve made her calls and her plan not to bring him into things went south. Fast.

"Bella, we have some serious talking to do when you get home, but for right now, I'm coming to get you. You said your final painting is done and now you are coming home."

"But there are loose ends to tie up."

"The only acceptable response is, yes, Daddy."

"But, I have to—"

"Bella Kaye, say yes, Daddy."

"Yes, Daddy."

"Good, now listen to Maeve. She is going to get you out of there and then she's staying to tie up your loose ends."

"Fine."

That was last night. Today, Bella was relieved she was finished. She'd sent a message three days ago, knowing Anthony and Jarl were out of the country. She said she was cleaning the studio, and the work was ready for him. Anthony said, through Jarl, that he'd be out of the country for a few more days, and he wanted to view the art when he got home. Jarl was with him, but not Bic. No, Bic was presently sitting in a vehicle within view of her row house outer door.

Anthony followed up with a message himself, asking her to stay in town until he returned so he could see the paintings with her. He posed it as a question. She heard it as the demand it was. She agreed, relieved that Jarl was with him. Maeve was doing some things on her own, leaving Bella to finish her packing.

"Don't look like you are packing a lot. Good thing you have done most of your moving already to my place. I'll get you your things. You just follow the plan."

"Okay."

Time to disappear.

The rest was obvious. She was a bit of a minimalist, so that helped. Time to go clean the studio so her tail would follow her back to the estate and miss Maeve clearing out any of the things she had piled at the door. The rest would be picked up by Allie's friend for another needy soul.

Her heart had been racing all day, and she'd been jumpy. One of the men who walked the estate for security and checked in on her hourly looked at her oddly several times. She smiled and shrugged.

"I'm not good with transitions."

The man had nodded and kept walking. She finished up and left out the side door before he returned. Not that every person in the place didn't know when she left the house and then left the estate, but she liked to live in the illusion that she wasn't watched twenty-four-seven. And she was out before Anthony and Jarl had returned.

Arriving back to the apartment with her expected tail in tow, Bella sighed her relief. Everything was done. Bella had noticed that Bic was once again hanging around the apartment building in a different car today. She was ready. Whenever she looked out, he might have moved the car, but he was always there. She was glad all this would be over in a few hours. She just had to show up to give them the final presentation and then she would leave. Without Maeve.

Returning to her apartment from the back stairs after leaving her friend's place via the back stairs, she heard Bic speaking near the top of the staircase and she stopped to listen. She had never heard or seen him inside or near her apartment before. The chill that ran up her spine had her biting her lip, so no sound released.

"She's inside. She didn't go anywhere the whole time you were gone except to the estate."

"Good. She'll be done with the boss' work once she presents it tonight, but she's just what I've been looking for in my girl. The boss wants her for business. I want her for pleasure. Compliant, pretty, and smart, with just a little bit of spunk."

"What does she think about it all? I mean, living in the boss' world isn't for everyone."

"Bella will do as she is told. I'll teach her that. So, when you pick her up for the meeting with the boss, just make sure you don't give anything away."

"You sure the boss will be okay with you taking her if he wants to go into business with her?"

"Who says it's against her will or that he's not going into business with her? You are assuming shit you don't know fuck all about. She hasn't told me that she isn't willing or turned down the boss's proposal. Come on, I have things for you to do before you come back to get her."

There was a pause. "But her tail."

"She is packing up her place or getting ready for tonight or both. She isn't going anywhere."

"Gotcha."

Both men left by the unreliable elevator that, for once, Bella hoped, got stuck. Bella crept to her apartment. Racing to the window that had long ago lost its glazing seal, she watched as she saw them head to their vehicles and leave. Oh God, oh God, oh God! What to do? *Call Callen*, was her first thought but then, if she did that, he would tell her to stay where she was and he'd come get her but it would be too late. Then he'd go to the estate. He could get hurt. Bella knew the men at the estate all carried guns. Cal never did except on the ranch when working the cattle. He'd bring his brothers, but they could get hurt, too.

Call Maeve. That is her job. But Bella had learned that Maeve would charge into battle without a backward glance. Not that she didn't have skills. The woman had kickass tattooed at birth, but Bella could just take off and stop all of this. Maybe. Stryker, of all people, spoke in her head. *Get help from those you trust. Trust those who have proven themselves.* Bella sent a group text.

Bella: Did you know that prey never flies home in danger in order to keep its family safe?

A quick response came back.

Maeve: In most cases prey would survive if it did. The odds are in favor in group than alone.

Callen: A Daddy always comes when there is danger.

Bella: Good to know.

Bella clinched her butt. She couldn't wait. She sent another text to Maeve only.

Bella: Things have escalated. Calling in sick.

Maeve: Understood.

She would have to do this on her own and hoped Callen understood when she showed up on his doorstep after he expected her to wait for him and their first elaborate plan set for after the presentation. Maeve seemed to go to plan "B" easily, but Callen would be angry if she did this part alone. How things got so crazy in a flash was more than she could answer, but he would take care of whatever the fallout was.

Who were these people that they thought they could just kidnap her and no one would notice? She'd already had that talk with herself and Maeve earlier. She set herself up. She knew it was her fault in one way, but Jarl had not taken "I'm not interested," well. Not well at all, it seemed. And Anthony. What kind of business would work with a captive woman?

She created a delayed send message on her email to go out thirty minutes before she was to be picked up, addressed to Anthony and Jarl.

"I'm feeling really ill. I'll have to postpone our meeting until tomorrow. I'm heading to urgent care, or maybe the emergency room. Not sure which, but one of them. I'll get back to you as soon as I can. The paintings are in the studio. Please, enjoy them tonight if you like."

Bella was under no illusions that these men had already perused her work all along the way but she chose to perpetuate the charade of waiting for the surprise by Anthony. She'd received her final payment this morning, so even though she wouldn't ever be in their midst again, she had told them where to find everything. Then she took her phone apart to make sure there wasn't a tracker on it like she'd learned in a women's seminar on staying safe. Even though she always put her cell in her back pocket, you never knew completely. No tracker. She sighed her relief. What about her car?

No, they didn't need a tracker because they were always personally tracking her, nonetheless she jogged over to her mechanic neighbor on the other side and asked if he could tell if the undercarriage of a car was bugged. His face lit up.

"I've got this cool tracer for GPS trackers." He started pulling his shoes on. "You're the blue car in the parking next to mine, right?"

"Yes. Here are my keys."

"Thanks. This little beauty works, but I don't get many calls to use it. I'll be back in a few."

Bella was glad she could make someone happy today. With her course determined, she waited for her neighbor to return. When he did, he had a dissatisfied expression. Oh, he must have found something. Did he remove it?

"Give me the bad news," Bella said as she met him on the landing.

"Bad news? Yeah, well, I didn't find anything. Not a whiff of anything. Good for you and a bummer for me."

Trying not to be irritated at his response, she said soothingly, "Sorry. Better luck next time, huh?"

"Yeah. Oh well, no worries for you. Have a good night." He walked dejectedly into his apartment, and Bella allowed that fear to slide off her plate. Now, if she could slide a few more off, it would be easier. But things were moving way too fast. Her anxiety that things wouldn't work was high.

Once again, she chose to use the back stairs and was relieved she had thought of parking in the corner. She was headed to the safety of Callen and the Red Eagle Ranch. Realistically Bella had no other options to explore even if she wanted to and she didn't. She hoped

Maeve was able to do the things she had said she would do, and that they worked. All Bella could do now was follow the modified plan and hope things worked.

Chapter 17

Escape

G rabbing her bag, she took it to the car and tossed it into her trunk, and now that it was getting dark, she was relaxing a little. She raced up to the stairs for one final look around and grabbed her second, smaller bag, her purse and slipped out of the door, with an immense sense of doom, fear, and urgency.

"They aren't coming two hours early. That has never happened before. They have barely arrived back at the estate, so there is nothing to worry about," Bella assured herself.

Bella crossed the parking lot a little quicker the second time. She hoped she was right and every logical thought said she was safe, but the fear that she hadn't gone yet and wasn't on the ranch still dominated her thoughts. Her whole goal from this second forward was to get under the protection of Callen. Unfortunately, knowing that anything could still happen was a strong agitator.

Climbing into her car, she drove to the other side of town and signed into the check-in sheet at the acute care counter. As soon as she sat down, she pretended she was looking for something.

"Oh darn, I left my phone in the car. I'll be right back."

"No problem," replied the receptionist.

Bella climbed into her little car, next to one that looked identical to hers, thanks to Maeve, and drove away. If Jarl or Bic found her somehow and followed her to that spot, they would see the car and might think Bella was in the back and wait for her or think she went to the emergency room instead.

Between the hour and a half head start before the message was released and the time it would take them to figure out, she was gone for real, she'd have made the just over two-hour run to the ranch further north and in the middle of nowhere. She wouldn't be found and if she was, there was plenty of protection. Yes, they knew about Callen, so probably the ranch but she didn't need to worry about the Red Eagles. Callen said they had plenty of clan protection on both sides of his family. She hoped so. Something was telling her that things would get ugly soon.

Bella hoped the snow was gone from the recent storm, or at least not too bad. Her little car was tough, but she wasn't good at driving in the snow at night. She drove carefully in the darkened areas between little towns. Bella was never so glad to pull into the small familiar town of Buffalo Township for a fill up, a bathroom run, and to stretch her legs. She hadn't felt comfortable doing that until reaching town. But it was definitely cold and blustery right now.

Again, she contemplated stopping and staying at her old home, but she just didn't feel like that was home anymore. She would need to add cleaning out the house to her list of things to do to get on with her forever. And to be honest, only one place was home now, and that was the ranch. She yearned to be folded into Callen's arms. She figured she had better tell him she was on her way early.

She tried to call Callen, now that she was in town and if, for some reason, the roads were too dangerous, she could hole up in the only motel overnight. The phone went directly to voicemail. Callen wasn't ignoring her because he was angry. He loved her, but she knew she was in for one hell of a spanking. She should have listened to him and stayed on the ranch the last time but the money she had made was good and how could she forfeit her work for free? So she kept her contract.

Callen wouldn't see it that way, but there wasn't anything she could do about any of this now. And his not answering made sense, really. She rationalized that he could be anywhere. Cell service in town wasn't great on good days and the internet either unless you had a booster. The ranch had one, but the roads between the bigger spreads and town were spotty at best. Talking herself down from her fears was harder than usual, but she was able to climb back into her car and head toward the Red Eagle.

"Great. More snow," Bella said to Pinky and Ping-Pong. "I didn't see that coming."

The wind was whipping the large flakes of snow, and it swirled around her car, reflecting her headlights making it even eerier. Bella turned on her wipers and her amber halogen fog lights so she could see the road and the surrounding area. No streetlights out here. A vehicle was coming. She checked to make sure her lights wouldn't blind the oncoming vehicle. A big pickup careened past her at speeds a race car driver wouldn't use on this very dark, very icy, snowy road.

While she had been courteous, the truck hadn't and his high, overly bright headlights hit her square in the eyes. She braked and immediately felt herself slide as the truck continued on its too fast way. She turned her wheel into the slide, as she remembered from her driver's education class too many years to count. Before she could have another thought, she sat in the ditch, upright but truly stuck in the snowbank.

"Damn it!" She stopped the angry, defeated tears that she felt tingling in her nose and filling her eyes. Her bags had deployed. "Pull it together, Bella. You have had worse things happen. Let's see how far we are from the ranch."

Thank goodness her engine was still running. She deflated the bag in her face and checked her GPS program. "Two miles isn't far."

Except it was in freezing weather, in the dark, with dangerous men looking for her, because by now they had to have received the email. She hoped Jarl would wait until tomorrow but didn't think it was likely. When he wanted something, he got it and he made it abundantly clear that he wanted her. Besides, Bella doubted Anthony took refusals well and any further association with either of them would be a hard "no".

Bella was tough. She was one to push through to accomplish her goal and she wanted to be that person, but she could feel herself slide back into that girl that looked to Callen to handle her problems. She hadn't felt that version of herself this strongly in years. Tonight, it might have been okay to give him her troubles.

That Stryker Red Eagle thinking came through again. Lean on those you trust. She shoved that weak person aside and started gathering her coat and gear. She took a deep breath, tried to reach Callen again and then the ranch without getting through. She left messages that who knew when they would receive them, and that wouldn't change the situation right now. Resigned to her fate, she turned off her car.

Putting on her coat, wrapping a scarf around her face, leaving only her eyes uncovered, and pulling her gloves on her shaking hands, she opened the door. She grabbed her purse and her paperwork bag, crisscrossing them over her body as she stepped out of the car and started walking to the ranch. No cell service this far out of town, so she debated whether to leave the hazard lights on or not and decided it wasn't going to help tonight to leave them on.

She shivered as the wind seemed to cut through her heavy coat. Bella was used to harsh winters, but this was really cold. "One foot in front of the other, Bella. It's only two miles."

"Just a little further," was her chant as she worked on raising her spirits and focusing on putting one booted foot in front of the other.

She focused on walking to the far fence post and then the next furthest fence post, hoping that it would allow her to get there in one, not totally frozen, piece. She could feel her legs getting colder.

She pulled out her cell phone as she trudged through the subzero weather, checking for the non-existent service.

She used the light to see her surroundings. She could see a familiar barn that wasn't too far from the ranch. Sorry that she didn't put another layer or even two of clothing underneath her outer wear, Bella put away her light and tried to ignore that she felt the cold through what she was currently wearing. She was keeping an emergency kit in her car from now on.

Bella wished she knew how far she'd gone. But, however far it was, she realized it wasn't nearly as far as she needed to go. She prayed that someone would find her along the side of the road, but she didn't hold out much hope at this time of night in this weather. Ranchers tended to go to bed fairly early because they got up so early, but it was Friday night, so hopefully someone had a night out.

She had really begun to worry as her feet became numb and thinking was slower. Her teeth had begun chattering for a while. Headlights that could only belong to a large truck came down the road but not barreling, as the previous truck had.

By the time Bella realized she was still walking in the middle of the road and should move, the vehicle had come to a shuddering stop. She was bathed in light. She heard the slam of a door and a male voice was fuming, spewing some not so nice words her way.

Chapter 18

Found

C allen hated coming home in the winter after a night of hanging out at the bar, as tonight turned out to be. It was his turn to watch the girls spend a few hours having a girls' night. The weather turned and several of the guys came to pick them up while Callen paid their tab and gathered the things the girls seemed to always leave behind like a glove, or a scarf.

Tonight, Teagan left her wallet. He sent a text to her, and she said thanks. "Don't tell Declan." He smiled. Yeah, he was going to say nothing when he handed it to her in front of his brother and walk off. Let her tell him. Right before he went to grab Bella. The only reason he'd agreed to watch the girls tonight was because he was antsy and this would occupy his mind.

All he could really think about was Bella and going to get her for good tomorrow. She'd had a hard time of it and this was the end of a chapter of their life that would never be repeated. She would be with him, living on the ranch, every day from now on. They would decide on and then build their house, so come the autumn of the year, they would be married, in their own cozy little house. Maybe working on another little Red Eagle. But together.

Callen was tired. His mind wouldn't stop thinking about Bella. His gut clenched with an unusual dread. He couldn't get it out of his mind that something was wrong. Really wrong. He told his Bluetooth to call Bella, but she was out of service somewhere. Damn it.

He was going to get a satellite subscription or something for her, so he could call her wherever she was.

He'd been careful not to drink the last few hours, and he'd had dinner at Cattleman's, making sure it absorbed the remaining alcohol, but damn, even sober he nearly hit her.

Callen swerved and slammed on his brakes. His big truck jolted to a stop. Thank God the ranch had bought them good vehicles last year. Who the hell would be walking on the side of a country road half-dragging what looked like a canvas bag behind them in the middle of the damn night? Someone must have had a fight, or worse, too much to drink. Friday night in cowboy country could sometimes end that way.

Callen couldn't see who it was but whoever it was would have some explaining to do when he got her back home. Wherever home was. And he might have to kick some cowboy butt when they got there. A man who cared for his girl would never let her take off into the night, not in winter or summer. He took care of his woman and made sure she didn't feel the need to scamper off.

Callen threw his truck into park and eased off the brake before he tossed his door open. His determined walk told of his irritation. It was obviously a woman and his need to chastise her for being unsafe felt odd to him. Only his Bella and the other women in the family got that kind of reaction from him. Usually, for the community females, he looked for the first place he could unload a woman in a situation like that.

There was no one here but him and her. So, it would have to be him taking care of her. Even as he had the thought, he followed that up with a faint feeling of familiarity. Did he know her? Likely. It was a few small communities in a large portion of real estate, and they employed at least one member of most families around here. His determination increased.

"Hey, do you know you almost got plowed over by my truck? What made you think walking out here on a country road after midnight was a good idea? Where do you live that you're walking out here, in the pitch of night, where anyone, hell, where I almost hit you?" The wind picked up and Bella couldn't contain a violent shiver.

"It w-wouldn't be th-the f-f-irst time t-tonight."

"What?"

Callen felt like he was losing the plot. And that voice, the wind was whipping the snow and freezing cold around, but he thought he might recognize that voice. Who was she? And whoever she was, she was obviously cold.

The woman, it was definitely a woman, shivered, as did he with that wind. She was likely numb from the cold. She turned and took a step into the truck's headlights, blinding her but giving him the recognition he needed.

"Bella?" He didn't know what was going on, but he understood he needed to get her in his truck as soon as possible.

"Callen? Thank God."

The words sounded faint and fragile, and he struggled to believe it was his girl. She was supposed to be with Maeve in town until he came to grab her the next day. Callen watched as the woman seem to crumble in place. He barely caught her before she hit the ground. His whole body lit up. He knew her. He didn't need to verify, but he did because he'd been thinking about Bella so much tonight that he could have been imagining her. He turned to her, so the light didn't blind him, but assisted him in getting a good look at the woman in his arms. She felt like his girl. His heart stopped. What the hell was she doing out here?

"Bella? Baby? Are you okay? Honey, I don't know why you're here, what happened or why you didn't call me, but I've got you now. We'll figure out the rest later."

He unhooked the canvas bag from her shoulder and scooped her up. Damn, she was lighter than he expected, but dead weight was still dead weight, and she was nearly unconscious, cold, and exhausted. He placed her inside his truck, put on her seatbelt, and resisted the urge to kiss her blue lips and spank her likely frozen ass before shutting the door. Not now. Now she was in some kind of trouble and every protective instinct he had was ignited. He had to get her to the ranch, get her warm and dry before he started to work things out.

"C-Callen?" she said when he threw her bag in the back. "M-my car is s-sitting in the ditch back there, s-somewhere." She shivered. "M-my clothes that I brought with me are there too. M-Maeve has the rest."

"Baby, it's covered in snow by now. I didn't see it as I passed, but I didn't know to look out for it. We can go back and get everything else in the morning. You can wear anything of mine you want. I need to get you to the house and warm you up. It's late for you to be out here and too damn cold for anyone. Why are you here? When I got to town, I tried calling you but no answer, then just a little while ago you were out of service range. I guess I know why now."

Callen cranked the heat up, turned on her heated seats, and started to pull back onto the road.

"Why didn't you tell me you were coming? I'd have met you partway, or at least in town."

Bella didn't respond right away. She plastered her gloved hands on the heat vents in front of her, then snuggled into the warm seat and accepted the blanket Callen dragged from the back seat.

"There's so much to tell. I'm scared. I didn't know what to do, and I didn't have anywhere else to go. I don't know where I'm safe."

"Hell, baby. You should have told me. I would have come and gotten you."

"N-no. It wasn't safe. Everything happened so fast."

"Then we would have all come. Never mind, we are nearly at the ranch. Let's get you home and figure this out. Things will be okay now. I've got you." He placed his hand on her thigh. He noted how cold her leg was through her pants. Too cold.

"No! Wait. I've changed my mind. I can't go to the ranch."

"You can't go to the ranch? Baby, you're just cold and you aren't thinking straight."

"I am and I can't go. Not when I could be putting people in danger."

"You are absolutely going to the ranch. I need to be able to take care of you, and that happens at the Red Eagle."

"He's dangerous. They both are."

"That Berg guy and Shaffer? No, hold on. Just wait until I have you warm and fed, at least before you start filling in some blanks. No one is dangerous enough to best the Red Eagles and many wouldn't even try, so whatever is going on, we'll take care of it."

They were pulling onto the ranch, and once they were through the security gate, he heard Bella sigh. She was really scared, and it made him feel good that he could offer her a place of protection, but what the fuck? He got her a bodyguard. Where was Maeve? Angry didn't even cover his reaction to her being fearful of another person. That Jarl guy and his boss were so insecure he couldn't take a *no thank you* from her? Callen was kicking his own ass because he allowed Bella to dictate how he handled things. Not again.

Callan's first instinct was to take her into the farthest part of the house, gather all of their people, have them load up their guns and rifles. Then they would take shifts on watching all the women while he went on a hunting expedition to find this Jarl character. Yeah, that was his first thought, but then his second thought was a bit more controlled. Até would never allow vigilantism.

He needed the whole story from Bella before he engaged and eliminated the threat. He needed to have a conversation with his brothers, and then they would plan because he was determined not to let Bella go again. She was his to protect, and she would just have to get used to that idea. She was his baby girl and that meant that she would come to him if she had a problem or needed help. Not do things herself. When this was all over, she would understand that. He'd make sure of it.

Bella moaned. "My legs and feet and everywhere hurt."

"Yeah. I knew that would happen. Sorry, baby, that you have to go through the warming process, but you need the blood to get back into those extremities. I'll get Seamus to look at you."

He looked over at the woman he'd never been able to get out of his mind from the moment he met her in his yard helping their gardener to today. No longer a teenager, but an accomplished artist who held her own beliefs and expectations of the world. She looked frightened and resigned to her fate, caught like a helpless rat in a trap, and he'd be damned if she would stay there. He couldn't love a woman more than he loved Bella. It was time to take the reins.

"Bella, we're here."

There was no response, and he wondered if she'd fallen asleep and then he saw her blink and he knew she was tired, cold, traumatized and he was expecting too much if he thought she would be able to do more than warm up and maybe eat something light and then go to bed.

He hopped out of the pickup, grabbed her canvas bag out of the back seat and soundly closed the door, walking around to open hers. Bella jumped when he opened the passenger door, as though she didn't hear the slam of the back door or the driver's door. She shivered and looked at him, almost shell-shocked.

"Come on baby, let's get you inside. If Seamus is home, he'll make sure you're okay and fed and Stryker will make sure you're warm and I'll make sure you don't get lost in the shuffle. I'll try to keep the women away from you tonight, but they'll want to coddle, because I guess that's what women do. Our women, anyway."

Bella just stared at him with a half-smile and a half nod before sliding around to exit the truck. "Whoa baby, let's get you out of the seat belt first."

Callen turned her back enough so he could unclip the seat belt, and then he brought her to the edge and lifted her out of the truck, bridal style. He finally got a response out of her.

"Callen Red Eagle put me down! I can walk. I'm just a little tired."

Callen laughed. Yeah, she'd be fine. His grip tightened. "Settle down, Bella Kaye, before I flip you over my knee and spank that sassy ass."

Bella went still and quiet. "You wouldn't dare."

Callen heard her words but felt the tremble he had learned long ago to associate with a turned-on Bella. Now wasn't the time to deal with their attraction, but he had every intention of following up on that soon. Right now, however, he had to take care of her immediate needs, which demanded his own arousal would have to wait. He was learning to be a patient man.

As he reached the top of the front porch stairs, the heavy oak door swung opened in a controlled movement, allowing Callen to continue straight into the living room. He was surprised when he saw it was Avery who held the door open, not one of his brothers.

"Hey, honey. What are you doing up?"

He dropped his tone just a hair to encourage her truthful response, although Avery was usually forthcoming all on her own. Stryker was a strict man, except when it came to the women. Avery could excite his brother's spanking hand and his indulgent hand faster than anyone Callen had ever met. Stryker and the rest of them had helped keep her safe from her brother and his associates soon after Stryker and she got together. Stryker and Avery had many over the knee conversations, but no one would argue they were meant for each other.

Seamus had found Kai after so many years apart. They had worked together to keep her safe from a greedy man. Declan found Teagan in the nick of time because of the connection they had and similar interests. Keeping her safe had been almost impossible, but they had done it because Declan claimed her and wouldn't let go.

Callen, like his brothers, used his father's teachings to center himself. He knew something was very wrong with Bella. He'd get to the bottom of it tonight, even if he had to call Maeve to do it. They would eliminate the threat and erase his girl's fear. That reminder killed his libido response.

Seamus walked into the family room, going straight for the fire to stoke its embers back to life. Without a word, Callen placed Bella in the armchair next to the fire and began to strip off her outer wear.

"No thermal underwear or flannel under clothes or anything? Baby, what were you thinking?"

"That I had to get to you. My car was in the ditch—"

"In the ditch? Are you okay?" asked Stryker from the doorway.

"Um, yes? I mean, yes. Please everyone, go back to bed. I'm so sorry I woke you up. Don't let me disturb your sleep." She grabbed her coat from where it lay over Callen's forearm. He stopped her from moving away from him. "I'll figure something out."

"You'll figure what out?" asked Seamus as he returned to the room with a large medical kit.

"My problem."

Declan walked into the family room, grabbed a thick fuzzy throw, and stood ready to cover her once Callen got her outer clothing off. "Sounds like Little Miss Bella is looking for a paddling," said Declan. Bella gasped her surprise at his announcement. Callen barely suppressed his grin.

"I'm not little," said Bella vehemently. "I'm a grown woman with adult problems that I am going to handle myself."

Bella watched all the Red Eagle brothers look at Callen. "Yes, I hear you, but understand that you are *my* Baby Girl, and that is all there is to it. I said we would handle things and we will. It has nothing to do with your independence, your abilities, or your stubbornness. It does, however, have everything to do with who you belong to and that is me."

"I'll start some soup and warm up the bread," said Avery before Bella could answer and get herself into more trouble.

"I've got the coffee," said Teagan, followed by a yawn.

Kai padded in with a heavy robe and boot slippers. "We still have plenty of dessert. I'll heat the peach cobbler for everyone."

The tears rolled quickly down Bella's face. Callen took the blanket from Declan and sat next to his girl, pulling her into his lap. He sighed with relief when she snuggled into his arms without resisting the comfort.

"Baby, what's wrong?"

She sniffled. "I woke everyone up."

Renee wandered into the family room, still fully dressed. "Why so late tonight, young lady?" asked Stryker.

"Because I'm an adult. No curfew, remember? I'm not a young lady to you, Stryker. I'm your sister. Your grown sister and I stayed out past your bedtime, not mine. Sorry, but it *is* Friday night."

Carson wandered into the kitchen door. "Why are all the lights on? It's after midnight."

All the men gave Carson various versions of a firm stare. "I imagine it's got something to do with the room being so hot in here, Bella sitting on Callan's lap, and a car in the ditch a few miles down the road."

"You would be right," said Stryker. "Why is your car in the ditch, Bella?"

"I was trying to get away and a big truck tried to run me over."

"What?" asked Callen.

"Well, I'm not sure, but he did road hog and made me slide into the snowbank."

"Can you describe the truck?" asked Carson. "Between us, we probably know every one of them in the district."

"It was almost as big as I imagine one of those monster trucks to be. Bigger than Cullen's and any I've seen being driven on the ranch."

"Color?" asked Seamus who, before her eyes, seemed to go from gentle giant to avenging angel.

"Well, it had to be a light color because I didn't really know the lights were that close until they were nearly driving over me." Bella shivered. Declan put another throw over her shoulders.

Nearly everyone in the room said, "Felix."

"You know who it is?"

Callen's expression hardened. "Yeah, baby. You described Felix's rig to a tee. I'm going to take him apart limb by limb."

"What? Callen, no. I don't want to draw attention to me being here. We have to let it go and get my car out of the ditch."

Renee shook her head. "Afraid that isn't going to happen. Not tonight anyway."

"She isn't wrong," said Carson. "The snow has almost covered it. I flagged it so its owner could find it later. Guess that will be us. We're going to have to dig it out. I'll get a couple of the guys to head out with me tomorrow with the snowplow and the tow. We'll get it out."

"I don't want to trouble anyone," said Bella, the distress heard loud and clear. "I had to leave because I believe they were going to kidnap me even before the unveiling, so I dumped and ran. Maeve had a backup plan, and it worked. Even if I'm a little worse for wear."

Avery and Mia brought in coffee and cobbler. They were followed by Teagan who carried a bowl of soup. She sat the soup on a side table and began to pull out the bed tray.

"Don't bother." Callen reached for the bowl. "I'll help her."

He proceeded to blow on the spoonful of soup and test it before holding the utensil in front of Bella's mouth. Bella took the bite without hesitation, then she froze, her eyes wide. Callen smiled but didn't comment.

"I can do it," said Bella quietly.

"Agreed, but I'm going to do it."

The next time the spoon was held to her mouth, she shook her head as though she were done eating. Callen leaned close to her ear. "We take care of our women, and you are going to let me do that. Tomorrow we can negotiate, but not tonight. You're having this soup, then we are going upstairs to a shower and bed."

"Callen..."

"And if you want to create a scene, I'll haul your cute ass out of here and paddle it, then we will come back and finish the soup. Got me?"

She blushed hotly but nodded. "That's my sweet baby Bella. Now open."

She obediently did and finished the entire bowl. Callen grinned. Bella seemed better.

"We need a plan. Since the exit plan we set up for tomorrow is obviously not in play now. Also, I haven't heard from Maeve, which bothers me some."

"Maeve! I forgot to call her." Bella tried to scramble out of Callen's lap.

Declan raised his hand. "But I didn't, so update. She is on her way here in the morning. She will text before she leaves and as she gets closer. Evidently, there was a shakeup when Bella left. There's a lot more story, but Maeve will fill us in tomorrow."

"Well, my girl needs a shower and a bed. We'll talk tomorrow. Not much to do but feed the stock tomorrow with all the snow we've gotten."

"Well, I've got paperwork to do," said Stryker.

Avery grinned. "You always have paperwork to do, but does this mean tomorrow is a snow day?"

"Yeah, except there's no such thing on a ranch. Not sure about the professors, though." Stryker looked at his brother, holding Teagan in his lap.

"Spring break next week and I don't do Friday classes, so all good. Teagan is working on a project so, no classes either."

Teagan grimaced. "I was nearly done. Guess I'll grade papers or something. It will be a bit before I can go to sleep."

Seamus looked at the wall clock pointedly but said nothing. Stryker did raise his eyebrow in question. Declan shook his head. "No papers tonight, baby. Let's work on getting you to sleep."

"Really, I can't...oh, yeah. I should try to sleep." She blushed, and the men grinned, including Callen. Declan kissed her on the forehead and squeezed her tight.

The rest called out goodnight, and everyone headed to their beds. Callen led a very tired Bella upstairs and walked her into one of the two hall bathrooms, turning on the shower. When he faced her again, she simply stood there as though processing was going to be a herculean effort.

"Baby, let me help you shower and get into bed."

She wasn't responding, and when she finally did, she agreed. "Okay."

"Right."

With clinical precision, against his cock's demands and his primitive brain's inclinations, he stripped her, directing what he needed her to do as she soundlessly did it. It hurt his heart to see her shut down like this. He hesitated, then followed his instincts, quickly stripping down. He waited for his girl to screech or tell him to get out, but she didn't. Bella stood calmly as he took care of her. She didn't seem to realize he was even in the room with her.

His ego might have taken a hard hit if it weren't that Callen knew how intensely his girl had tried to get to safety, and she'd decided he was her answer. He would always be her protector, her lover, her man, as she would be his reason for existing. She wouldn't always like how he took care of her, but at least she would have company in her irritation. The other women would likely be under the same restrictions when things needed to be held close to the vest. Like now. The one thing she would always know, though, is that she was his everything.

He walked her into the shower with calm, nonsensical words as he followed her in. He watched her shower for a few moments and thought he'd never seen a more beautiful woman. It was close to eight years since they had broken up. He'd missed out on all her maturing, physically, mentally and emotionally. She's missed out on his but they would make up for it by being primary in each other's lives.

His hands wanted to linger, learn her body, revel in the feel of her, but she had experienced one traumatic day and night. He would never add to her ordeal. He hadn't even heard the details of this last installment and knew he wanted to go on the warpath, like his ancestors, and protect his family. Like his ancestors, he was going to take control of what was his.

"Bella, just hold the bar while I wash you."

He knew Stryker was Avery's daddy, and Seamus was Kai's, yet he hadn't really been drawn to that dynamic with anyone but Bella. Right now, as he took intimate care of his girl, he could see some of the advantages. He didn't need the designation to take care of her like his brothers did their women. He wanted that part of the dynamic but calling him daddy didn't really do it for him until now. Spanking, on the other hand, was definitely his thing and his girl needed her gorgeous ass heated for doing things on her own without including him from the beginning.

Once he had Bella washed and himself cleaned, he left her holding onto the shower bar under the warm spray while he stepped out and dried off quickly. Tying the towel around his waist before grabbing a second towel, Callen turned off the water, then held a towel up for her to walk into, which she did. He then began drying her carefully but vigorously because she didn't have any clothes in the room.

"Callen, can I stay with you?"

"Of course, baby. You are staying with me. You're on the ranch."

She nodded, then asked, "Staying in your bed?"

"You aren't ever sleeping without me again."

She nodded again. "I don't like to be alone."

"That isn't going to happen unless one of us is gone from the ranch on business. We are a couple."

"Forever?"

She was killing him here. "Forever."

"And we can snuggle."

Snuggle? Hell yeah. "And snuggle."

She whispered her answer. "I can't be alone."

"You won't be alone, I promise you. We have a lot of things to figure out tomorrow."

"Okay."

He hurried to grab his sleep shorts and a tee shirt for Bella and when Cullen opened the door; he saw she was curled up, fast asleep. He stood and just watched her for a few moments. He could have lost her tonight. The thought was like a punch in the gut. Right now, his girl was the most relaxed he'd seen her since she started this commission. Taking the opportunity, he left her naked in the bed while he threw their clothes in the wash. He'd toss them in the dryer in the morning.

Next, he slipped the tee shirt over her head and grinned when she murmured something about being too early to get up. He slid in behind her and spooned his baby. God, this felt so good. She'd been gone so long, months right after years. He would do everything he could to make sure she was comfortable with him because this was their new sleeping norm. Hell, it was going to be their new norm, period. The planning for building their house had begun and would get into full swing when all this Shaffer and Berg shit was over.

He was never so glad that his parents had built a large home as he had become recently when his brothers and now, their forever loves were here. His mom had wanted more kids, but once Renee was born, they decided they had enough. Having four brothers was tough for her, but when Carter and Jacob joined the party, Callen thought she just gave up.

Bella was in trouble, and it killed him inside. She hadn't asked him for help when she felt unsafe until it was almost too late. That Jarl guy with the funny sounding name had done something to his girl to make her so fearful that she had risked herself to get to Callen. But brave enough and reckless enough to jeopardize herself. That would stop now. He had no intention of her ever needing to do that again. Ever.

Chapter 19

At the Ranch

Bella woke up to Callen whispering his kisses over her face and lips while simultaneously running his hand up and down her exposed bicep, then moving onto her hip. She moaned, but he only chuckled. "How do you feel this morning?"

Rolling over, she answered with a yawn. "Is it even morning?" She glanced at the window through sleepy eyes. "It's still dark."

"Yep. Get up, baby. We have things to do this morning with the family before some of us head out to get ranch work started. Yesterday may have been a snowy day but today is a workday. Family always comes first, and sometimes that means early rising, so up you get. You can take a nap later." Bella moaned and complained a little but got up when Callen moved the blankets and patted her ass lightly. Her bare ass.

"I thought you were going to make it worth my while to get up so early. And I hope you don't think I'm going to be okay with you smacking my ass again."

"I'm patting your ass. You know the difference between that and a spanking."

"Which you won't do."

"But it's such a gorgeous backside. I can imagine it becoming more beautiful, colored a delicate pink."

"I bet you do. I don't remember it being a thing with us in high school, but it won't become a habit now. You got your bit in, but I'm not having it any longer. No spanking this girl."

"What is with you this morning? We agreed this was part of our dynamic with or without Daddy/Baby girl play. Honey, talk to me."

"I worked hard for my independence and when I give into you, I sacrifice myself at the altar of us."

"Oh, baby, is that how you see this? That submitting to me for discipline is giving away your freedoms? Leaving your personhood at the door?" Bella nodded. "I promise you nothing could be further from the truth. It is not something that I assume you do. That you will submit to me. I cherish the trust and autonomy it takes to do that. That strength of character is something I never take for granted. Not ever. And I know that I am a lucky man to be honored by you."

"Really? You don't think I'm weak because I give into you and let you take over when things get tough or overwhelming? It doesn't make you lose respect?"

"I fucking love that. It feeds my need to be that protector and nurturer for you. I can be a man without it, love and cherish you every day without that component but with it, you fly higher when we make love, you trust me more and I can openly adore you in every way without causing you or anyone else distress or embarrassment. Do we have to have this dynamic in our lives? No. Are we so much freer and happier with it? I believe so. What about you?"

Bella wiped her eyes and sniffed. Callen brushed her hands away and used his thumbs to wipe them as his hands cradled her face. He gently kissed her lips and then leaned back.

"Are we good?"

"Yes. We're good. I thought this was just something you enjoyed, not that had any significance, or that you saw it as so much more than I ever knew. I do love and trust you, and I understand you better."

"Well, after I settle your punishment, you can start again and not be naughty because I was very honest when I said I spank for naughty. Come down to the kitchen when you're dressed."

Callen kissed her lips until they were red and puffy, which made everything south of her neck react, including her slickening sexy chamber. Then he tapped her nose, tweaked a perky nipple, and admonished her to get moving before his long, muscular legs took him from the room, quietly closing the door behind him. She licked her still tingling lips and images of his cock inside her made her belly twinge with desire.

Bella thought briefly about going back to sleep. She had a busy and possibly long day ahead of her and the thought of tackling it without adequate sleep made her sigh and consider just how important this was to Callen. She groaned as she rolled out of bed. Family was everything to her guy. Yeah, he was her guy, and she wasn't letting go, so she walked into the bathroom to start getting ready for whatever they had in mind.

Breakfast was already cooked, and on the table to be served family style when Bella arrived. She hesitated. She was not a breakfast eater, but evidently everyone in this house was. Callen pulled out a chair for her and she took his lead, sitting next to him. She took a glance at a sound behind her and found Maeve wandering in, not a second of hesitancy in her entrance.

"Hello, Maeve," said Stryker. "Wasn't sure you were going to make it to breakfast."

"The sooner we finish this, the sooner I go home. Besides," she grinned, "I like eating at a table of appetizing food eaten by scrumptious men."

Callen shook his head at Maeve. "Behave, or I'll tell Uncle Kiernan that you were flirting with his nephews."

"You would, too. Okay, I'll play nice if someone will pass me the coffee."

While Declan filled Maeve's cup and Avery dished a healthy portion of the omelet casserole into Maeve's plate, Callen quietly asked Bella, "Do you want a little of everything?"

"I'll just have coffee and toast." Bella felt the air change at her answer.

"I bet you don't eat this early. Artists keep their own hours, right? When do you usually have breakfast?" asked Kai.

Bella smiled, grateful that Kai was trying to save her more explanation. "I don't usually have breakfast, per se. I just eat whenever I'm hungry, without much of a timetable, I'm afraid."

"Meals are a regular time around here, as I'm sure you remember, because it's usually the only time that we are able to catch up with everyone," said Seamus.

Callen placed her plate in front of her with a small amount of breakfast on offer. Avery placed a steaming cup of coffee next to her plate, indicating the cream and sugar in the center of the table. Callen leaned down and spoke softly in her ear.

"Your creativity may not be on a schedule, but at least one meal a day will be. Today it's breakfast. Eat a little. You've lost too much weight. From here forward, I'm going to make sure you eat healthy food at proper intervals, among other things."

Bella graced him with a withering look, which he met with a grin. He nodded toward her plate and frowned when she grabbed her cup of coffee instead of her fork. Callen raised his eyebrow and Bella huffed her dissatisfaction. She watched everyone eat and banter back and forth as she pushed her food around the plate. One small bite of omelet, a bite of toast and pushing the small amount of hash brown potatoes seemed to be all Callen could handle before he leaned over again.

"I'm not only going to spank that perfect-for-me ass, but I'm also going to feed you breakfast if you don't stop playing and eat. Your last warning."

"I'm an adult," she hissed back.

"Then act like it. Otherwise, I am going to bring out your Daddy and let him handle this. What did you eat yesterday besides that cheese sandwich?"

"Plenty."

"What?" His voice was dark, and she knew she was wandering into dangerous territory with him. This was a Callen she was familiar with.

"I don't have to tell you," she whispered back.

Yeah, really grown up. Bella realized she didn't feel as in control as she usually liked, and his tone had her tingling in all her sensitive parts. Turned on? Really? Again. Damn him.

"Oh, my baby Bella, you are about to know what being protected and claimed by a Red Eagle when you are an adult is all about. Now eat."

Bella opened her mouth, then closed it and picked up her fork. No one said a word when she started eating, keeping her concentration on the plate. She was surprisingly hungry once she started to eat and was embarrassed when she cleaned her plate.

"More coffee?" asked Teagan.

"Yes, thank you. I can get it."

"I'm getting up, so I'll grab it. It looks like your guest status has changed, though. Since Callen has laid claim, you're family now," said Renee.

Stryker took the lead. "Since it looks like we've all eaten, Bella, would you and Maeve like to start filling in the blanks here? Let's go to the family room. Girls, sorry, but the cleanup is going to have to be you."

Libby came out of the kitchen. "Shoo. I don't need anyone in my kitchen. I've nearly finished the cleanup, anyway."

"Good, because I really want to hear what happened," said Kai.

"We'll fill you in later, honey." Seamus kissed Kai. "Promise."

"Shay, please."

"There will be a penalty."

Kai, who was always the more polite and compliant of the women, smiled. "Deal."

In the family room, Callen settled into one of the large armchairs and pulled Bella into his lap. Maeve sat in the chair next to Bella, facing Stryker. The women stationed themselves on the sofa and chairs around the large room, flanked by Carson, Declan, and Seamus. Avery sat in Stryker's lap. Bella knew Avery did that sometimes as a deterrent for Stryker's overprotective responses. A nice way of keeping his anger responses in check, too. Avery was smart that way. Declan drew her attention back to the subject at hand.

"What changed that you altered the pickup plan so drastically?"

Callen held Bella's hand in silent encouragement. Bella took a fortifying breath and began. She shared about everything she heard and saw in Rapid City. Maeve filled in what she knew, what she had heard and observed and what made them decide to change the plan.

"I hadn't ever accepted a commission with this large amount of work, but Anthony Shaffer seemed legit, and his business seemed to consume him. He only ever checked in on things once a week and only then to make sure I had all I needed in the studio he provided. I was required to work on the art there at his studio, but not to work on it every day. My timetable, his venue."

"Like he was worried you were going to share his painting with others and he didn't want that," mused Declan.

"Possessive and paranoid," said Renee.

"I am never going against my instincts again," said Callen. His voice carrying that deep warning rumble that seemed to come from his belly. It made her tummy wiggle and her sex to tingle. How could she be turned on now? Callen, that was how. Hell, and damnation, that man.

"Then Jarl began to pay attention to me."

Maeve attested to the strange fascination he had with Bella and then Shaffer began to show interest, but in a different way. "I kept Kiernan in the loop, and he was getting suspicious that something else was going on besides the paintings."

Callen gave Maeve a hard look. "Why didn't you tell me? I would have pulled her out. I'm the one who asked for you."

Maeve returned an irritated stare to Callen. "I report to Kiernan, and I did my part. It was up to Bella to share what she wanted with you."

"But she didn't." Callen turned his question to Bella. "Why not?"

"I told you. He would have hurt you.... will hurt you, or worse. And if I'd said that, you would have brought some of these guys," her hand waved the air encompassing the room, "and they could have gotten hurt."

Callen grunted. He leaned down to speak close to her ear. "We will be talking about that later, baby girl." His hand tightened on hers briefly as he lifted his head. "Go on, baby."

Maeve continued instead. "Kiernan said to keep an eye and hang tight. He also had us formulate a second plan if our first exit plan didn't work." Maeve shrugged. "It usually doesn't."

"What the fuck? What do you mean 'it usually doesn't?'"

Bella nodded. "And when I overheard Bic and Jarl talking about how they were going to not let me leave, aka kidnap me, then we knew going for the unveiling wasn't going to happen. It was too risky."

"But Baby, you should have called me. I could have been there ready."

Bella shook her head. "Not enough time to wait until I could get hold of you. You were out of range. I was out of time. So," she shrugged, "Plan 'B'. Jarl wouldn't leave me alone. He was everywhere, making suggestive comments. Then Anthony was overly kind.

It drove me crazy, to be honest. But then they became more controlling, and I felt like they had slipped a noose around my neck and were slowly tightening it."

"Son of a bitch. I'll kill them."

"Quiet Callen." Seamus spoke gently. "Bella, what did he do, exactly?"

Bella took a fortifying breath. "At first, I thought Jarl had Bic sit outside my place and watch me, follow me, for safety. Later, recently, I decided that it might not be Jarl who thought of that, but Anthony."

"Honestly, I think Jarl wanted Bella for herself. Still creepy, but Anthony seemed to want her for her talents. Like he was going to get some benefit from her being such a detailed painter and he loved her sketches. More than the average art lover should."

"Fuck! How long has this been going on?" asked Seamus.

"I don't know how long they had me followed or watched, but a long time, I think."

"Okay," said Declan, who seemed deep in thought. "Go on."

Bella explained how she and Maeve began to really worry several weeks ago and created the escape plan everyone else was in on. "Sorry, but my sister might be on her way here, too." She looked a little sheepish.

"Why would Tracy come now?" asked Stryker.

Maeve answered. "Jarl began to make reference to Tracy, like he knew about her, and it felt to me as though he was gearing up to use her to control Bella if necessary."

Callen sat Bella on the sofa and paced. "Don't worry, baby, we can handle a little sister."

"Then we can handle these assholes," growled Carson.

She nodded. "This week, Anthony went on a business trip and since Jarl was his second, he went, too. That's when I found out things were much worse than I thought. Shaffer is some kind of gangster or something, and I overheard Bic and Jarl talking in the hall outside my apartment. They said that I was going to be kept at that mansion after I showed up that last night to present the art to Shaffer."

She then filled in all the information about faking her illness and finally getting out of town.

"Okay, girls, you know the drill. No one leaves the ranch without escort and prior authorization," announced Stryker. He left no doubt in anyone's mind that he meant what he said.

"What? Callen, I didn't want to disrupt lives here. If I can just get my car, I'll be on my way. I'll come back after things have cooled down. I don't know what I was thinking."

"You were thinking you didn't want your ass beat for going off grid," Seamus said. "Callen, don't forget to add this to your list of things that need to be addressed." Seamus was not happy.

Bella's mouth opened in disbelief. "I thought you were my friend."

"Nope, your brother and keeping you safe means you do your part and we do ours, or there will be consequences."

Bella felt sassy. "What if you don't do your part?"

The men in the room laughed. "You're cute," said Seamus. Bella huffed.

Declan spoke. "You were thinking that we could and would protect you when you set up the plan to come back here. We can and will, but it includes safety measures. You aren't the first to send us into protection mode. You won't be the last with this many people on the property."

"I understand where they are coming from," said Renee, "but it isn't reasonable. I have things to get in town, and Teagan must work. Jacob is gone for a while longer, but Sage has to run the feed store."

Stryker shook his head. "We will work it out like always, but you know there isn't any other way. Bella is ours now and we will protect her the same as we have done for all of you."

Avery nodded. "He's right. We'll figure it out. We always do. Don't worry about things around here, Bella, just listen to Callen and we will be fine."

"I need my car."

"Your car is in the yard and Callen has the keys, but neither are going to be at your disposal until we have things handled. Someone will drive you where you need to go," said Seamus.

Bella turned her inquiry to the man sitting and holding her again. "Callen?"

"Yep. You don't go anywhere unless I know about it, and even then, someone drives you. Someone besides one of the girls." Callen gave the women a stern look.

"You can't do that. It's kidnapping."

"It's protection."

"Get used to it," said Kai with a shrug that communicated *it is what it is*.

"We've all been in your spot. Luckily, there aren't any more brothers to find women," laughed Teagan.

Avery said quietly, "Except we still have Renee."

"Oh, God, she's right," said Seamus with a groan. "She isn't allowed."

This time, the women laughed. Renee simply rolled her eyes. "I really have more brothers than I need, Shay-Shay. A girl needs a man to stand up for her, not that she needs to stand up to."

"Shay-Shay. I kind of like that," said Kai with a grin. "It's *mo' bettah da kine*."

"None of you repeat that unless you want a hot ass," said Seamus as he pinned each woman with a look, then his gaze stayed on Kai.

"And you, my girl, look so good wearing a bright red backside. *That will be mo' bettah da kine.*"

"What?" asked Callen.

"Hawaiian Pidgin English. Basically, in this context, it means *this is better, or this is best,* but it can mean a lot of things."

Callen shook his head. "No offense, but I'm not sure if I can add another language to what I already have."

Kai laughed. "No problem, *brah.*"

"You aren't thinking clearly," insisted Bella. "I should go because I would never cause any trouble for you if I could stop it. And I can. Just take care of Tracy when she gets here and don't let those assholes get her."

"Yep, she needs her ass smacked," said Declan. "Callen, take care of that later."

"You can't stop anything without putting yourself in even more danger, and that won't be happening on my watch, young lady," said Stryker in an ultra-stern tone.

Bella looked at Callen. "Cal?"

"You heard Stryker. I told you we take care of our own. That includes you because, You. Are. Mine."

"Right," said Maeve, "we need a plan."

After working out what everyone was doing and where they would be until at least lunch, the guys left the house for the ranch offices and put in a conference call to Ireland. They brought Bella and Maeve in with them. It was time they called Até, and he joined in the discussion. Callen could tell Bella was glad for the vote of assurance, but also worried about what the family patriarch would say. Callen had no such concerns.

"Até, how are you?" asked Callen as he spoke to their father.

"We're good, but I'm beginning to think about coming home soon. Your mother is anxious to see her soon to be new daughters, and I just want to put my feet under my own table. How are all of you? Kiernan has mentioned Bella has a little trouble going on."

"We're good and yeah, Bella has run into an issue."

The men each told their updates to Até and then sat back while Callen explained what was going on with Bella.

"Bella?"

"Yes, sir?"

"Sweetheart, it's nice to hear your voice. I can't wait to tell my wife you are back on the ranch. We've been worried about you painting away from home. Kayleigh had hoped Callen would have kept you in high school, but that wasn't the time for you. Is it now?"

"I think so, sir."

"You remember I prefer all the children to call me Até. I imagine we will be seeing much more of each other in the years to come. I hear being a well-known artist isn't all it's cracked up to be."

"Well, I'm at least known to some, sir... um, Até. And no, it isn't always easy."

"I'm so proud of your dedication. Maeve, I hear you are there too. Good girl. I'm glad Kiernan kept you near our Bella, but I think he is getting antsy to get you back home. Now, what shall we do about this problem, hmm?"

Each gave his opinion while Até listened on the other end of the call. Finally, he spoke.

"Bella, usually I speak with the guys without the women because they can translate the information to the girls the way they see fit and we can be a little raw on here, but I think it is important that you stay and hear my words. First, you are part of us now and so if Callen or any of the men in the room, Jacob as well, tell you something is for your safety or your health, that is to be followed. You are not to answer back or ignore their words. This is vitally important. Maybe the most important thing you will ever hear me say, other than we love you."

These men and her Callen must have learned their sternness from their father. He gave her no doubt that disobedience would be frowned on and punished. Yet he never used one word of a hint that punishment was an outcome.

"Yes, sir, but I don't want to cause any trouble."

"Até, Bella. Others call me sir. My family calls me Até. Be assured that if you leave the ranch unsupervised, you will be in very deep trouble. We back each other up and protect our women at all costs. But your job is to do as you are told for safety. Do you shoot a gun?"

"Not really. I mean, Callen showed me a little a long time ago, but... I don't really like guns."

"And we don't like you with one, but sometimes it's necessary. Callen, you'll take care of that."

"On my list."

"Heighten your security. Call the sheriff if you need him. Brief the men on duty. Call Jacob and Sage home and keep Carson in the loop. I trust him with everything."

Seamus said, "Carson is with us. I'll call Jacob after this. We were thinking about running spotlights at night but don't want to spook the cattle so close to calving."

"No, just put guys out in the little cabins. They will be more ears to the ground that way. We need to get this problem taken care of so we can get down to the ranching business. Welcome to the family, Bella."

Até and his sons spoke about other things concerning particulars on the ranch and then they signed off right as Bella yawned.

"Time for a nap, baby."

"No, I'm fine. I just sat too long."

"Come with me. We have things we need to discuss as you get ready for a nap."

"But I thought I'd..." the rest of the sentence died on her lips when Renee opened the door in a rush.

"Some pretty impressive black SUVs have asked to be allowed on the ranch. They are sitting at the gate."

"Shit. How did they find me already? Callen?"

"Not hard baby. I'm a Red Eagle. Renee, Bella is with you in your office. We'll take care of this, Bella. Stay with Renee."

Bella's expression darkened. "Did you order me to stay with Renee like I'm a dog?"

Callen hesitated. "My wording was unfortunate. I meant to say that I want to keep you two as safe as I can while we deal with whoever is sitting at the gate. Please stay with Renee while we do that."

"Not sure that was a good save, but I'll accept it."

He dropped a quick, hard kiss on her lips before giving her a warning look. "I mean it. Do not leave this office."

Callen stood for a moment and gathered his thoughts. It was important not to lose focus on the prime objective: family safety. He watched Renee usher his girl inside and shut the door while the guys made a quick decision as to what to do. Declan put on his poshest tone and answered the gate intercom bell. Seamus checked in with Carson, who left as soon as he heard there was trouble at the gate and was assured they had eyes and guns trained on the three vehicles in the motorcade.

"What can I do for you?" Declan asked.

The response was unexpected. No demands. "We have booked accommodation at the Red Eagle Inn."

"Name?" asked Declan.

"Gerald."

Stryker sent a text to Renee, in the office. Callen took down the license plate numbers spied through the security cameras that he sent to Jacob's office assistant, Raj. He could do security checks, including license verification.

"Hey, Raj. Do me a favor? We have suspicious visitors at the front gate saying they are booked for a stay at the inn. Could you look up these license plates and tell me who owns them?"

"You got it."

Renee responded. "I have a single reservation under Bickley Gerald in the system. There is no reason for him to have more than himself and the reservation was made last night. Pretty odd to make a resort reservation less than twenty-four hours before you check-in."

Raj rang through to Callen. "All vehicles are registered to Silo Investments, Inc."

Stryker asked Renee to pass the phone to Bella. "Does Silo Investments sound familiar?"

"That is one of Shaffer's holding companies. I know only because that is where my payments were drawn from."

"And that was your third mistake, Shaffer," said Stryker. "We'll be done here shortly."

Within a few more minutes, the four brothers re-entered the office along with Carson. Bella took a few seconds to process. When a teen, she had longed to be part of this big family of hard loving, working, playing people. Her yearning hadn't lessened, but their distance from where she stood in life still made them out of reach, or so she had thought. Before, she had been the artsy kid that no one really cared about. Now she was the artist that was in danger. A danger so intense she couldn't expose these good people to any more than she already had, except they didn't see things the way she did. Were they that good or that arrogant? She looked around the room. Maybe both.

"Stop right there, young lady. No matter what you may be thinking, you stop it immediately. You are not saving anyone. You're not playing the heroine in your own subplot. We are in this together. You are my girl."

"Meaning?" The smart response came out entirely too quickly.

Callen raised his eyebrows in question. "Meaning, my little sassy one, that you stay with me. If you even attempt to leave this ranch unescorted, you'll learn what going against my rules and the ranch rules gets you."

"You are not keeping me prisoner."

"Nope. You're complying because you know we have your best interests at heart and it's time you settled into your new life. With me."

"Callen, I'm not going to be bound to your hip. I have things to do. And I don't want to risk you, any of you, getting hurt or worse," she ended in a whisper.

Callen drew her into his arms. Bella didn't know when everyone left them alone, but they were the only ones in Renee's office. "Not going to happen, baby." He kissed her temple, then pulled her close again. "We'll figure this out and protect everyone. We told Mr. Bickley Gerald his reservation was for only one person and unless the other cars left, he would be refunded his reservation fee."

"That's Bic, Jarl's right-hand man. He was the one who kept an eye on me most of the time."

"So, Shaffer's right-hand man has a right-hand man?"

"Unfortunately. So, what happened?"

"They decided to leave. We decided to let them. This time."

Bella shook her head. "They'll be back. Jarl will believe I'm here until they come back. You can tell him I left. Everyone will be safe."

"Stop being selfish. You leaving here, unprotected, will make me come after you and really put us both at risk. The guys wouldn't allow me to go alone, then Maeve would have to follow, Uncle Kiernan will be pissed and send more people after us and all because you took off on your own."

"You guys have this down to a science, don't you?"

"Not yet but we're learning. So, stay here and save the mess. It's your home, Bella. Your family."

Callen heard her words and knew she was struggling to do as he said, and she wanted to comply, believe, but she was still trying to figure out her martyr mentality. Trying to reconcile both sides of her and he knew she couldn't. She'd have to accept or reject him and what he offered.

"But they will be back," she repeated.

Callen nodded. "I hope they do, but we'll be prepared next time." His voice quieted, becoming spine rattling intense. "And if you think I would ever let you stand alone against Jarl or anyone if I had the power to prevent it, then you have a lot to learn about me, Bella. You are one of us. More specifically and importantly, mine." His tone softened. "I know we have a lot of untangling to do, a lot of re-routing and re-writing of who we are together, but I will do that gladly. I will do what it takes to have you with me. To be able to show you that my feelings have resurfaced in a dramatic way. I love you. I always have. Now, I need to deepen that love to reach the depths of the feelings I have for you. That I'm positive I have, but it's going to take time and work. This is the next step to that future that I see for us."

Callen was so earnest, so intense and in a way, entreating her to agree with him.

"For so long, I allowed myself to push my feelings of hurt and rejection down on top of my all-consuming adoration of you. My love was a young love. Then, my hurt and anger made it easier to deny that I loved you in a more core deep way. Even when I was doing the paintings. It was easier because I kept allowing myself to not focus on forever. Trying not to be vulnerable enough to believe it. Just in case. But right now, I see you vulnerable. Raw. Laying all your feelings out, no matter the consequences."

"I love you, Bella. I would do anything for you, willingly. Don't deny us by putting yourself in danger uselessly. I'm a protective asshole and possession isn't nine-tenths of the law with me, it *is* the law.

I see why Berg wants you, but I'm selfish and I don't share. Ever. I must know you are all in with me so I can concentrate."

"I do love you, Callen. In some way, I always have, but what are we going to do about this situation? I want to be with you, but I can't see a way out of this mess with me still here."

"You let us worry about that. We've had some pretty good practice in finding ways to overcome the roadblocks in our way. Let me take care of this, of you."

Bella nodded. "Alright. But if things get too intense, we have to reassess."

"We'll be fine. You let me do what I have to do and promise to stay on the ranch."

Her sigh was loud. Her body language was clear. "Fiiine."

Callen's response was to swat her pert bottom as she crossed her arms in protest and turned toward the door from Renee's office. Her squeal of surprise was answered by chuckles in the front office. When Bella crossed the threshold, her face was hot, and she was sure, flaming red. Thankfully no one was there to see her. She headed straight out the front door into the chilly outdoors. She'd forgotten her sweater in Renee's office, but there was no way she was going back for it right now.

These Red Eagle boys may have grown into responsible men, but there was still the tang of immaturity when it came to dealing with their women. Spanking. Really. Bella was glad no one saw the knowing smile spread across her face, unbidden.

Chapter 20

Revelation

The ranch was a fortress of tension, the air crackling with the undercurrents of impending danger. The Red Eagle men were on a mission, their expressions grim, as they spent a lot of time scanning the horizon for the threat they knew was coming. Bella leaned heavily against the sturdy frame of the house, her eyes flicking from the beefed-up security to the ever-present group of brothers scattered about the grounds. She took in the determined set of their jaws as they talked in the yard.

"Should have known they wouldn't let it go," muttered Callen, his voice a low growl that conveyed both frustration and readiness. His hand rested near the holster at his hip, a silent vow that no harm would come to Bella on his watch.

Carson's "Fuck," echoed as he yelled, "They've been sighted a few miles away."

Callen pushed Bella into the direction of the house as the men disbursed like some Old West show. As if summoned by their fears, a cloud of dust appeared in the distance, growing larger as vehicles charged toward the ranch. Jarl's henchmen, no doubt, each one as ruthless as the last, were closing in fast, driven by their leader's obsession with Bella. Men who had smiled and treated her well until now. Now that she was their target.

"Positions!" barked Stryker, his command cutting through the tension like a blade. The brothers scattered, moving to their preassigned locations with practiced ease, forming a protective barrier between their loved ones and the oncoming threat.

Callen kissed her hard and fast. "House, now!" He slapped her backside to hurry her along.

At that same moment, the first vehicle barreled onto the property, its tires churning up dirt and gravel. Bella's heart hammered in her chest, each beat echoing through the thrum of engines as more cars followed. Callen's grip on her hand tightened, an unspoken reassurance that he wouldn't let go—not now, not ever.

"Too late," she said.

"Stay behind me," Callen ordered, positioning himself in front of Bella, his body a shield.

"Yes," she replied, her voice steady despite the quiver that threatened to break through.

It happened in a flash—the once peaceful ranch erupted into chaos. Shouts filled the air, mingling with the sound of screeching tires and revving engines. Then silence.

"What can I do for you? Make another reservation?" asked Seamus.

"We are here to talk to Bella Gregoria."

"Who are *we*?" asked Stryker.

Callen eased Bella back out of sight of the vehicles. "Now go in through the kitchen door." Bella ran but tripped on rope left partially unrolled on the ground. She stood, but Callen was there, standing guard in front of her.

The women watched the security cameras from Até's office. No one left the cars. No one made a move. Callen's brothers and cowboys, ready to leap into action, stood waiting for the next move. After a few moments, when those in the vehicles did nothing, the air crackled with tense expectation.

Renee screamed into the cameras' communication device, "Gun!"

"Get down!" Callen shoved Bella toward the ground, covering her with his body as a warning shot rang out, splitting the air. She gasped, the scent of gunpowder and earth filling her lungs.

"I've called the sheriff," roared Seamus.

"Think you can scare us off?" sneered a henchman, emboldened by Jarl's instructions. "We just want to talk to Bella."

Callen answered. "If all you wanted to do was talk to her, you could have texted or called."

Jarl stood out of the vehicle. "Ah, Mr. Red Eagle. We meet again. It seems we are always vying for the same prize. Where is Bella? We have a bonus we would like to pay her."

"Thanks, but she declines. Now go home."

"We would prefer to hear Bella speak for herself."

Stryker called back out, "Suit yourself." Sirens echoed across the open land.

Callen looked around to see Bella was no longer behind him. He had to pray she slipped into the kitchen. The confrontation reached its peak, neither side yielding, each tossing barbs and threats of some kind or other at the other group. One side stalling the other hoping for police help. The frenzy of motion was a blur to Bella's eyes. She spoke out loudly into the security com system, ignoring the gasps from those around her and the Red Eagles' angry tension.

"Mr. Berg, this is Bella. No, thank you. My association with you and Mr. Shaffer is now terminated."

"Bella, I just wanted to thank you personally. It is Mr. Shaffer's request."

She didn't respond. Thankfully it seemed either Maeve or one of the others got her away from the speaker control or she came to her senses. Whatever it was, it worked. Callen could feel his anger rise to fury. He would discuss this later with Bella looking at the floor, his hand doing most of the talking on her bared backside.

"Well, Berg, looks like you have your answer. Now those sirens are pretty darn close. Decide whether you want to meet our country sheriff or if you are ready to leave."

There was some discussion and suddenly the doors closed, and the vehicles left just as the sheriff's department was pulling in. Stryker pointed toward the exiting cars and one county car stayed while the rest escorted the vehicles out of their county.

CALLEN TURNED AWAY from the sheriff's deputy, who was talking to Stryker and marched into the house. He intently scanned the room and then, finding it empty except for Libby, he headed to the family room where he found her on the sofa. Grabbing her hand he led her upstairs.

"What's wrong?"

"Don't talk. I am about to blow and I need to calm down but while I do, you are stripping down."

"Why?" she asked cautiously.

"I don't think that is really a question you need answered, is it? What you need is your man to settle himself before he takes his leather to your backside. You want me calmer for that."

"What are you made about?"

"Bella, quiet."

This time, she listened and stood silently while he closed the door to the bedroom and locked it. "Strip down, baby."

"Callen."

"Nope. I'm not ready."

Bella silently removed her clothing and since he was still not saying anything, she folded them carefully and laid them on the dresser. Finally, when the tension was too thick to breathe, Callen said, "Corner." He pointed to an empty space.

"Um, I don't... know how to do that."

"Walk to that corner. Face it. Stand there. No talking. I have to pull myself together and settle my mind. I think you do too."

Bella walked slowly to the place that he pointed to and stood facing the wall. She kicked it with her foot. Callen ignored her. She kicked again. Still no response. She sighed heavily and kicked it again. Hot breath swept across her cheek.

"I know you're here, and I know you're confused. But if you kick that wall one more time or give me another dramatic sigh, you will not be sitting easy for dinner or breakfast tomorrow morning. Understand?"

"Yes."

"That isn't your safeword."

"I don't know if I want to use it or not. Callen, I don't know if I can do this. Maybe it isn't for me but I can't stop this. I can't safeword. It doesn't feel right." He kissed her cheek.

"Okay baby, then we play this out until things change. How do you answer me?"

"Daddy. Yes, Daddy."

He kissed her ear. "That's my baby."

She trembled. Her entire body was on fire with her need for her very upset man. "I'm sorry," she whispered.

"Do you know why you are sorry?"

"I somehow made you upset. Maybe because I used the speaker."

"Turn around, baby. I'm angry because by talking to them, you verified you were here. Where on the ranch you were, and that someone wasn't watching you or you would never have been able to reach that speaker let alone use it. All of that puts you in grave danger. What is the biggest rule we have?"

"Don't jeopardize health and safety."

"Yep." He led her over to the bed and pulled her between his legs as he removed his belt and arranged himself.

"Callen, what are you doing?"

"Daddy. You get five with the belt but I'll warm you up first. I think twenty should do it."

"Twenty? Spanks?"

"Yep and if you want to debate it, I'll add five more for every time you argue with me about it. Baby girl, you scared the breath from me. I can't let this go. You are too precious to me not to show you how much."

Bella stared at her daddy, who she had scared and dropped her head. "I'm sorry, Daddy. I didn't mean to cause you so much trouble."

"Baby, not trouble, real fear for your safety."

She nodded her head and crawled over his lap. The first five were a shock but not unbearable, but by the time the second five swats had landed, Bella was sure she wouldn't make it to the end. Callen placed his hand on her stinging cheeks.

"How are you doing baby?"

"If I said not good, would you stop?"

"Are you safewording?"

Was she? No. "No, Daddy."

"Okay then we will continue." The next five were blistering, and the last five smacks were enough to draw screeches and kicking feet. Tears were streaming.

"These last five are going to make that lasting impression that I hope stops you from making an unsafe rash decision."

Bella nodded, the tears still rolling down her face. Positioning her over the edge of the bed, he took no time laying down five swats with the belt. She found herself in his lap, her daddy loving on her and kissing her cheek as her tears subsided. She snuggled in as Callen pulled up the comforter over her. She fell asleep with his sweet words of praise and love in her ear. Yeah, praise was definitely a kink, and she owned it.

After dinner, Bella took a little walk outside within sight of the security cameras. Callen and the others were working on something.

Bella wasn't as optimistic as Callen that things would work themselves out, but she was thankful he and his family were her family
now. She just wasn't sure she believed they understood the full extent
of the problem. It was a good thing to have confidence in your abilities and that of your family, but it would be a huge mistake if the Red
Eagle men thought Jarl would give up easily. The man wasn't used to
not getting his own way. In fact, Bella never saw anyone deny him
what he wanted. Except her.

The wind whipped around her, carrying a bite of stinging cold. It
was time to move a little quicker. By the time she reached the house,
she was chilled to the bone and looking for some tea. She loved coffee, but tea was a comfort. She wished she could get some comfort
for her bottom. Callen had never been that firm with her, and she
never wanted a spanking like the one he gave her today. She still
ached. But she understood. She put everyone in danger even though
he only focused on her danger. She was sorry for the others, more
than her own exposure.

The guys were talking as they exited the ranch offices and Bella
turned to see them, hoping one of them had good news about this
situation. She heard the whop-whop overhead, almost a whirring of
rotor blades cutting through the air. It appeared as though it was flying over the ranch and continuing on its way, so she was surprised
when Callen and his brothers began swearing. Carson came out from
the horse barn and yelled in their direction and pointed. Renee came
up and nudged Bella to go to the house, but she resisted. The guys
were motioning them to go inside.

"We can watch from the window," said Renee as she hurried Bella up the front steps.

Bella nodded. "What is going on?" she asked as Renee pushed
her through the front door.

"Hell, if I know. But this is where you have to let the guys and
the hands deal with this stuff. They have hired on some really good

extra men. I have a feeling those goons from a little earlier are trying another approach to get onto the ranch."

Kai and Teagan came to the front room. "What's going on?" asked Kai.

Renee answered. "I think it's Bella's not-so-secret admirer. Let's go look out of the upstairs windows. We'll get a much better view of things."

Kai half shook her head. "I'm not so sure Seamus will be happy to see me in the window gawking at the goings on. He is kind of touchy about me being around trouble. Can we do the security cameras again?"

"Can't. It won't be good enough to see everything. Upstairs windows will give us a panoramic view."

Teagan bit her lip. "I haven't gotten spanked in weeks and I'm needing a little love, so I'm game."

"Wait. Don't do anything that will get you in trouble, Teagan." Bella's face was scrunched.

Renee patted Bella's right arm. "She loves them. Don't rob a woman of her guilty pleasures. That's just mean. Come on, before things are all over."

Renee ran up the stairs, and the other three followed her. "Kai," said Renee, "You can peek from behind me, so Seamus doesn't see you."

"He'll know."

"Yeah, probably."

Teagan stood front and center and Renee stood beside her but while Kai could see through the space between them, Bella didn't see as well so she went to the other window facing out. Almost immediately, something hit the window frame, cracking the window Bella was looking out of. She screamed and hit the floor, her hands over her head. The other three followed suit, just as another projectile hit their window.

"God Almighty, that was too close for comfort," said Renee.

"I think someone was shooting at us. Who would do that, and where are they?" Teagan sounded angry. "I thought you said he was into Bella. Looks like his affections have changed."

"We need to stay down and crawl from this room. I'm confused but something is happening. Something is wrong."

Renee led the way, but Bella seemed to be frozen in her spot. Kai noticed as she started to follow the other two and turned back around to grab Bella's hand, giving it a tug.

"Bella, come on. We have to get out of here." Bella nodded but didn't move. Kai pushed her forward ahead of her. "Crawl." She slapped Bella's ass. "Now."

Bella seemed to snap out of it and crawled out of the room with Kai fast on her heels.

Renee opened the gun cabinet and unlocked the ammunition drawer. Every woman had either grown up shooting guns or had lessons from a Red Eagle. Bella knew that because she had been taught by Callen and his father years ago, and if she had to, she would, but she hadn't had the chance to practice with Callen again.

Bella took a step back from the pistol Renee held out to her. "Renee, I haven't shot in a long time. Callen hasn't practiced with me yet, so, in all good consciousness, I can't carry a gun."

"Right." Renee held one out to Kai, who shook her head. "Look I don't mind getting in trouble for peeking out the window, but Seamus would skin me alive if he thought I reached for a gun at the first sign of trouble. He has stressed, in an emergency only. The guys are out there and seem fine. They aren't shooting anything or anyone." Gunfire opened up in a short burst.

Bella sneaked a look out the window just as Sage flew in through the kitchen door, slamming and locking it. "Lock all the doors."

Teagan scrambled to do her bidding. "Where did you come from?" asked Renee.

"Jacob's truck. We just were pulling in through the north entrance when we heard shooting. He drove up to the kitchen door and practically threw me inside. I don't know what is going on, but we need to make sure everyone is safe. I'll take one of those if you are passing them out."

Sage grabbed a box of ammo and the rifle. Renee seemed satisfied that at least one other woman had protection. Teagan had gone very quiet, staring at the front door. Bella watched through the kitchen window. Where was Maeve?

"Wait, the sheriff is here. Several police vehicles," said Teagan. After a few minutes, she added, "The guys are all escorting someone to the cop car."

Kai spoke after another few moments. "Now they're all standing and talking, like it's a social gathering."

Sage walked with purpose and put her unloaded gun back in the case and the full box of ammo back in the drawer. Renee followed suit and had just locked the case when the front door opened. The men seemed to know something wasn't right. Bella raised her eyebrows in realization. The Red Eagle menfolk didn't likely want their women to handle guns when they were available to handle the trouble.

She was glad she'd not touched one, but Renee was a woman to dance to her own tune. She thought Renee was likely very familiar with the act of standing up to her oversized, bossy brothers. Sage was like Avery and Renee. She was a woman who marched to her own beat.

Stryker led the rest of the men in. Each headed for their girl and interestingly enough, Carson made a beeline for Renee, who didn't reject his presence. Bella was never so happy to see someone as she was when her eyes landed on Callen. He reached for her and after quick confirmation that she was unharmed; he kissed her hard. His second kiss was more controlled, gentler.

Stryker sat with Avery on his lap, and the other men did the same. Renee sat next to Carson rather than on his lap. A response Carson seemed not too happy about. If Renee noticed, she didn't show it.

Seamus spoke. "All four of you," he pinned all but Sage with a stern look, "Have some explaining to do."

Bella straightened her spine, and Callen rubbed her back in a soothing manner. Bella figured he was trying to settle her irritation, but this didn't make sense.

"Why?" she asked.

Seamus stared hard at Bella for a moment, then rubbed his hand over his face. "That was dangerous, Bella. The window you were standing in was shot at. If his aim had been a little better, we wouldn't be sitting here have a debrief, we'd be at the hospital or worse, the morgue."

Callen made a deep, throaty sound. "Careful, Shay."

Declan spoke next. Bella figured it was because he wasn't as blunt as Seamus. "It wasn't safe to stand in a window when we had intruders on the ranch."

Bella pursued her questioning. "But how were we to know someone was going to shoot?"

"Why did you assume there wouldn't be any danger, given what you already knew before coming inside?"

"Dec," she used the name she and everyone had called him when she had spent so much time on the ranch with Callen in high school. It didn't seem to work as well as she had thought. "I can't live my life trying to second guess when something is going to turn dangerous or when I should and shouldn't stand in a window."

"Bella, baby, I don't think that is what Declan is trying to say. It was a risky situation and you of all people should not have shown yourself because there was every possibility that Jarl was trying to verify where you were and find a way to kidnap you. He is obsessed."

Bella didn't respond. Stryker took over. "Regardless, you all know that putting yourself in the middle of an argument, fight, or any kind of conflict is not acceptable. We protect, you stay safe."

Carson continued as he looked directly into Renee's eyes. "And standing in the upper windows so you could be easily seen is never going to be okay."

"What are we supposed to do when something is going on outside? You guys could be in trouble. Do you want us to be in here twiddling our thumbs and hiding? We could have helped. We could have identified where the intruders were." Bella was building a head of steam.

"Baby, I'd stop while you're ahead."

"You don't get to be the only ones with the answers."

Stryker must have had it with the discussion. "Here is how this is going to go. When we have trouble of any kind on the ranch where anyone could be hurt or put in an unsafe situation, you stay low. That means no taking the trouble on, no standing on display in the upper windows, no arming yourself with pistols, rifles, and shotguns."

Renee scrunched up her face. "How did you..."

"One is put back wrong," said Declan.

Sage shrugged her shoulders with an *oops* expression. Jacob patted her thigh, which she answered with a sigh. Carson was talking close to Renee's ear. She leaned away from him, but she had obviously heard him because her expression turned sour. This family seemed to have a communication frequency that no one outside of them could understand or tap into. Other people like her.

Callen came into her line of sight. "Bella Kaye, when this is all over, there is going to be one heck of a comeuppance, so be prepared."

Bella hissed back, "You aren't spanking me again."

"We'll see. I took you at your word and you agreed to take me with all that I am. I thought we had crossed this bridge already. I'm not debating it every time you earn a few swats on the ass."

"But I didn't do anything on purpose."

Callen graced her with a look of incredulity. "Bella, what you did was naughty and damned dangerous. You will be punished."

"It's not fair. Besides, don't you believe in natural consequences?"

"I do. In this case that would be getting shot or worse and that isn't happening."

Bella huffed her defeat. "I wasn't trying to be seen or get hurt."

He snagged her at the waist and drew her close. "Standing in a window and being seen is not a surprise, baby girl and you have to concede that. Again, I could have lost you and at this rate, I'll be feeling like an old man by the time we are done with this mess. But make no mistake Bella Kaye, I am going to make damn sure that putting yourself in danger or risking my baby's life will be the one thing you run in the other direction from. I believe in making that lesson last." Wrapping his arms around her, he hugged tight.

"I get it but it's still not happening. Not again. But butt is still sore."

He hugged her tightly. "Fair or not, you know I spank for naughty. I spank hard for dangerous behavior. And you did both, so expect it when this is over."

And for some crazy reason that she didn't want to explore right now, Callen gave her the best feelings of being special and loved. But he wasn't going to spank her, no matter how tingly she got at the prospect. She was still feeling the burn from earlier. She'd come up with another, less humiliating, punishment. She was smart enough to divert him. Stopping

Chapter 21

Calling in the Cavalry

"**M**aeve, what happened to Maeve?"

The Red Eagle family huddled in the spacious living room of their sprawling ranch house, a fortress against the encroaching peril that Jarl represented. Callen stood by the stone fireplace, his posture rigid with frustrated anger. And fear. He never hesitated to take the lead in things, be the authority when called on to do so, but he could feel the lines on his forehead etched with new worry. Bella might take off to protect others, and that would make his life much harder. He'd have to go after her because he wasn't letting her go or allowing her to become a martyr for the family.

He watched his siblings, who were sitting in front of him. Each one knew the weight of the situation. The air was thick with tension, and the worn leather couches and oak wood furniture seemed to absorb their collective anxiety. They were all getting antsy, but Callen noticed Bella the most. He watched as her tells became more pronounced. She was approaching meltdown status, so changing the direction of thought was essential.

"She was in the kitchen a while ago, but then we had all the trouble, and I haven't seen her since," said Avery.

"Who is Maeve?" asked Sage.

"Someone Uncle Kiernan sent to help take care of Bella while she was at Shaffer's house," said Callen.

"Was she with you upstairs?" asked Jacob.

Renee shook her head. "I didn't see her."

"Fuck." Seamus was not happy. "Where would we even start looking for her?"

"I have her phone number," volunteered Bella. She pulled out her cell from her front pants pocket and tapped a few keys. "It's ringing." She put the speaker on for others to hear.

"Bella, are you okay?" asked Maeve.

"Yes, but that isn't the question. The question is, where are you and are *you* okay?"

"How is Callen? Nice to hear you are okay, too. All the rest unharmed? No hospital runs?"

Callen spoke. "I'm fine. One of us just got a little injury in the gunplay and got a ride with one of the deputies to get it checked out. Nothing to worry about. Now stop avoiding the question. Where are you?"

Maeve's voice lost some of its tenseness but still sounded avoidant, wary, and that was so unlike Maeve. "I'll stay in town tonight. I would appreciate a ride back in the morning if any of you cowboys have a little time."

"Hell, honey," said Seamus, "you need to let someone know when things happen to you. Kiernan expects us to watch out for you. How did you get to town?"

"I drove, of course."

"Exactly where did you drive to, Maeve McCleary? The actual place." Declan stood up to make sure he could be heard on the cell phone.

Maeve hesitated, but then her flippant confidence emerged. "Just your local clinic here. I thought I could handle things, but I had difficulty stemming the trickle of red, so I decided I'd better get things checked out. You know, get a little help."

"Damn, Uncle Kiernan isn't going to be too happy about this. We could have taken you in and stayed with you. I'll come now."

Stryker pulled his keys out of his pocket, the jingle alerting Maeve to the fact that Stryker meant what he said.

"No, they said they were keeping me here, so I'm not going to argue. The sedative they gave me is making me tired. They removed the bullet pretty easily, no vital organs or bone, so just flesh. I might be limping for a bit. I'll fill you all in later. Oh, and don't tell Kiernan. He is such a helicopter boss. I'm feeling a bit tired, but I'll call you when I'm being released." Maeve ended the call.

"I'll gather some clothes and we'll grab her in the morning when they release her," said Kai.

"I'll ask if a deputy can stay with her tonight. Just don't like her being alone," said Callen. He pulled out his cell and made the call. He looked up after the call. "She's getting round-the-clock protection."

Bella giggled. "She isn't going to like that."

"Tough," said Callen, but he smiled at the thought of Maeve complaining. "It's all good. She'd likely blame it on Kiernan."

"Okay, then Maeve is taken care of for now. Ending this for Bella is our primary goal and keeping the women all safe."

"Jarl's moving fast, and he isn't stopping. Safety is non-negotiable," Carter grumbled. "We have to revamp our responses and our going forward plan. We need to jump back in the driver's seat and stop reacting."

"I think we can all agree on that, so what's our next move?" asked Callen.

"Até might know a way through this mess." Renee's words cut through the uncertainty, offering a sliver of hope. "Let's call him."

Callen kissed Bella as he and the men stood to go to the office. He strode decisively to the front door, grabbing his Stetson hat from the rack. The others followed. Including the women. Callen stepped out onto the porch, the vast Dakota sky stretching endlessly above him. The cold wind whispered across the land they loved so much.

"You ladies stay here," said Stryker as he followed his brothers.

Avery shook her head. "Yeah, not happening. If we are in danger, we are part of the conversation."

Declan nodded. "It's reasonable. They aren't children, they're our women. They should come."

The other men agreed and put the women between them as they headed out. They walked with purpose to the ranch offices and the conference room that would hold them all with space to all talk to the head of the household. With a steady hand, Jacob dialed the familiar number and set up the video call. This time they needed to see the man who had more wisdom running through his veins than all the men he had a hand in raising. Callen's heart thudded against his ribs, a drumbeat of anticipation for the counsel only his father could provide.

"Come on, come on," he muttered under his breath, willing the call to connect across oceans and time zones. The ringtone buzzed in the room, a lifeline reaching out to the rugged coast of Ireland, where his father would be waiting. The line clicked, and Callen braced himself for the conversation that he hoped could change the tides of their struggle.

"Até," Stryker said.

"You boys are calling more frequently. You have more trouble."

Callen answered. "Yes, sir, we do." His voice was steady despite the hammering in his chest. "We've got another layer of trouble."

Renee spoke up. "And we are all here this time, Até."

"About time you all got tired of sitting in the background. Good to hear your voice, sweetheart. Now, what's going on?"

Callen paced the length of the room as his father's voice, rough like weathered stone but warm like hearth fire, filled the room. "Listen, son. Jarl, and his employer are snakes. You can't grab them by the tail. You confront them head-on, or not at all."

"Até, we're cornered here. If we don't face him down, Bella's in grave danger," Callen said, his words slicing through the distance that separated them.

"And the girls," added Seamus.

"Ah, Callen, but there's a fine line between bravery and foolhardiness. Remember, to protect your love, all of you, that is your goal. But to do that, you must be thinking clearly, not just with your heart but with your head too."

"Understood," Callen responded, his jaw set.

Stryker was pacing. Something unusual for him. Carter joined him.

"Até, we're stuck between doing what we need to do and staying within the law. I'm not sure we can do both," said Seamus.

"Let's get sure. Tell me what you're thinking."

They shared their worries and concerns and their ideas of the responses they want to initiate if they are pushed to the wall again. Then they listened intently as their father laid out a strategy, wisdom weaving through his counsel like threads of gold in a tapestry of war.

Jacob rubbed his neck. "The thing is, the sheriff is doing what he can, but his response is too late. The distance is too great. And the danger is too real."

"His hands are tied by the law but mine aren't," said Seamus.

"It's my home and I am allowed to defend it and my family," said Stryker.

"Be cautious, my boys. And remember, no matter how far this goes, your family stands with each of you. Tell me if there are more developments. This is beginning to sound more like a life challenge to show that you are worthy of your women. Don't take it as such. Know we are proud of each of you and your women love you. Talk soon."

"Até's advice is clear," said Callen.

Declan spoke solemnly. "We meet Jarl head-on. It's the only way to protect our women and our property."

"We end this so life can continue," said Callen. There was no quiver in his tone, only the steely certainty of a man who had made his decision, come hell or high water.

"Before we confront Jarl, there's one more call to make," Stryker continued, already fishing his phone from his pocket. His thumb hovered over the contact list, a tremor betraying the adrenaline coursing through him. He pressed the screen, selecting the name of someone who could tip the scales in their favor.

"Hello, Uncle Kiernan. It's Stryker."

"Aye. I wondered if you would need some help from me after learning a little about your troubles there. Maeve keeps me up on things, but she hasn't called me in a couple of days. Is she there with you?"

He listened and put the phone on speaker. "I've put you on speaker. Yes, Maeve is fine. She got a flesh wound and is overnight in the clinic with the Sheriff's office keeping watch until we bring her home tomorrow."

The rough voice spoke with absolute authority. "I'm going to thrash that woman. I told her not to get into any fire fights so far away from me. She's going to stay home for a while."

"She is a firecracker. But we have a situation here... we need your help."

He listened intently, nodding as he paced a short line in front of the call they projected onto their video screen. Their father liked to see and hear his boys when they called. Uncle Kiernan didn't make video calls, but he did for his family and Maeve.

Kiernan sat, leaning back in his chair, the leather creaking under the shift of weight, his fingers tapping a steady rhythm on the polished mahogany desk. An emblem of order and power. He listened intently, the bronze statue on his desk catching the sunset filtering through the blinds.

"Anthony Shaffer and his man, Jarl Berg, is pushing us into a corner, Uncle," Declan explained, his voice a low rumble of contained fury.

"We've got to make a stand, but we need some leverage on our side. We're worried about keeping the girls safe," added Seamus.

"Tell me a little more about this. Maeve made it sound as though it wouldn't be a problem. Another thing she is good at," he grumbled, "downplaying the danger factor." A wicked smile spread across his face. He nodded. "Good, I have another reason to scorch the lass' ass." They filled Kiernan in as he thought through what would work best in this situation.

Callen spoke. "Uncle, there is one more problem. Maeve is coming here until things have concluded. She isn't going to be happy that she will be on ranch lockdown like the others. I know she has skills that we will use if she can be safe while doing so, but how do we get her to stay where we put her and not place herself at risk?"

"Like today?"

"Yes."

"You leave Maeve to me, but don't underestimate her abilities. She's a brilliant bodyguard, so give her something to protect. The lasses."

"Excellent," said Callen. "She kept Bella safe. We can do that."

Seamus nodded. "And what about our problem? Any ideas of how to get to them where they hurt?"

"Which is?"

"Hell, if I know," answered Seamus.

"Leave this to me. I know people who know people." Kiernan's reply was calm, a cool hand reaching out through the chaos. "I have contacts who owe me favors. I'll make calls. But remember, keep your women safe at all costs, and don't worry about cleaning up. If it becomes necessary, that is. I'll take care of that. I know your Até would want me to remind you to stay within the boundaries of the law. Those would be Até's words. Protect what is yours. The world is run on survival of the fittest would be mine."

"Understood," said Stryker. The video call ended abruptly.

It was hard to feel calm and not restless after such a long, over stimulating day, but things did settle and after a quiet dinner, they cleaned up for Libby and went to their room. Everyone except Carter and Renee. They opted for the front porch to breathe in the late winter night. As each couple headed to their rooms to relax, Bella could hear the men murmuring to their women as they walked up the steps and down the long hallway. She wondered what they were all talking about until Callen started speaking quietly to her.

"Take your shower, baby, and then we can deal with your behavior. After which, I plan on making love to my girl until she can't walk straight."

"What do you mean? Not the sex part. I get that. I want to make love, but what does 'deal with your behavior' mean?"

They walked into the room they were sharing, and Callen kissed Bella's neck, right at the sensitive curve where her shoulder met the slender column of her neck. It brought on racing chills across her skin causing her to step closer. His lips made love to hers, showing punishing dominance and then gentle caresses. His tongue slipped into her warm mouth, advancing and retreating like the waves that crashed on the beach, then sedately returned to the sea.

Feeling the familiar tingling between her thighs and the ache that called to her deepest need, Bella whimpered when he retreated and hummed when he advanced while mimicking the mating dance. He moved down to take her breasts, one at a time, in his mouth to tease and torment. Just when she was about to bring his hand to her wet channel and reach for his zipper, he groaned and leaned back, releasing her nipple with a seductive pop. Leaning his forehead on hers, his hands raised to her cheeks to give her one last, firm kiss before taking a half step back.

"What are you doing?" she gasped with indignation while still in a pre-orgasmic state. She believed she could come with just his kisses.

"We need to shower before taking care of today. Then we will make love to your heart's content. That was just the prelude. I intend to have you until we pass out from exhaustion."

"So why are stopping? You can't kiss me like that and then stop before... before getting somewhere."

"Normally, I wouldn't, but we still need to deal with the behaviors that almost got you killed." He paused while he got himself under control. He could feel that violent fear he experienced when the window she had just been standing in front of was shattered by a bullet.

"Fine, but after."

"I'll always deal with the lesson first because your safety is the most important thing to me. It might take some uncomfortable times to get the idea through to you, but you are it for me and I intend to keep you happy, healthy and safe." He took a cleansing breath. "Now get in the shower and don't bother to dress afterwards."

Bella stomped into the bathroom and slammed the door. "That's another five, baby. I'd recommend you take care. I'd hate to postpone our sexy times because your backside is too sore to enjoy it."

Callen heard her grumbling in the bathroom and smiled. His girl was pushing back as he had expected. Bella had gone too long without someone around that cared about her choices and intended to keep her safe because she was important to them. He had her now, and it was going to take some getting used to for both of them. Bella had trouble trusting others, and she was determined to do most things on her own. He was determined to allow her those freedoms, but within the circle of his love.

Bella walked into the bedroom with a towel covering all the sexy bits. Callen couldn't believe that his younger self had let her go so easily. She was so perfect for him that she took his breath away. He was constantly amazed at the intensity of his feelings for her. Those days he wasn't with her, while she was fulfilling the contract, had been pure torture.

Now that he had her with him every day again, he was constantly reassessing his decision not to have pushed her to stay on the ranch when the opportunity had first arisen. Now, she and the other women were in danger every day that Shaffer and Berg and their goons were not contained. He hoped Uncle would figure out a way to make this end for their women's safety and so he and Bella could go on with their forever.

He smiled at his girl. "Come here, baby."

"Hmm, I like that look in your eye."

"Do you? Then you'll love what I plan to do to you tonight, but first, we need to deal with your punishment."

Bella stopped her approach, a touch too close. Callen reached out to grab her hand and draw her to stand between his legs.

"No, we don't. I thought I made myself clear that I didn't mean to become a target. I was watching to make sure no one got hurt."

"Huh. How were going to do that in the second-story window?"

"Well, I had a bird's eye view of the area."

"And?"

"I..." she closed and opened her mouth as if to continue speaking, finally keeping it closed with a sigh.

"Okay. So, here's the deal. You were unsafe, putting yourself in danger, standing in that window for all to see, and nearly got shot. That is never going to be acceptable, therefore you have earned a punishment to the tune of twenty swats."

"Wait, that's too much, Callen. Way too much."

"Bella, I could have lost you forever. You could have died in my arms. I keep remembering how close that bullet came to you. That if you hadn't stepped away from that window when you did..." He inhaled deeply and blew it out. "How many do you think you've earned?"

The tears streamed down her face. Callen took another deep breath as he rubbed her hands, keeping a connection while waiting for her response. He felt a little like crying himself when he thought of how close he came to losing his Bella. His gut clinched every time he remembered seeing her standing in full sight of Shaffer's men.

"I thought I would be able to help but I guess I didn't think it all the way through. That is an error in judgement, not purposely putting myself in danger."

"I know, baby. I do understand that. Give over, Bella. Let Daddy take this from you."

He sighed when she simply laid across his lap. He loved her so much. He moved the towel to uncover her perfect bottom. He rubbed and leaned down to kiss her pale globes. No hint of her earlier spanking. "Tell me your safe word, baby."

"Zucchini," she whispered back.

"Right. Now promise you will say it if you truly need to. I am going to be as cautious as I can, but I might miss a cue. Ready?"

"Yes."

He raised his hand and laid down five swats in quick succession, peppering her entire bottom. He paused to run his hand over her perfect, rounded, lower cheeks. "How are you, baby?"

"Good. I'm good."

"Okay."

The next round of five were equally quick, solid swats only to be followed, again, by his tender touch. Another five was laid down decisively leaving Bella crying quietly, her backside a solid deep pink. The final five were delivered to her tenderest bit of skin stretched between her thighs and the underside of her bottom. Her tears were no longer spilling quietly. Callen kept her on his lap as he soothed and spoke nonsense to her as she slowly calmed down.

His finger swept down through the crevice of her pussy, sliding through her hot, slick channel, and entered her heated opening. It was sexy that she got off on spanking, which meant he would no longer pay attention when she said spanking was not for her. It was entirely her. His girl simply didn't want to acknowledge it. She wasn't hiding from it any longer. Nope, he wouldn't let her. Owning how you felt was freeing. She'd soon find that out.

It was important that she felt the consequences of her actions, but he didn't have any intention she spend one more moment in her regret. Spending a few moments plunging into her sexy sheath, igniting her desires, heightened his own. Time to make his girl feel so good. He pulled her up and kissed her salty tears and laid his Bella out on the bed.

Bella smiled, her face soon showing her arousal, and then pouted in anticipated rejection. "Do I get to feel good?"

"As in, do you get to feel good and orgasm?"

"Yes. I don't care if you're helping me or having full on sex. I'm so horny I can find my way if you aren't into it."

"You were very naughty today."

"But you punished me and it's over." Bella was good at pleading with her eyes. "You promised."

"True. And I could do with some relaxation."

"With me."

"Always with you."

"But Bella, baby if you ever bring yourself pleasure without me, I will edge you for hours. Then I'll find my pleasure and you will watch. Got that?"

"So mean."

"Yes, Daddy."

She pouted. "Yes, Daddy. Now can we get messy?"

Callen laid his girl out and simply looked at her. Her hair was still damp from the shower and beginning to curl, her beautiful breasts, shapely thighs, and glorious expression of adoration and desire was all he needed to come on the spot. He had thought to have her suck him off, or at least a little, in preparation for the finale, but honestly, that was not going to work today. He was too touchy. Calming everything the fuck down so this was good for her was going to be his biggest problem.

He pulled out the condom from the side table and kissed her hard, gentling his touch along her neck and jaw before returning to her mouth and deepening his kiss again until both were breathless. Callen ran his hand through her channel, gathering her arousal on his finger. He tweaked her clit for a few seconds before moving on to push in and out of her entrance full of liquid heat. Bella's arousal set her muscles to contract and flex in response to her need and his continued digital penetration.

"You're drenched baby. Daddy's good girl is ready for me to take her."

"Mmm hmm." She tried to place herself for easy access. He slapped her inner thigh, leaving a panty-melting sting behind and an even higher need in her belly.

"Who is in control here, baby?"

"You, Daddy, but I need more."

"I'll make you feel so good, I promise, but you need to remember who the boss is right now." Repositioning Bella, with her adorable squeaks and moans, into position with her still pink bottom up and presented to him. He loved taking her from behind, no matter where he put his cock. It was all he could do to take the necessary time to put on a condom. "We are getting you on birth control," he said through gritted teeth.

"I am on birth control," she whined as her body began to sway toward his cock that was jutting out in front of him. "I told you that."

He gave her a look of disbelief. "I don't think you did, but I'm glad to hear it." He grabbed his erection and slid his hands slowly up and down the length of her wet channel. It was so hot.

"Are you good with me going bareback? I promise I'm clean."

"Me too. I checked after the last time I... I'm good."

"So, I can dispense with the raincoat?"

"Yep, looks pretty sunny here."

And that's all it took for Callen to slide home, safe, warm, and secure. The muscles of her core rippled around his cock, and he gritted to hold on. She was going to be the death of him, but what a wonderful way to meet his demise.

She could feel Callen enter her easily with the lubrication she had been producing. She'd gotten a gander at his cock the first time, months ago, when he had taken her. They had never done more than heavy petting in high school, but Callen wasn't about to let her go without taking and claiming her soon after she came back to town. She hadn't wanted to wait, either.

Now, that broad purple headed cock was taking her, and somehow the meaning was deeper. Each time Callen had taken her, it had seemed a little more of her was claimed. This time, it was as though she was not only fully claimed but being made love to.

"I love you, Bella Kaye. Let me make you mine in every way."

"Can you first just finish staking your claim? I love you too, but I need you to fuck me right now. We can change the pace soon. Move, cowboy."

"Yes, ma'am."

He began to pound into her, just as Bella longed for him to do. Then, as though he remembered she was his girl, he eased and was more sedate.

"Callen, no. I need hard. I need fast. Please don't treat me like porcelain. Take me, claim me."

Bella was in confusion when the first two spanks landed on her backside, but by the third she was screeching. "Hush." His deep, calm, commanding voice seeped into her outrage. The voice she knew to focus in on.

She did stop but then demanded in a stage whisper, "What are you doing?"

"I'm heating things up. Well, I'm heating you, anyway," he answered as he rubbed in the heat from his spanks. "I am in control and if you won't remember, then it is up to me to be the reminder. And quiet. We aren't alone in the house."

"I'll try."

Callen kissed down her back. "Now where was I?" He played with her clit, then gathered some of her copious liquid arousal and pushed a finger into her darkest entrance. "I'm going to make your come, then I'm going to take this glorious anus when I'm sure you are ready. When I've prepped you enough. For now, feel my fingers as they slide inside you as I take your pussy and spank your bottom. Then pinch your clit. Just let it happen, sweetheart."

He hadn't been that dirty talking since high school and this man treating her to sexy times was no teenager. He was everywhere. Touching her bottom hole, occasionally pounding into her core while kissing her, touching, tweaking her nipples, then back to her pussy and twiddling her clit, intensely then softly. She couldn't believe how he surrounded her completely. Then it was all gone except for his fast, deep and satisfyingly hard.

"Come, baby, because Daddy is close behind."

He leaned down and changed his angle where his hot breath was in her ear, his sweaty body laying over hers, and his hand pinching her clit. The shock was all it took to fall over the cliff of ecstasy. Callen grunted almost immediately after Bella. She was exhausted, would swear she saw stars, was breathless and wondering when they could do it again. No harm in asking.

"Wanna do that again?"

Callen landed a hard spank on her butt. "When we can breathe again, my greedy brat. But this time I make love to you. And you don't direct."

Her exasperated sigh got a raised eyebrow from Callen, encouraging her sedate, "Yes, sir."

Chapter 22

Showdown

Bella woke to yelling and swearing. In her half-awake state, she didn't immediately respond, but once she heard Stryker say, "Wherever the girls are, they need to head to the basement. Where is Bella?"

Callen answered, "Sleeping in. I tired her out, but she's going to need to get up."

Declan called out to Teagan. "Teague, go and get Bella up and help her find the basement."

Jacob was grabbing out the guns for distribution. "I think we've got everyone going in the right direction. Libby and Avery have already started to bring some supplies."

Stryker asked, "When is Seamus back with Maeve? Can we call him and leave her in town? It would be safer for her. Maybe hang with the sheriff?"

Kai knocked on Bella's door with intent, not like the timid knocks she had done before. Teagan followed her in. Bella was already zipping up her pants. "There's trouble."

"Before breakfast? That's new. Where is everyone?"

"This is real trouble. The guys are gearing up. Libby and the others are taking things to the basement. Jacob said he thought that was the best place for us. Safe and defendable." Teagan shivered.

Kai nodded. "I guess Renee and Avery will split the bossing duties. Better them than me."

Bella grabbed a jacket out of habit, her phone, her keys, and her tablet, grabbing Ping-Pong and Pinky more for her feelings of security than for their safety. She tossed all inside her backpack.

"Just in case," she said to Kai, who nodded. Teagan grabbed her hand, and they headed to the kitchen basement stairs.

By the time they had reached the first floor, Jacob was steering the women to the basement. The guys were all prepped and kissing their girls before reassembling back in the family room.

Callen kissed Bella hard. "Bella, get downstairs and no leaving until one of us comes to get you. No letting anyone in except Maeve. Seamus couldn't convince her to stay in town, so she will be here any minute. Uncle Kiernan has already been in touch with us and her. He isn't pleased. Evidently, Kiernan put people in place to watch Berg and Shaffer and they saw Berg and the same three cars load up, going in the direction of town. We are holding them off until we get back up from Uncle's people."

"But he's in Ireland."

"Not him specifically, but those he pays to do things and don't ask me what things."

Bella was beginning to think he and Shaffer were in similar professions, so she didn't want to know more than what she needed to know. The man was Callen's family, after all. Besides, Maeve was her friend.

As they started down the steps to the basement, Seamus was shoving Maeve in the kitchen door. Carter came in and handed his brother a gun as Seamus was hanging the truck keys and steering Maeve to the stairway behind Bella and Kai.

"Do not come out for any reason. That's meant for all of you." His meaning was clear.

"Don't I get a gun?" asked Maeve.

"Can I trust you to stay downstairs and defend the group from that place? No more going off on your own." Obviously, Seamus was privy to what actually happened yesterday.

"I promised Kiernan."

"Great, now promise me," demanded Callen.

"Maeve, you promised to let us handle things on the ranch, but you decided you were going off to do your own thing and look what happened? We work together around here. No one goes off half-cocked. There's something you need to learn no matter where you are; family is together in their efforts for the common good. Always."

"I'm not part of your family, Seamus."

"You are Bella and Callen's friend, and you work for Uncle. That makes you part of this family and, as such, bound by our rules. Now move."

Bella hadn't heard Seamus get so fired up, but then, she hadn't spent as much time as she had wanted on the ranch. She hoped that was about to change. She was glad there was a light over the stairs, because Seamus handed over a pistol and shut the door soundly. Bella had no doubt they would have been in total darkness if it weren't for the lights because there was nothing but a painted black window that had any hope of shedding light on them. A shiver ran through her body at the thought of total darkness.

Callen watched as the men in his family took up different positions on the property, all situating themselves to the best advantage to cover the road and entrance to the ranch. The gate was locked but bullets could easily penetrate the air and find any one of them between the wrought iron bars. Callen had just taken up his position at the side of the barn closest to the house and had identified each of the hands and his kin in their respective places when the black SUVs arrived. Game on.

The first vehicle pulled to the head of the drive, and the inhabitants stayed inside. They were smarter than he had thought. What he imagined Jarl and his goons didn't know was these men could wait them out. In fact, he could wait longer than they could because ranching was another word for working your patience and faith. Callen had plenty of both. He'd felt antsy all morning until now. Now he was focused on the task at hand, as his father had taught him. Stalk your prey. Look for the best opening to take them down. Then strike.

The air was thick with tension, heavy with the scent of protective, raw aggression. With no words exchanged, Jarl's men released the first shot, dinging off the side of the paddock and diverting off. Callen's muscles flexed in readiness to return the challenge, but he held back. That wasn't the plan. Back up would be here soon and heroics weren't called for right now. He waited to see if Stryker would speak. He didn't. He stood quietly behind the closest outbuilding flanking Jacob and Carter. Stryker had gone hand to hand with Avery's brother, but the situation was different. Avery was there, and a gun was pointed at them, close up and personal.

There was a single return fire released by someone in the bushes inside the ranch boundaries. Damn, one of their younger hands must have lost his fight to hold fire. They would have some conversations on orders and practice on that later. The wait was agony and he could understand the loss of control. The car door opened. Out stepped Jarl.

"Let me have Bella. She's mine. This bloodshed can all be avoided if you just gave me my property."

Callen couldn't hold his tongue, but before the words of denial rang loudly, a tire was blown out by a shot that must have come from a tree. Who was up there? Declan? A hand? Another shot, another tire, this time on the second vehicle. The third vehicle's driver began to maneuver his car further away, but a third shot took out his front passenger tire. Callen wasn't sure that was a good move because now they couldn't leave. But, then again, they couldn't leave.

The sheriff would be happy to have a captive audience, but everyone knew what happened when wild animals were held against their will. Callen wasn't disappointed. The doors flew open and shielded the men inside, who began to fire on the ranch in earnest.

A helicopter could be heard in the distance. The Red Eagles had agreed not to return fire unless necessary, and right now, they could all still stay behind cover. Whoever was on that roof or tree perch was about to catch the wrath of Stryker when this was over. Callen was glad it wasn't him that had to deal with the hand, because he might not disagree with the choice...maybe.

The helicopter drew closer. Jarl and his men were quiet as though waiting for the chopper to pass them. Maybe they were. Fewer witnesses to their attempted storming of the ranch for his Bella. There was gunfire from the chopper. Hell, who was this and whose side did they belong? And where was the damn sheriff?

"Enough!" Anthony's voice cut through the tension like a well-honed blade. "Who is that?"

He stepped forward, flanked by associates whose loyalty was unwavering, but they were following the wrong person. They were his silent enforcers, men who spoke the language of strength and blind obedience without uttering a word.

Jarl's followers, scattered around the edges of the front gate, shielded by the cars, shifted uneasily, recognizing the authority encroaching upon their temporary playground. A crow cawed in the distance, the sound mocking the sudden change in power dynamics. Men poured from the helicopter and the second one that landed beside the first. Callen waited for them to show their hand and then he saw Kiernan.

His uncle never came to the ranch. He stayed in Ireland, where he ran his own syndicate of sorts. Callen wasn't positive, but he was confident that his uncle had power no one had yet quantified. What was he doing here?

"Fucking stop, I said," Anthony snarled when another one of their associates fired a random shot.

Callen was confused as to what was going on. "Just give us Bella and we will leave." Jarl angrily demanded.

"Over my cold, dead body," replied Callen.

He could hear the sheriff's vehicles, but sound carried across the plains, and they were still some distance away. He counseled his inner defender to at least bank the hotter coals of his protective anger for now.

"Shaffer," yelled Kiernan as he approached with his own associates, "why are you bothering with my family?"

"What do you mean? This has nothing to do with you, Kiernan."

"The Red Eagles and their women are my family."

"Fuck off. You don't have family."

"Ah, but my sister does," came Kiernan's cold, menacing words spoken quietly.

If possible, Anthony turned even paler. "Your sister's family? Here?"

"I can see your goons didn't do their research. Pity. I'd address that if I were you."

A heated conversation between Anthony and Jarl grew as Kiernan walked closer to the house. Callen could hear a little of what was being said as three lackeys were changing the tires on three vehicles.

"Stand down," Anthony growled at Jarl, his eyes narrowing into slits that promised retribution. "Or you'll find yourself in a world of hurt that doesn't end with a few bruises. And you'll be on your own. I can't have anyone going against that man." Anthony pointed in Kiernan's direction. "This is Kiernan Donahue. *Uncle Kiernan.* We are not messing with him. You understand me?"

Jarl's jaw clenched, and for a moment, it seemed as though he might lash out, unwilling to yield under the scrutinizing gaze of his boss. But the flicker of defiance in his eyes waned, replaced by a cold calculation as he weighed his odds against the wall of muscle and authority that was Anthony Shaffer. He seemed to be gauging the power of Uncle Kiernan and weighing it with his desire to possess Callen's girl. His better sense or Anthony's seemed to prevail, and he turned away.

"Fine," Jarl spat out the word, the taste of defeat bitter on his tongue. He straightened his jacket, brushing off the invisible lint with deliberate slowness. His retreat was not an admission of weakness, or so he tried to convince himself; it was a strategic withdrawal, a pause to reassess and possibly plan his next move. But the fury that smoldered in his gaze spoke more of wounded pride than tactical prudence.

Anthony's towering presence commanded the space, his eyes leaving Jarl and fixing on Bella. That is when Callen noticed his naughty girl was not in the basement but beside the house. His irritation was tempered with concern for her well-being. Her chest heaved with shallow breaths.

"Bella," Anthony's voice carried. It rumbled, a surprising gentleness tempering its usual demanding authority. "You're safe now. We had no idea you were part of Donahue's family. We won't bother you again. You have my word." The firmness in his tone left no room for doubt.

Bella's gaze flitted past Anthony to Jarl, who stared at her with a hardened expression before he stalked over to the first vehicle. She shifted her focus, seeking Callen, who was watching her. He was a tempest barely contained, his jaw clenched, stance still ready for battle. Yet, his stormy eyes softened when they met hers, silent encouragement echoing in their depths.

Callen took that moment to move, each step measured, controlled—a predator's careful prowl. But it was the fierce protectiveness radiating from him that drew Bella's attention, her heart responding to the unspoken bond between them.

He stopped between her line of sight and Anthony. Callen didn't speak. He didn't have to. His stance spoke volumes, a testament to his unwavering love and commitment. In the aftermath of chaos, his proximity was her fortress, his silent pledge louder than any spoken oath.

The dust swirled in the wake of Anthony's intervention, settling slowly as he assumed command, his presence a bulwark against the chaos that had just threatened to continue. With an authoritative sweep of his hand, he directed his remaining associates on alert to step forward, their movements precise and deliberate. Jarl, his face a mask of barely contained fury, met Anthony's unflinching gaze, the air thick with the finality of the standoff.

"Finish taking care of the tires. We are done here." Anthony instructed. His voice was low but carried the weight of finality. Two of the associates stepped toward Jarl and his henchmen, their approach signaling the end of any resistance. Jarl's shoulders tensed, then dropped in resignation, his defeat palpable even as he allowed himself to be led away, his glare lingering on Bella like a dark promise unfulfilled.

Bella appeared in full view of everyone from the side of the house. Kiernan saw her and grinned. "Looks like your lass is as disobedient as mine, nephew." He nodded in the direction of the corner of the house. Kiernan chuckled when Callen swore and stalked in Bella's direction.

"It appears so. I had no idea about Maeve and..."

"Aye. My family isn't privy to all my secrets. She is in denial. For now." The men watched Anthony and his entourage leave. "You won't be bothered by this group again. Anthony Shaffer doesn't have enough clout to tangle with me." The brothers came closer. "Do you know what they wanted with Bella?"

"No," said Callen who pulled his girl close, kissing the top of her head.

"Forgery. He wanted Bella to create sketches and forgeries of original masterpieces. It's his stock and trade. Imitations made and sold of real articles."

"Damn," said Stryker.

"Yes. He would have kept her like a hummingbird in a gilded cage, all the luxuries but no freedoms. And that second of his? Jarl? You can't have a man like that in your organization and do well. He will either decide to put down the rabid dog or find a corner of his organization that needs a rabid dog."

"Thank you for coming and ending this terrible mess," said Bella.

Kiernan looked down at Bella and took her cheeks between his hands and dropped a kiss on her forehead. "It was my pleasure lass. I'm thinking Callen will be having a talk with you later about risking your safety. As I'll be having with my girl." Uncle looked up. His next words aimed at the roof inhabitant. "Get down here, Maeve Eilís McCleary. Now." His tone was no longer slightly amused. He was pissed. "You're due a thrashing, me-girl. Get down here and gather your things. We're going home."

"I'll be finding my own way home, Kiernan Donahue. Same as how I came. Now go on and get in your whirly-bird and fly away home. I'll be there in me-own sweet time."

Maeve's accent, that was barely detectable at times, colored all her words now. Callen thought it was telling. Yep, there was something big between Kiernan and Maeve. He'd love to be a fly on the wall to find out what. Then he smiled. His girl was all he could handle at the moment. He pulled her closer as Kiernan spoke again. Calm, authoritative and with definite affection.

"You'll be coming with me, or I'll be taking off my belt. You have had enough freedom for a while. You've got no more than ten minutes." Maeve began to swear and climb down from the roof. Kiernan just leaned against the paddock as he smiled and waited.

"Thank you," Bella whispered to Callen, her voice a fragile thread in the silence between them. Callen's eyes softened, the rigid line of his jaw easing as he regarded her. "You are always welcome. I told you I would always be there for you." Callen nodded in Kiernan's direction. "He isn't wrong, though. You earned a big punishment for being so naughty. And putting yourself in danger...big trouble."

"But you aren't going to punish me. You're too relieved no one got hurt. And I waited until Kiernan had things under control, so no danger. You won't."

"Am I just? I wouldn't place any bets on that, baby girl, because I've got it on good authority that you are getting every bit of the spanking you earned."

BELLA SIGHED WHEN THEY finally entered the cabin. Callen had called home before Bella's return. "Hungry, sweetheart?"

"Starved."

"Good thing I have the makings of a good breakfast."

Bella hated that things between them were a little awkward, stilted. "Are you really angry?"

Callen turned from pulling out the food he intended to cook and placed it on the counter before he responded. Reaching for her hands, he drew her near and placed his chin on her head as she wrapped her arms around his middle. They stood there a moment before he kissed her temple, then her cheek, and finally her lips.

"Yes. I was angry, more scared when I realized what could have happened. There was no way to predict what Jarl would have done when he began to realize he wasn't going to get you. The look in his eyes was approaching desperate and that kind of emotion in anyone is dangerous. In the eyes of a man who killed without thought, it produces serious unpredictability. It was that understanding that brought on my fearful anger."

"I didn't even think through things. When Maeve slipped up the steps so quickly, we decided to follow. No, I decided I had to follow her."

"Ah, so you had company in the decision to disobey."

"No. It was just me following Maeve. I couldn't climb the roof behind Maeve because of my fear of heights, but I did find a place to watch what was going on without being in the middle of things. I guess I was already caught, though, when Kiernan looked at me when he started to talk to Anthony. Then I was worried about you getting hurt and I stepped out without thinking about what the consequences might be."

Callen kissed her firmly before stepping away from Bella. "Yep, and that is something I'm not ever going to be okay with—you placing yourself in harm's way, no matter the reason." He turned to begin cooking. "And that is why you are getting a spanking. I was very clear what was expected of you, you disregarded me. Not okay. I intend to make sure you understand that after we enjoy some breakfast. Do you need to have a shower? It will take me a little to finish cooking."

The hot steamy shower washed away all the morning's worries but one: her punishment. She walked into the kitchen in just a robe. No use putting anything on until Callen had finished her punishment. He looked up and smiled so lovingly, that Bella knew things would be alright if she could just get through this morning. Callen's cell rang.

"Could you grab that, baby? My hands aren't clean."

"Sure." She wished she'd let it go to voicemail when she saw who was calling. Ma. Kiernan's sister. His baby sister and Callen's mom. She was probably calling to tell him to find a better mate. She didn't blame her. "It's your mom."

"Well, answer it. She likely is checking on you."

Bella didn't respond to him, but answered the call with a great amount of trepidation. She felt vulnerable today, and that wasn't going to make this any easier to hear what his mom had to say.

"Hello?"

"Bella? Oh, darling, you're who I was checking on. Kiernan said you had a rough morning, and I wanted to reach out, but I didn't have your number. How are you? Has my family been taking care of you? Callen has been good to you?"

The relief was so tangible that Bella had to sit down at the small kitchen table to continue. "I'm fine. Thank you for asking."

"Oh, well, my love, if you are fine, that possessive son of mine hasn't had a go at your backside yet. I'm glad I got you before he did. It seems that all is over, and you are out of danger. I can't tell you how my heart is relieved. Atè nearly climbed aboard with Kiernan yesterday. I'm glad he didn't, but sometimes these men are so protective that nothing will hold them back.

"Remember that is the heritage Callen was born with, Bella. He loves hard, plays hard, works hard, and he defends what belongs to him even more fiercely. You, my darling. He will defend you and if you don't safeguard yourself as much as he believes you should, well, our men get itchy palms. Better to let him satisfy himself than you not have this intensity in your love. It makes everything spicier."

"I guess, but I really think I should make my own decisions."

"Of course. When we return in a little over a month, after the weddings, I'll start showing you how to get your man to do what you want and keep yourself out of trouble. Well, mostly." Callen's mother chuckled and then murmured to someone.

"Bella?" asked Atè.

"Oh, hi Mr. Red Eagle."

"Atè. I'm glad you are all right. Ma has already started your wedding plans, so you better get online soon and keep her doing it all the way you want. My Kayleigh is so excited to do these weddings, I'm not sure I can even keep her reined in. We are glad things are going to settle down now and don't forget, let Callen do what he needs to do and then let's get these wedding plans started. All my sons getting married to women I know we love already. Okay. Take care and stay out of trouble, young lady. We'll talk soon."

Callen set her plate in front of her and a cup of coffee. "They didn't want to talk to me?"

"I guess not."

"I expected as much. You okay?"

"Yep. I really like your parents, but did you know they know you, um...?"

"Spank?" He ate a bit of bacon and smiled. "I don't doubt it, but we haven't ever had that discussion. It's our business, not anyone else's. Now, eat all that. I don't want my girl hungry when I'm spanking her naughty backside for disobeying her daddy and taking ten years off his life."

Bella rolled her eyes and laughed. "You can be such a drama queen."

Thirty minutes later, Bella was worried she would be the drama queen. His spanks were not the sexy kind. No, sir. This man was intent on roasting her butt to red-hot and she was worried sitting would only be a fond memory.

"Callen, I get it."

"Obviously not enough. What do you call me?"

"Daddy! Daddy, please, I know you mean business and I was wrong. I promise not to take my safety lightly or go against you. Not ever again. Promise!"

Callen stopped his spank cadence of left, right, left, right, and center, leaving his hand on her hot backside. "You ignored my instructions to you. You disobeyed me and put yourself in harm's way. That Jarl Berg could have easily decided to make sure no one could have you and aimed a gun at you. It is unacceptable and every time I think about it, I want to spank you all over again. Then wrap you in bubble wrap and put you away so no one can find you."

"Daddy! That's a little creepy."

Callen sighed. "I know and I also understand it isn't something I can do, but I do feel like I want to. It's going to take me a while to get over this, so don't expect me to allow you many freedoms for a while."

"I know. I get it. Can I get up now?"

"Nope. This round is going to count." His hand landed and while his palm stung, he knew her bottom stung more. He meant it to and to make sure she remembered what could have happened. And Callen wasn't kidding about locking his girl down for a while. She could interact with everyone at the ranch, but leaving to go somewhere else was going to be off limits for a bit until he calmed down. She could paint.

"Final round, baby. You are doing so well."

But he knew these last ten would scorch her already blistered backside, and he felt better about things, even if she would be standing a lot today. Her tears used to affect him, and they still did when it was something that made her sad, but right now, they meant he was getting through to her and that was music to his ears.

Helping her onto his lap and holding her close as she finished crying, her tears wetting his shirt, he kissed her temple. Callen pulled out his shirttails and wiped her face, kissing her salty, wet lips. "I'm sorry I had to be so harsh, but damn, girl, you do know how to get my attention."

She sniffed. "I know. I just wanted to make sure Maeve was safe."

"And you were nosey. There was no way you thought you could keep Maeve safe when it had been her job to keep you protected when I wasn't there."

"I guess I didn't think about that too hard."

"I aim to make sure you think about your safety all the time."

"I promise I will. I don't want to repeat this again."

"Good. That was my intention. Now, are you too sore to give your daddy some love and let him give you some?"

"I thought you'd never ask." Callen chuckled. "No, really, I'm serious. I thought I'd have to endure the need without being satisfied."

"Well, let me start satisfying my baby. Don't want to be too cruel, right?" He swooped in with a seriously focused kiss, his hands touching, caressing her everywhere. This was going to be a good day, after all.

Epilogue

Forever

Luckily, the ranch didn't have any cowboy guests or *duders* this last week, but the hotel did have guests. A few were on a hiking experience when the morning exploded with gunfire and helicopters. As Teagan chatted with one guest as she was gathering her bill, she noticed the excitement radiating from the young woman.

"Happy to go home?"

"This was like staying in the old west this week with gunfights and modern cowboy ranching using helicopters. I'm booking for next year. I can't wait to see what new excitement will be going on. You should start a blog with all the goings on around here. It would be a hit. Well, goodbye ladies. See you next year."

"We do. Here is the website address."

Teague just smiled. "Glad someone had fun this morning," she said under her breath.

Their relationship was stronger than ever, but after the heavy events of the last few months, Bella was ready to start her new chapter. Even Callen proved to be true to his word and keeping her on the ranch.

"Callen, I have to go for painting supplies."

"Order them."

"And for my sanity."

"I'll take you later today. I have some things to pick up as well. We'll go together."

"When can I go alone?" Callen simply stared at her with a raised eyebrow. "Need me to freshen up that spanking from last night?"

"No, thank you. And you spanked me for no reason. Then, putting in that plug," she continued in a stage whisper, "was mean and wrong on so many levels."

Pulling her into his arms, he walked back to the house. "I love you. You are my *Mo shtorghrá,* as ma would say. My forever love. Or as Atè would say, and I'm sorry, I don't know if I'm saying this right, but you are my destiny. I love you. Thečhíĥila. You are it for me, baby. Will you consent to be my wife and share my joys and sorrows, my children in my youth, my grandchildren in my old age and my eternity in death?"

Bella teared up. "That may have been the most romantic proposal of all time. I love you so much. More than I ever thought possible. You have a sweet way with your words, my cowboy."

"Does that mean that you are saying yes? We can get married in June when my parents are back and when the rest of this motley crew is getting married?"

"Um, as lovely as your proposal was, I'm not sure. How about I take it under advisement? My acceptance of contracts has been a little faulty in the execution and outcome lately. My boyfriend might object if I jump into another one so soon without discussing it with him and reading the small print." She grinned as she danced a distance away from Callen.

He raised his eyebrow in mock anger. "Take it under advisement? The small print? The small print is I will love and protect you as long as I live and beyond. Now, about the rest of this contract business," he stepped closer.

Bella squealed, stepping further back as she watches Callen begin to unbuckle and pull off his belt while walking toward her. "Don't forget baby girl. I spank for naughty."

Bella tried to stifle her laugh without much success. "I'm kidding. I'll marry you! I thought a person could say no."

"Oh, you can. Just not to me."

When he stalked closer, Bella giggled and leaped into his arms. Callen's arms caught her to himself and wrapped around her tightly.

"I love you so much." She watched as his head lowered deliberately, kissing her hard, then more gently.

"I love you more, cowboy."

Later on...

"I've been watching Renee and Carter. Are you sure they don't have something going on between them?"

Callen sat on the porch in a chair and snuggled her close to his chest, settling in with her in his arms as though nothing could be better than this. Bella noticed Callen did not look surprised or concerned about Carter and Renee. Was it a fact she hadn't picked up on until now?

"Why do you think something is going on?" Callen asked. Bella felt he was being cagey.

"Maybe the question is, why don't you? He gravitates to her, is protective, bossy, and so much more. She responds to him. Not always in a compliant way, though."

Callen smiled. "I'm not sure if Saoirse Renee is going to be compliant with anyone, always. You have to hand it to the man who chooses her as his bride. He will have to be made of stern stuff."

"Or love her completely."

"I'm thinking he will need to be both. Our girls are kinda sassy. Takes a gentle hand and stern voice to keep them in line."

"We like it."

"Thank God."

CALLEN WATCHED BELLA as she snuggled in and relaxed in his hold. If he could stay here all day, every day, he would be a happy man. He loved the ranch, and he loved working on it. The Duders were often good help and usually great people to be with. No one would question his love for his family, but Bella coming back into his life was something he had never expected and would always be thankful for. Callen dreamed of the family he wanted with her. She greeted him every morning with a smile, and her sassiness entertained him throughout the day. At night, the time they relaxed and dreamed together was all he had ever wanted in life. Except for a real house instead of this cabin and the family they were now discussing.

The family had a conversation last night, with Atè and Ma on video. Next week, the first groundbreaking would start. The permits came through and they called their contractor this morning. They'd run two crews and start putting up the first house, then go from there. Callen put him and Bella last on the list because they had a cabin. It was small, but they had a place to be alone. Stryker had been waiting for the longest. It had worked well with their parents in Ireland this past year, but now, since he and Avery were soon to have a little one and the year abroad for the elder Red Eagles was ending, it was time to build their own place.

The subject of babies came up again at the dinner table last night.

Teagan smiled at Avery. "I love you are having a baby, Avery, so I don't have to right now."

"Why?" Stryker asked. "Other than the obvious."

"Because then I won't have to change my life for a long time."

"I don't see it that way," said Sage. "Ma is going to see how much she loves grandchildren, and we will all be hounded to give her one or five."

"Ugh. Do you think so?" moaned Teague. "I'm waiting so the rest of you better decide who goes next."

Seamus smiled as he leaned down to kiss his Kai. "We don't mind when the time comes, do we sweetheart?" Kai smiled back and shook her head.

"Super, that takes care of the next one," said Teagan. "Any takers for number three?"

Declan spoke calmly. "You can't line baby parents up like an auction or a lineup for some kind of program. Next! You have to let nature happen and let people decide when they are ready. Like I am doing for you."

"Declan, you don't get it. If I can get others on board, then I can wait a few more years."

Carter spoke up. "Then wait a few more years. When or even if you have a baby is up to you and Declan. You don't have to jockey everyone into place."

Stryker laughed and slapped Carter on the back. "I know you are ready to settle down, so why don't we look for the prospects and see what there might be out there for a stud like you?"

Carter laughed and joked, but Callen saw him look at Renee and her eyes immediately dropped as though she was worried someone might catch the look. Someone did. Several someones by the looks of it, but no one said a word. He wished Carter would just lay claim to his sister already. Renee had spent the last few years trying to find a guy that would be what she was looking for when that man was having dinner with her most nights.

Carter was already so protective, they argued often. Bella and Avery both mentioned that they believed *the lady doth protest too much*, but Renee would never admit her attraction to Stryker's best friend and Seamus' co-manager. Maybe it was time he and his brothers worked on getting those two together.

Callen watched when Renee, who hadn't shown any interest in the women they all dated before, became very invested in their love life this last year. There was something there, he was sure of it. Time to turn the tables on her and get them all settled. Renee would never be free of her brothers, if that was her intent, but if they knew Carter had her under his wing, they could rest much easier. He'd have a talk with the guys and the women would have to be on board or it wouldn't work. Their women could smell a fishy deal a mile away... so they would have to agree. Yep. This just might work.

Bella yawned. Callen leaned into her and spoke close to her ear. "You ready to go home, baby?"

"I think so. I wanted to start a new piece tomorrow, but I don't seem to be getting enough sleep. I mean, I am according to the clock, but I'm tired a lot more that I should be."

"I'll start paying more attention to you and let's see if it's anything we can easily fix. Otherwise, you will be going to the doctor."

"I'm sure I'm just needing more sleep and to eat better. Honest."

"Okay, say goodnight and let's go home."

Bella walked back to the cabin with Callen's arm wrapped protectively over her shoulder. She snuggled in and kissed his neck. She loved this man with all she was. He would make a great husband and an incredible father someday. And he was all hers.

The End

About the Author
Alyssa Bailey

USA Today Bestselling Author of Diverse Romance that is realistic and sensual with a touch of suspense. A dyed in the wool Texan living in Alaska for half her life, Alyssa now divides her time between the beauty of Southeast Alaska and the piney woods of East Texas. She enjoys taking from her own experiences to create series that tease the reader's palate and invite them to sink into exciting adventures.

Alyssa enjoys writing consensual power exchanges between intelligent, sassy women who are not afraid to make a stand and loving men confident enough to give his woman space but masterful enough to keep her safe despite her choices. Whether it's Daddies, Professionals, Military, Cowboys, or more, there is *always* a happily ever after.

Visit me online and sign up for my newsletter:
http://alyssabailey.com
Join my Facebook Group for fun and prizes:
https://www.facebook.com/alyssabailey.romance
Find me on Social Media:
https://linktr.ee/alyssabailey

Red Eagle Series
Stryker's Girl
Declan's Girl
Seamus' Girl
Jacob's Girl
Callen's Girl
Carter's Girl

Other Romances by Alyssa Bailey

Safe and Secure Series: Contemporary, suspense, spicy
Saving Sharlee
Saving Jessie
Saving Ivy
Saving Mallory
Saving Callie
Saving Becky
Saving Oakley
Saving Finley
Clearwater Daddies Trilogy -Contemporary, Spicy
Piper's Plan
Camille's Second Chance
Josie's Refuge
Red Eagle Ranch:
Stryker's Girl
Declan's Girl
Seamus' Girl
Jacob's Girl
Callen's Girl
Carter's Girl (TBD)
Darling Duchesses: Regency, Daddy Dom, Spicy
The Devil Duke's Little Distraction
The Daring Duke's Little Impulse
Lords and Little Ladies (Historical Daddy Doms)
Lord Thayer's Choice

Lord Ashton's Distraction

Guardians of Refuge (Contemporary, Military, Spicy)
SEAL of Refuge
The Strategy of Love
The Tactics of Love
The Mandate of Love
Sage County (Cowboy, Contemporary, Spicy)
Deep Waters
Still Waters
In the Spirit of Christmas -Contemporary, Sweet
Christmas Wishes and You
Dear Santa-A Christmas Wish

Don't miss out!

Visit the website below and you can sign up to receive emails whenever Alyssa Bailey publishes a new book. There's no charge and no obligation.

https://books2read.com/r/B-A-MXIL-KVTWD

BOOKS 2 READ

Connecting independent readers to independent writers.

Did you love *Callen's Girl*? Then you should read *Stryker's Girl*[1] by Alyssa Bailey!

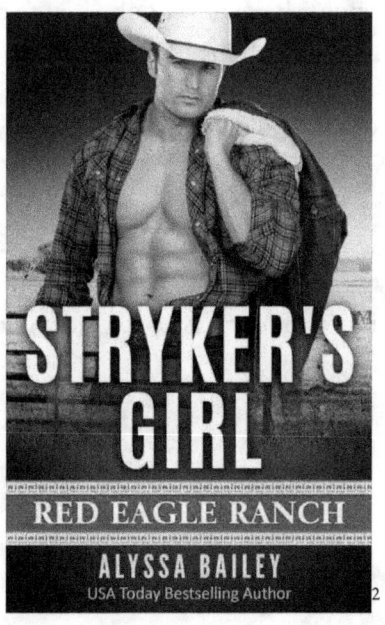

[2]

"You'll like your brothers again once they each find their true love. Their women will tame them for you."

Young adult, steady job, parents in Ireland for a year, sounds like heaven, right? Not to Saoirse Renee, who is bound by a promise to live at home with her four nosy, intrusive brothers. Their need to run her life with hot Irish tempers and immovable Nakota rules, has gotten completely *out of control.*

Renee, the youngest of five children born to an Irish-emigrant mother and a Nakota Sioux father, often finds reconciling her parents' worlds with her own challenging. The cultural diversity is, at times, explosive. Richard Red Eagle expected his sons to watch over

1. https://books2read.com/u/38QyVL

2. https://books2read.com/u/38QyVL

their little sister, while his wife, Kayleigh, does damage control with their daughter.

With a little help from providence and some strategic orchestrating, Renee intends to help each of her brothers find their true love. She can smell sweet victory and see her freedom just around the corner. Time to get to work.

First victim on the list? The eldest: **Stryker.**

Read more at alyssabailey.com.

Also by Alyssa Bailey

Lone Wind
Reclaiming Clover

Red Eagle Ranch
Stryker's Girl
Callen's Girl

Safe and Secure
Saving Sharlee

Watch for more at alyssabailey.com.

www.ingramcontent.com/pod-product-compliance
Lightning Source LLC
Chambersburg PA
CBHW070921260626
47162CB00007B/2752